THE HAPPINESS PROJECT

A laugh-out-loud and utterly feel-good romance

HELEN BRIDGETT

The Mercury Travel Club Book 2

Choc Lit
A JOFFE BOOKS COMPANY

Choc Lit
A Joffe Books company
www.choc-lit.com

This edition first published in Great Britain in 2024

© Helen Bridgett 2024

This book is a work of fiction. Names, characters, businesses, organizations, places and events are either the product of the author's imagination or are used fictitiously. Any resemblance to actual persons, living or dead, events or locales is entirely coincidental. The spelling used is British English except where fidelity to the author's rendering of accent or dialect supersedes this. The right of Helen Bridgett to be identified as author of this work has been asserted in accordance with the Copyright, Designs and Patents Act 1988.

Cover art by Dee Dee Book Covers

ISBN: 978-1781896990

For Angus,
my constant writing companion
xx

CHAPTER ONE: THE ODD COUPLE

Never move in with your best friend. Things can get rather weird in a very short space of time.

'Oh look, there's a thirtieth-anniversary showing of *Four Weddings and a Funeral* coming up at the Savoy,' Patty is saying. 'If you go dressed up for a wedding you get a free glass of prosecco.'

'And what do you get if you dress for a funeral?' I ask, yawning.

'Oh, that funeral scene, do you remember it? I cried my eyes out — just beautiful. Shall we go?'

I sit up in bed and take my iPad out of her hands.

'Patty, I'm really tired and I've got work tomorrow. Is there any chance of you letting me get some sleep? We can talk about this in the morning.'

'All right, don't get your jammies in a twist,' she says, switching off the bedside light.

I turn over and snuggle under the duvet, waiting for her to move. She doesn't.

'And do you think you could possibly get into your own bed?' I groan.

'But I've warmed this side up now.'

'Out!'

Much harrumphing follows but Patty does eventually throw back the duvet and get out of the bed, stomp across the room and slam the door behind her. I spread out, and although I'm glad to finally have some peace, I must confess the space she's left is really very cosy.

* * *

Come morning, she's turned from acting like my partner to sounding like my mother.

'You can't go to work on the first day of a new year on a yoghurt. I'll make you a bacon sandwich.' She's already pulling the ingredients out of the fridge. 'Your brain needs proper food.'

'I don't want one and I don't have time anyway.'

'Why don't you have time? You part own the place — you can hardly sack yourself.'

I'm lifting a spoon of yoghurt to my mouth as Patty reaches across me to get the milk and nudges my arm, causing me to spill some down my chin and blouse. Before I can reach for a piece of kitchen roll for myself, Patty has one in her hand and has wiped my chin. Then she starts dabbing the drip on my blouse, making a stain that was quite small rather large.

'No point crying over spilt yoghurt,' she says cheerfully. 'Anyway, I've ironed your blue blouse with the little flowers and it suits you much better than this one.'

I shake my head in disbelief, suddenly reminded of all those odd-couple sitcoms that used to be on TV. They often lived in houses like this too — big Edwardian semis with huge windows and spacious rooms. I always thought they were completely unrealistic — no one could ever live like that — and yet here I am. Patty leaves the kitchen and returns with a blouse that is ironed far better than I could have done. This situation might be ridiculous but it has its upsides.

I've moved into Patty's while I find somewhere of my own. Last year I had to sell the family home when my ex-husband upped and ran off with a caterer, so I rented a little starter home to begin with. Then, just before Christmas and with very little notice, my landlord decided he wanted it back, which meant I would have been homeless if it hadn't been for Patty. Well, not exactly; there was always the unthinkable option of moving back in with my parents for a while, but Patty suggested we become roomies (although at the time I hadn't realised that would mean she would be in my room *all* the time) and I agreed. It wasn't a hard choice, as she and I joked when we agreed to give it a trial run; I'm allowed to bring boys back for the night here. Not that there is a boy to bring home — not yet anyway.

But there could be. Just as I was moving out of my old place, I finally met one of my neighbours, Michael. Practically running over his cat was not the best of introductions, but the cat was fine and he seems to be a really nice guy. I took the plunge and invited him to Patty's New Year party; astonishingly, he survived meeting all my friends and left promising to call me. That was two days ago.

'Come on, get your coat,' Patty is saying as I tune back in. She's also dressed to go out, which puzzles me.

'Where are you going?' I ask.

'With you. I'm heading into the office to do some of my own paperwork.'

She stands behind me holding out my coat while I slip both arms in, then she spins me round and starts buttoning it up until I come to my senses and bat her off.

'The first week after New Year is always really busy, Patty,' I tell her. 'I don't think there'll be space for you to work or anyone to help you.'

'Oh, you won't even know I'm there. I'll just sit in my office and get on with stuff.'

'You don't have an office,' I remind her sternly. As much as I love Patty, she does have a tendency to distract everyone and this is genuinely one of the busiest weeks in the travel industry. 'This is *my* place of work — not yours.'

'Semantics,' she says with a dismissive wave of the hand. 'Now, are you going to get in the car or not?'

During the drive to work, Patty gets a call from Jack, the ship's doctor she met on a cruise last year. Her face lights up when his name appears and she has to tell him that I'm in the car with her so no dirty talk. That's a relief as Patty's version of pillow talk would have made Hugh Hefner blush. I smile as I listen to them laughing together and think about the bizarre circumstances of their meeting. Patty is the lead singer in an eighties tribute act and is so good that she was asked to join the entertainment crew of a cruise we went on. While compèring a Rick Astley covers show called Rock Astley, she was trampled by some hardcore fans — Rick-Rollers as they like to call themselves — and in her words '*ended up under the doctor all week*'. Why Patty and I can't meet men under normal circumstances, I'll never know.

Jack is telling Patty that his rota means that he'll be at sea until summer but home for some shore leave after that.

'Oh, I hope I'll be joining you before summer,' says Patty.

'So there's no news yet?' asks Jack, to which Patty says no but she should hear soon.

Patty has applied to join the entertainment crew and has said that she'll take any length of assignment as long as she's on Jack's ship. As much as we wind each other up, I'll certainly miss her if she goes.

She continues to chat, asking Jack whether the purser recovered from his laryngitis. It's strange because although I've done some amazing things in the past year, I can't help but feel a little left out as she chats away to Jack about cruise liner details I'm not involved in. I'm delighted for Patty — both that she has this new singing career and that she's found the man of her dreams — but it feels like my best friend has another life now, one that I'm not really part of. We've been together for so long and through so much — the death of her husband and the infidelity of mine — that it's strange to have this other person making her happy and knowing her secrets. That was always my job. The call finishes with kisses blown and promises to keep the bunk warm.

'I can't wait to meet him properly,' I say, deciding that I'll make a real effort to get to know this man who makes my best friend smile.

'You could bring Michael and we'll have a foursome — it'll be a laugh,' she says.

My first thought is that it won't be as much of a laugh as it would have been with just us girls, but I can't think like that now so I bury the thought and just smile and nod.

'If he ever calls me,' I add with a shrug.

'This is the twenty-first century, you know.' That was Patty's schoolmarm voice. If she wore glasses she'd be looking over them and giving me a hard stare. 'You are allowed to call him.'

'I know, I know. It's just that I don't know if he wants me to call or if there's a protocol about these things — how many days should I wait? Do I invite him somewhere? I invited him to the New Year party so you'd think it would be his turn to do the asking.'

'You really overthink things — have I ever told you that?' says Patty, pulling up into a parking space.

'Once or twice.'

We park and Patty pulls down the vanity mirror, applies lipstick and declares herself gorgeous. Then like two cowboys in a one-horse town we stride side by side towards the still-empty high street, where the Mercury Travel Agency sits. It will be buzzing soon as we live in one of the few places where small independent shops still thrive. Across the street the florist already has blooms out on the pavement and the coffee shop has its regulars streaming out with their eco-friendly takeaway cups. I recognise some of the customers as we're always here at the same time most days. I get a buzz out of waving hello to them and really feel that I belong here. Through the windows of the agency I can see that my co-owner Charlie is already there changing some of the posters. He spots us and sticks his tongue out comically; I return the gesture and laugh.

Although it's been months since I used some of my divorce settlement to become a partner in this fabulous business, my heart still leaps when I think about the place. It hasn't just been a business to me, it's been a lifesaver, and we've made so many people deliriously happy. And here we are, at the start of a new year of travel and excitement. I can feel little tears of joy starting to form when Patty grabs me by the shoulders.

'Are you ready for this, Bo?' she asks. Bo-Peep is the nickname she gave me over thirty years ago when she found out my name was A. Shepherd.

'I most certainly am. Come on, let's make some memories.'

CHAPTER TWO: DANCING QUEENS

Charlie greets us with a double hug when we walk through the door.

'The terrible twins! The Ant and Dec of the travel industry! Welcome back to work!'

'Which one is Ant?' I ask.

'Definitely you,' says Patty, placing her hand coquettishly under her chin. 'I'm the little cute one.'

'Anyway, we were always Cagney and Lacey.'

'And I was the cute one of them too,' Patty whispers to Charlie as we take our coats off.

'I'm not even sure which one that was,' Charlie says. 'Anyway, to what do we owe the pleasure of your company today, Patty-licious? At a loose end?'

'Of course not,' she says haughtily. 'I'm going to do some setlist planning for my next assignment — just in case it comes through quickly. I thought I might as well do it here. I need to catch up with Sheila, Kath and Frankie to see how they've been coping without me. It must have been hard on them.'

I snort, getting a very sharp look from the diva in the room. Sheila and Kath are part of the comedy cover band the Granny-Okies. We met them at a karaoke night and somehow

Sheila, Kath and Patty went on to make a career of it. They've played several gigs together, including the cruise ships, and I have to admit that they're really very funny. Everyone has a brilliant night out when they're around. They're managed by Frankie, an ex-airline steward who now books bands for concerts and festivals; he also happens to be an old friend of Patty's, so he has no choice but book her for any open slots.

Patty heads out to the break room, where I've no doubt her first point of call will be the biscuit tin. Charlie is obviously thinking exactly the same. 'She's going to be disappointed back there — I haven't filled the tin, so there's not even a soggy rich tea to go at.'

Sure enough, she's straight back and putting her coat on.

'Don't know how I'm supposed to keep my energy up without any sustenance in the place. I really don't know how you two cope without me.'

With that, she heads out the door and disappears into the convenience shop across the road. I use the moment of peace to talk business.

'Have we had many enquiries over the break?'

Charlie nods, taking me over to his desktop.

I look at the Mercury Travel inbox and see it's absolutely chock-a-block; I clap my hands together in delight.

Last year we launched the Mercury Travel Club, aimed at creating a loyal base of customers for the business — after all, it's pretty tough working in travel and online aggregators can always undercut us on prices. We developed something a bit different, producing a calendar of events and trips that brought people together for an adventure. After my divorce we realised that all of us working for the agency were single. None of us particularly fancied singles trips — we wanted more of an amiable, inclusive group where you could travel with local people who would then become friends. So we book holidays for people, but then we might also go to a local wine bar together and get to know them better. It's the antithesis of internet booking and it seems to have worked for us so far. One of us occasionally travels with the group to ensure everyone has a good time — and to make sure we all get some pleasure from working in the industry. Today, our assistant manager Josie flies out to Finland to go dogsledding with a group of people who seem okay with the idea of minus thirty degrees.

Just before Christmas we advertised trips for the first half of the year and that's what people seem to have responded to. Charlie and I sit down at our desks and begin to look through the emails, ready to convert these enquiries into sales. First and foremost we have to process all the final payments and passport details for our February trip to Athens to celebrate Aphrodite, the goddess of love (and prostitutes, apparently). This trip was one of the first ideas I had when dreaming up the Mercury calendar all those months ago and now the reality is but a few weeks away. I get a little shiver down my spine as I complete the passenger manifests, knowing that I made it happen — with the help of Charlie, of course.

'You're smiling to yourself,' he says to me.

'I'm just remembering when we first put together that scrapbook.'

If I really think about it, I'd have to admit that it was probably the most ridiculous business plan ever developed — a scrapbook with *The Mercury Travel Club* blazoned across the front and a picture of a destination for each month of the year. Alongside the actual holiday, there'd be a local business idea to involve the community. So, just before the Athens trip, everyone booked will be getting together at the local Greek restaurant to get to know each other. We've also had trips to ghostly castles — reading Wilkie Collins for the book club — and a Monaco trip for the classic car enthusiasts.

'How much has changed since then,' Charlie observes.

I know what he's thinking; his partner Peter works in finance and before they got together, Peter offered to look through our plan/scrapbook. He gave us the thumbs-up, we put our heart and souls into making it a reality, won a People's Champion Award for our efforts and, of course, Charlie and Peter became inseparable.

'Well, not everything has changed,' I say as Patty comes barging through the door with her arms full of packets of biscuits.

'Are we expecting a coach trip on a rest stop?' asks Charlie as she offloads them all onto my desk.

'They were buy one, get one free,' Patty explains. 'These supermarkets know what they're doing don't they? It's January, so everyone's on a diet but after a full day of self-denial they're now completely fed up with it, so what happens? They saunter into a shop, pretending they're there for a lettuce or something, and bingo — they see this bounty on the ends of the aisles. I mean, who can resist? They've even got these ones that are advertised as low fat — if you restrict yourself to two, but who does that? Anyway, we now have supplies, so who'd like a cuppa?'

We put our orders in, mainly to avoid a further rant about biscuit offers, and within ten minutes she's back with a tray of hot drinks and a plate of the aforementioned confections. Ignoring the fact that Charlie and I are heads down, deep in work, Patty pulls up a chair at Josie's empty desk and takes out her phone.

Mornings are when we get all of the admin done as customers tend to drift in over lunchtime and into the afternoon. As much as I enjoy talking to people about their dream holidays, I find these few hours really satisfying knowing that all of the loose ends are tied up and that the holiday will be as stress-free as we can possibly make it. I take care over the important details — how much luggage people can take, what visas are needed or jabs are recommended, which trips are better booked while they're still in the UK and which phrases they should learn in the local language. I like to send customers a little link to videos teaching them how to pronounce simple things like please and thank you. Some of our customers even get together to do language courses, which I think is really lovely. So yes, this is my quiet time — or it would be on any other day.

Patty has her earbuds in but she's nodding away to a tune and mouthing the lyrics. I'm dying to know what it is but have to focus, so I shift my screen just a smidgeon so I can't see her. I manage a few moments of concentration but then the track obviously changes and her nodding turns into dancing; within moments she's doing the hand movements that are only associated with one song — Madonna's 'Vogue'. From the corner of my eye I can tell that Charlie has spotted her too and he's trying to keep a straight face. I know it won't work as he's an absolute superfan when it comes to her royal Madgeness, and before I can say anything he's up and over at Patty's desk. She whips her earbuds out and turns up the volume, filling the shop with the chorus while Charlie attempts unsuccessfully to synchronise the dance moves with her.

'You've got it wrong,' Charlie shouts above the song. 'It's hand out, out, cross, cross, side, side, round the head and round the body.'

He does each move as he calls it out over and over again. A customer comes in and stands transfixed before eventually succumbing to the inevitable and joining in. Then Patty begins to get it right and I think, *Well, if you can't beat 'em, join 'em*. I get up and fall into rhythm, enjoying the little livener. It disintegrates into a freestyle dance-off when the chorus finishes and by the end of the song, we're all exhausted.

'Well, I wasn't expecting that,' says the customer, collapsing on a chair. I bring both of us over a cup of water. 'It has to count towards today's step count though doesn't it?'

'It beats Zumba any day,' I reply. 'Someone should invent Madonna-robics.'

For a millisecond Patty looks up, the idea apparently flashing through her head, but just as quickly she scrunches up her nose and shakes it away. There's no way she'd actually commit to an idea that involves ongoing exercise.

My customer has come in to enquire about our September trip to Seville, where we're going to try Flamenco.

'You obviously enjoy dancing,' I say. She was certainly better than the rest of us at it.

'I really do,' she says. 'But since my divorce, it's so difficult to find others who do. I'm hoping to meet people on the trip.'

I smile and tell her I'm sure she will. I don't matchmake on our trips but they are full of like-minded people and I get a frisson of excitement when I see two of them getting together. I really hope it happens for this lady. I remind her that everyone going on the trip is meeting up beforehand at a tapas bar and wave her goodbye.

'So is "Vogue" on the new setlist?' asks Charlie. 'I would love to see the Granny-Okies doing that but what would be the angle?'

'Well, technically Madonna is older than all of us,' Patty says. 'So there has to be an angle there — maybe one of us could say that we're too young to do Madonna songs.'

'And there's the conical bra — you could do something with that,' I add, getting a laugh from both my friends.

'You could wear one on your chest and one on your head,' says Charlie.

'We'd look ridiculous,' says Patty with a grin. 'And heaven knows we wouldn't want that, would we?'

Charlie and I join in with a giggle, then Patty picks up her phone and dials a number.

'Frankie!' she calls out to an answerphone. 'It's your favourite act here — call me when you get this. I want you to organise a warm-up tour.'

CHAPTER THREE: AS TIME GOES BY

Lunchtime is as busy as we anticipated and we don't stop, but the buzz of sending customers away with smiles on their faces sustains us until just after two, when we finally get some breathing space. Patty has been worth her weight in gold during this rush. When Charlie and I have been occupied with one customer, she has sat and talked to others about where they're hoping to go and generally kept them entertained. She's been gushing over their holiday plans and telling them *she* wishes *she* was going there, so that by the time the customer gets to booking something with me or my partner, they've been nicely warmed up and the sale goes much smoother.

'We should hire you,' Charlie tells her as he accepts a coffee. That's the other reason she's been a godsend — endless hot drinks delivered to the desk.

'I doubt you could afford me,' she says with a coquettish flick of the hair.

The phone rings with Josie telling us that everyone for the Finland trip arrived at the airport and they're just getting ready to board.

'Can you even imagine how cold it's going to be?' she says.

'I'm trying not to.' I unconsciously rub my arms warm even though it's toasty in here.

'I can't anticipate what it's going to feel like. I mean, I've seen movies with deep snow, but they say there's gonna be at least two feet of the stuff.'

Josie is Australian by birth and came over here in search of love and adventure. She found both after snagging Matt at a speed dating event we went to last year. Inevitably I came away empty-handed. I tell her to enjoy it and to send lots of pictures. A big part of our success is our social media posts, and being practically half my age, Josie is the best at them.

Charlie looks up as I end the call so I tell him that all is okay with the Finland trip. We decide that now is as good a time as any to have a lunch break, and before the words are out of our mouths, Patty has her coat on and is out the door. She returns with a selection of sandwiches, crisps and chocolates, which after that morning's biscuit binge really isn't ideal for so early in January.

'Are you deliberately rebelling against the healthy-eating brigade or something?' I ask, tucking into a crusty ploughman's roll, which is absolutely delicious.

'There is more than one way to health,' she tells me, wagging her finger. 'You get serotonin from chocolate and serotonin makes you happy. Happiness is good for the soul, ergo chocolate is actually a healthy food.'

'I'll drink to that,' says Charlie, raising his coffee mug, 'but I really do need to shape up a bit. Peter works out all the time — he even went for a run on Christmas Day and I don't want to risk losing him to some Olympian.'

'I don't think that would ever happen, and besides, running on Christmas Day is just not normal,' Patty says. 'You should have tied his laces together and told him to get back into bed. Morning delight is the very best way to start the day. That's how Jack and I exercise.'

'*Waaay* too much information,' says Charlie. 'Nope, I'm thinking of signing up for one of those January challenges — you know, run a hundred miles or do a hundred press-ups for charity, that kind of thing. I know I've already missed the beginning of the month but would you sponsor me if I started soon?'

I tell him I will as long as he doesn't try and make me take part too. I really don't like starting things in January (and very much doubt Charlie will start anything now). I think they're doomed to failure as it's such a long, miserable month. Why would anyone deny themselves pleasure when it's consistently cold and dark? I start any resolutions in February, which is usually three days shorter and means that I nicely avoid even having to contemplate Dry January. I shudder at the thought of coping with Patty without a glass of wine in my hand.

The lunch things are tidied away as a customer comes into the shop to discuss a surprise getaway for his anniversary and Charlie leaps at the chance to talk romance. It's far more his bag than mine. I'm about to use this moment of calm to call one of our hotel chain partners when an ear-piercing screech and the window-rattling crash of the front door sends our romantic customer cowering behind Charlie while Patty and me duck under the desks.

'ANNNNGGGGIE, you have to see this!'

I decide to take one for the team and raise my head above the parapet — well, I raise one eyebrow first, but on seeing it's only my mother in full meltdown mode, I declare the territory safe and one by one the whole shop slides out from their hiding places like a scene from an action movie. If Private Benjamin had emerged from the stationery cupboard in full combats I wouldn't have been surprised.

'Mum,' I say when my heart rate returns to normal, 'what on earth is the matter? I thought we were being raided.'

'Why on earth would anyone raid you?' Mum asks, plonking herself down on the chair opposite. 'What's here to steal?'

'We have an almighty stock of half-price biscuits,' says Charlie. 'Your daughter and her friend have them stashed but won't give away the hiding place even under torture.'

Patty and I turn in unison and tut at his crazy scenario — neither of us could ever withstand torture.

'Sometimes, I swear you two are like those twins from *The Shining*,' he says and gets back to his customer.

'Morning, Mrs Shepherd — what's got you so excited on this January afternoon?' Patty pulls up a chair beside us.

'And whatever it is,' I say, 'can this crucial news possibly wait until the travel agency closes? We'll probably have more customers in soon.'

'Absolutely not.' Mum adds that any customer would want to hear what she has to say. I shrug. There's no point resisting when she's in this mood.

'Go on then,' I say with a sigh. 'What's happened?'

'I'm going to die,' she says, placing her phone in front of me, but the screen is blank.

'What's your pin code?' I pick it up.

'1234 — it came with that and I thought it was very easy to remember.'

'Mmm.' Typing the number in, I get a screen showing a gravestone. 'What's this?'

'It's called a death clock,' Mum replies. 'Jackie was telling me all about it when I had my roots done. You put in information and it tells you when you're going to die.'

Jackie has been Mum's hairdresser for an eternity and Mum visits her every month without fail even if it doesn't need doing. There are definitely weeks when I swear Jackie just makes scissor sounds behind Mum's head as you really cannot tell the difference.

'Jackie put in all my details and look — I've only got four thousand days left!'

I've never heard of this website before but it seems pretty grim. You enter your age and some health details and it basically calculates when you're going to pop your clogs. Patty takes it out of my hands and reads the information.

'But you're going to live until you're ninety,' she says to Mum. 'That's not a bad innings.'

'I want to get to one hundred.' Mum looks annoyed rather than distressed. 'Tell the website it's wrong.'

'Don't think it quite works like that,' I say. 'It's just making a guess anyway — based on general statistics. They can't possibly take into account your robust constitution.'

Patty is typing in her own information.

'Woohoo,' she says. 'I beat you — I'm making it to ninety-four. But I've only got twelve thousand days left, that's no time at all. Blimey, if I have four bottles of wine a week, how many do I have left in my lifetime?'

'Nearly seven thousand,' pipes up the customer from the other side of the room. 'Which sounds far too much for one person.'

'Oh I never get a bottle to myself,' swipes Patty, adding in a loud comical whisper, 'Angie always takes more than her fair share.'

I snatch the phone from her. Patty's result has a helpful clock counting down the time she has left on earth. I toggle back to where you input the information, snort and start typing.

'What are you doing?' asks Patty.

'Putting in your real information,' I tell her. 'You've said you have a BMI of less than twenty-five and never drink? Let's see what happens when we tell the truth . . .'

I finish typing, look up at her with raised eyebrows then stand and pick up my coat.

'Where are you going?' asks Patty.

'I'm going to need a black dress sooner than we thought,' I tell her, then can't hold back the giggle. I sit back down and tell both her and Mum to ignore this website as it's only a bit of fun.

'What did it say with . . . you know, more *up-to-date* information?' ventures Patty.

'Up-to-date? Do you mean accurate? I've put in those four bottles a week you mentioned instead of your original "teetotal" answer. And I'm not telling you — suffice to say it estimated that you wouldn't make it to ninety.'

'Wow,' she says. 'So less time than I've already had? I suppose that's obvious really but it's a bit shocking to see it in black and white. I need to get on with life, don't I?'

'We both do,' pipes up Mum. 'We need one of those bucket list things and we need to get on with them quickly.'

'Good idea — Angie could book us one of those trips to go swimming with dolphins,' says Patty.

'I can't think of anything worse,' says Mum, as I guessed she would. 'And why would dolphins want to swim with us?'

'They're supposed to be very intelligent creatures and they like human interaction,' Patty tells her, sounding like an authority on the subject.

'If they were that intelligent then they'd organise a petition and stop people bloomin' swimming with them,' replies Mum. 'We're intelligent creatures and we like interaction — how would we feel if a bunch of crocodiles suddenly turned up to go swimming with us?'

The dolphin debate is becoming ridiculously heated considering how, well, ridiculous it actually is. I raise my palms to signal them to calm down.

'Okay, no swimming with dolphins,' I say. 'Mum, if you decide there is something that you'd like to do then let me know and I'll try to book it for you, although I have to say that you both have more adventures than most people I know.'

Mum looks placated and tells me that she's going home to think about the rest of her life.

'No matter how short it's going to be,' she adds with dramatic mournfulness.

She leaves the shop at the same time as Charlie's customer, who despite all of the interruptions has settled on a stunning resort in St Lucia for his romantic retreat.

Now that the three of us are alone, Charlie and I cannot resist doing our own death forecasts and are delighted that we'll both outlive Patty. While we laugh and joke about creating the Mercury Nursing Home, Patty is actually silent for a moment and you can hear the cogs whirring. That's never a good sign.

'What are you thinking?' I ask, hoping that our jest hasn't upset her.

'About those numbers.'

'I've told you, don't take them seriously — you'll still be on stage way after we're gone.'

'No, I was just calculating — if I stop drinking and go on a diet to reduce my BMI I get a couple more years, don't I?' says Patty.

I nod at her.

'Two or three years,' she says contemplatively, 'and they'll probably be bedbound with someone feeding me blended food. Not really worth the sacrifice, is it? Better to go out with a bang — shall I stop off and pick up a curry and some wine for tonight?'

CHAPTER FOUR: WRAPPED UP IN BOOKS

It's book club night and I'm looking forward to seeing the group again. Joining them was one of my first attempts at rebuilding my life last year, and although Patty scoffed that book clubs were for older people, this group is fun and we've had some great times together. Even though it's held in a pub, Patty has no interest in coming along, so I pop on my coat and make my way to the Rose and Crown. It's a cool dark night and the fresh air is invigorating. Our first week back at work has been tremendous and we've been inundated with bookings, but I've hardly had time to look up. Happily, after the first day, my mother hasn't been back and I haven't heard from her either. I get a pang of guilt, hoping that she's not feeling too down, and decide that I'll pop over and see Mum and Dad at the weekend. But right now, this is my time.

The pub is quiet when I get there, probably the result of people doing Dry January. Although I feel yet more guilt for not ordering something alcoholic with potentially more profit for the licensee, I really don't want alcohol so order crisps and dry roasted nuts with my tonic water. I didn't want the snacks either but at least I feel I've made a decent contribution to the coffers.

'She brings food,' exclaims Ed as I plonk my purchases down. 'Excellent antidote to all the salad I've endured for the past couple of days. Why do we do it?'

'Because we've overindulged right through December?' suggests a new member I haven't met before. 'I know I have.'

She introduces herself as Sarah, and as I take a seat we all welcome her and give our names.

'I think it's just about retaking control,' says Caroline. 'Deep down, none of us want to be unhealthy — we want to be well and this is a core value for us. When we've a sustained period of overindulgence, we're acting against our own values and our subconscious doesn't like that so we try to get back to acting in the direction that we actually want to go.'

Caroline has trained to be a life coach and has been very supportive to me, but her words now just leave the table in a stunned silence.

'Or it could be that we just can't fasten our trousers anymore,' says Peter, getting a gentle laugh from the group.

Peter is Charlie's other half and there couldn't be a more loving, gorgeous couple in the world. They're perfect for each other and I'm delighted to have played a role in getting them together on one of the Mercury trips. In fact, I've been the matchmaker to everyone here. Caroline and Ed have started seeing each other too and although it's very new, they seem well suited. Caroline wasn't sure about getting together with him after my own failed relationship with Ed, but I could see that they would be happy so encouraged her right from the start. I wish I were as good at sorting out my own love life.

'Shall we start?' asks Ed, and we're all keen to start talking books.

We aren't discussing a particular book today; instead, we're putting together a list of titles to read over the first half of the year. We have diverse tastes, so it isn't always easy picking something that everyone might enjoy. We often choose the classics because most people know the story but haven't actually read the book. Over December we read the Dickens classic *A Christmas Carol*, which I must have seen a thousand times but never read. While I kept imagining Alastair Sim as Scrooge, Peter told me that he had the muppet version in his head!

'I know I'm new,' says Sarah with a little trepidation, 'but do you mind if I make a suggestion?'

Everyone instantly says 'of course, please do' — although there's a definite edge of unease as we have no idea what genre she enjoys. I'm mentally practising a positive facial reaction just in case she picks something I hate. Which is exactly what she does.

'There's a book called *Only Love Can Hurt Like This*,' she says. I note our group taking discreet glances at each other. 'It's about finding love after losing it,' adds Sarah. 'Although it may be a bit of a weepie.'

Ed clears his throat. 'I'm sure it's good but I probably wouldn't enjoy something too sad, if that's okay with you. Do you have any other ideas?'

I can almost feel the collective sigh of relief as Sarah nods her understanding.

'I do have a more uplifting idea,' she says. 'There's a book I've been planning to read for ages, about a couple who hit rock bottom and find their way by walking the South West coastal path.'

'I know that one and it's always among the bestsellers in my bookshop. It's called *The Salt Path*,' says Caroline. 'It's by Raynor Winn and I've heard fabulous things about it.'

I've relaxed a little now I know for sure it isn't sci-fi, but I have to say, a book about walking doesn't really float my boat any more than a weepie. It sounds a bit dull but I hold my piece, waiting for the others' reactions.

'They just walk? For the whole book?' asks Ed, echoing my thoughts again. 'That wouldn't normally appeal but if you think it's worthwhile then I'm happy to give it a go.'

'Charlie will be terrified if he sees me reading about a long-distance walk,' says Peter, laughing. 'He'll think I'm going to be inspired and drag him out to buy hiking boots.'

'You'll definitely have to pretend you are,' I say. 'I can just imagine him panicking because none of the walking gear flatters his colouring.'

'Worth reading for that alone,' says Peter. 'Okay — it's a thumbs up from me.'

And so I add my vote and it goes on the list.

'Did anyone get any good books for Christmas?' I ask. 'There might be one that a few of us got or we all want to read. I got *Demon Copperhead*, which I can't wait to start reading.'

'Hmm,' says Sarah. 'I'm not sure I fancy that. I know it's won awards but that's not always a sign that it's good, is it?'

I frown at her and am about to say that, actually, it is usually a sign that it's good, but around me I notice a muted murmur of agreement, suggesting that Barbara Kingsolver isn't going to make it onto our list. Although I love her writing, I already know that Ed is far more of a murder-mystery buff, Peter is a fan of historical fiction and Caroline enjoys romance. However, in the spirit of the club, I'm still sure that it would have been at least considered without Sarah's comment.

'We should pick something to tie in with another trip for later in the year,' says Caroline, moving the conversation on and obviously trying to throw me a bone after my idea has been rejected.

'Angie runs a travel agency,' Ed explains to Sarah. 'And last year we picked a couple of books linked to a location and we all went on a trip there for the actual meeting. It was great fun, so we've decided that we'll do two a year and the first is at the end of the month.'

Sarah gives a quiet nod but says no more.

'We try to support each other's businesses,' I add. 'We buy our books from Caroline too. What do you do?'

'I run a tea shop not far from the canal,' she says. 'It's just a small place but you'd all be welcome and I'm sure we could do you a discount on the cakes.'

That gets a far more hearty response than any book is likely to tonight.

'Sounds wonderful, and we should definitely hold one of our meetings there if you want us to,' says Caroline. 'But there's no need for a discount — we're all small-business owners and we know how tough it can be.'

'Then I'll just give you all bigger slices,' Sarah says with a smile. She raises her glass and we clink a toast. I think our new member might fit in rather well.

Ed picks up the thread of travel again and I realise he's been determined to get one of his choices onto the list. There's an obvious theme as he suggests several Dan Browns and Umberto Eco's *The Name of the Rose*.

'I'm guessing you're after a trip to Italy,' I say, to which he holds his palms up.

'*Mea culpa.*'

'I like the idea of Rome but I find Umberto Eco's writing style really difficult to read and I've finished all of the Robert Langdon series so I'd like something different,' says Peter.

'And does it have to be a thriller?' I ask, knowing this genre is Ed's passion. 'After all, we're already reading a dark crime for the Lake District trip.'

'Okay,' sighs Ed. 'If the group is keen on Rome then I'll research something other than crime and come back to everyone later.'

He gets a nod of thanks from everyone and we move back to our list, putting on Caroline's choice — a romantic comedy — and a historical fiction novel about the burning of the Pendle witches for Peter.

'That's quite a range for the start of the year,' says Sarah. 'I wouldn't have chosen any of your books myself, so I'm really looking forward to them.'

I know everyone's taste in books, so the only real surprise for me is Sarah's choice. I'm not sure when I'm going to get the chance to enjoy my beloved *Demon Copperhead* with all these others to read — I'll probably have to get the audiobooks and listen in the car.

Having completed our task, we order another round of drinks and conversation turns to finding out more about Sarah.

'Are you married?' asks Caroline.

'No, not anymore. My husband and I divorced last year,' she replies. 'I decided I needed to get out and about more — hence coming here.'

I empathise immediately and explain that I was in the same boat not long ago.

'It's hard, isn't it?' she says, and I nod. It really is.

'But no matter how it feels now,' I tell her, 'it does get better.'

'In fact, Angie bagged herself a new man in time for New Year,' Peter tells her and I feel myself blush.

'Not entirely true,' I say.

'He stalked her for a year doing her garden,' he continues. 'Imagine having Monty Don hiding in your bush.'

I give him a slap on the thigh as the others laugh at his innuendo.

'He's just a friend,' I tell everyone, protecting myself in case I never hear from him.

'Well, you're welcome to bring him to the café,' says Sarah.

I think that might actually be a good suggestion if I ever do speak to Michael. After all, supporting a new friend's business seems a harmless enough 'date'.

As the evening draws to a close, I swap numbers with Sarah so I can put her on our WhatsApp group, then I give each of my old friends and my new one a kiss on the cheek and head home. I walk slowly and find Michael's contact details on my phone. But although it's illogical as he's probably still up, it's late, and there's always that thought at the back of my head that a phone call late at night means bad news. I think I got that irrational fear from my mother — alongside the many superstitions she drilled into me, like saluting magpies and throwing salt over my shoulder if I ever spilt any. And even though I get really annoyed with myself for having to clean up even more salt from the floor, I can't stop doing it. My mother has a lot to answer for.

I put my phone away but promise myself that I won't let it go a full week before I call Michael; deep down, I hope that he calls me first. I've realised that I'm not great at reading romantic signals and I'm scared of making that call and him not actually remembering who I am. I close my eyes tightly then tilt my head to the sky, and on the first star I see, I whisper the rhyme I used to say as a child, 'Star light, star bright, grant me a wish tonight — let Michael call me.'

I laugh out loud at my own ridiculousness and check to see if anyone has been watching. Fortunately I have been allowed a solitary moment of madness. I look back up at the star and it seems to twinkle back at me as if saying, *Are you five or fifty? It's your love life — you sort it out!*

I reach Patty's house and before I've even put the key in the door, it swings open and she's standing there, looking jubilant. I can hear music blasting from the living room behind her. It's Cher's 'If I Could Turn Back Time'.

'Are you having a party?' I ask as she ushers me in, pulling the coat from my back.

'We both are,' she says with a huge grin. 'The Granny-Okies got the cruise gig!'

CHAPTER FIVE: LET'S GET PHYSICAL

On Saturday evening we're out with Charlie and Peter to celebrate a successful first week back at work and Patty's triumphant return to the stage. As well as being a great time for bookings it's been an interesting week with other minor victories, including the refill of the biscuit tin and my mother not re-enacting the scene from some great Shakespearean tragedy on dying young. Ninety years young. Although I very much doubt that the Grim Reaper will have the courage to take her, even at that age, I can't help but picture the scene.

'It's your turn,' says the towering black-cloaked figure tapping my mother on the shoulder with his scythe.

'It's bloomin' well not. Go pick on someone your own size. And stop poking that thing at people, you'll have their eyes out.'

I'm brought back to the moment with a toast led by Patty.

'To a new year of Mercury Travel, which if this week is anything to go by, will be another year of fun and frolics,' she says, clinking her wine glass against each of ours.

'And to your return to the high seas,' adds Charlie. 'We'll be selling plenty of cruise tickets now.'

'So sales went well all week?' asks Peter.

'They did,' I say. 'And Josie seems to be having a fabulous time out in Finland. She's sent a video of the snow around the hotel and sounds completely giddy with excitement. It does look beautiful.'

'And our February trip is sold out completely,' adds Charlie. 'We'll have a full complement of Mercurians accompanying us on our romantic trip to Greece.' He leans across and kisses Peter.

'Don't you mean they'll have to put up with you two smooching for the whole holiday?' I get poked in the arm with a breadstick.

We're in a local Italian, the same place that Ed and I came to last year. It was my first attempt at dating after the divorce and it was going well until we went back to my place. I'd managed to put that excruciatingly embarrassing memory to the very back of my mind until I walked in here and the whole debacle was triggered by the sight of the red-checked tablecloths. Thankfully, no one else mentions it, so I simply put that memory back in the archives, hoping one day I'll laugh at it.

The waiter appears at the table and we all flick through the menu as if we don't come here all the time and we don't already know exactly what we want.

'I'll have the sea bass,' says Peter and I order the same. I love my pasta but after all the bread and biscuits this week, I'm not sure I can face any more carbs. It doesn't seem to be bothering Charlie or Patty, who both opt for pizzas.

'As good as that looks,' I say when the food arrives, 'I'm not sure I'd have anywhere to put it after the buy-one-get-one-free biscuit frenzy we've been having all week.'

'Oh, Charlie is building a little bunker to keep his in,' says Peter, patting Charlie's rounded tummy. It's said affectionately but I know that no one likes to have a bit of extra weight pointed out in public and I spot Charlie flinching and doing a double-take of the Prosciutto Funghi Feast in front of him.

'Wouldn't that be the best thing ever invented?' says Patty, who is still high as a kite and suffering no guilt whatsoever about her food choices today. 'To be able to just tuck away all the impact of food you shouldn't really eat in a little separate bunker? Rather than getting fat, the bunker would just get bigger.'

'It could be like a wheelie suitcase that you drag around with you,' Peter adds. 'Your body stays slim but you move from a carry-on to an excess baggage warning.'

Again, he's joking and so is Patty but Charlie is beginning to look uncomfortable. He picks at the topping of his pizza but leaves the crust — and I know he loves a crust.

'I think you might have been right,' he says to me. 'That was a bit much. But this is my last hooray — the fitness regime starts tomorrow.'

'Really? I might join you — what are you thinking?' I ask.

A discussion about the pros and cons of various exercise options ensues.

1. Running — easy to get started but too hard on the knees and exhausting

2. Swimming — better for the knees but boring and you have to get into a swimming costume before you've lost all the flab — which seems to miss the point of exercise

3. Weights — too many testosterone-fuelled Schwarzeneggers mocking your puny efforts to lift 2 kg

4. Squash — way too fast and it really hurts if the ball hits you

That last point was made by me remembering my one and only attempt at the game with my ex-husband. As I now know he was in the full throes of an affair when we played, I do wonder whether he did it on purpose.

'The key to exercise is consistency,' says Peter with a lean person's complacency. 'If you don't enjoy it, you won't keep it up and you'll get nowhere. Don't do what other people do or what some social media post says is "guaranteed" to lose the flab — just do any activity that you enjoy and do it regularly.'

It's very rare that a serious point is made during any conversation between Charlie, Patty and I, so we're struck dumb for a few moments.

'So what do you enjoy?' asks Peter to his stunned audience.

'Food,' replies Patty, finishing every inch of her pizza.

'You did that military fitness last year,' I remind her. 'To get fit for being on stage, remember. Could we not all go to that?'

'Oh, he was good,' says Patty. 'Shouted a lot but you couldn't get away with just hiding in the corner and breathing like I did when we tried yoga.'

'She fell asleep,' I tell the group.

'The instructor told us to relax,' Patty protests.

'And she snored,' I add.

The waiter takes our plates and asks if we want to see the dessert menu. Given the conversation we're having, it's only surprising to him that we all say no in unison.

'I could give military fitness a try,' says Charlie. 'Shall we book ourselves in?'

Peter and I immediately agree — and after a bit of coaxing, Patty does too.

'I know I have to get back in shape but he'll take one look at me and know I haven't kept up any of the exercise,' she says. 'I'll have to say I broke my leg or something.'

'Tell the truth,' I suggest. 'That you met someone and became more interested in lurve than lunges.'

She clinks my glass, smiling. 'And to be perfectly honest, I still am.'

* * *

Leaving the restaurant, we say our goodbyes to the boys and head home. Once inside we both get straight into our slouchies, make hot drinks — chocolate for her and camomile for me — then take up position in our usual spots: Patty stretched out on the sofa and me snuggled up on the big armchair. As I said, it's amazing how quickly you can get into a routine with someone.

'What do you think will be on your mum's bucket list?' asks Patty. She's flicking through videos of eighties and nineties bands on the TV, making notes as to which might make it onto the Granny-Okies setlist.

'I have no idea,' I answer truthfully. 'She's never been the shy and retiring type so I've always thought that she and Dad have done everything that they've wanted to. They've certainly seen the world and are still travelling.'

My parents often come on Mercury Travel trips and they've been to many of the big places people dream about, including the Grand Canyon, Niagara Falls and the pyramids. My mother described them respectively as 'big', 'wet' and 'sandy' in her postcards home. Even now, Mum will seek out a shop selling postcards, and getting one always makes me smile. It's such a lovely tradition and I think it's quite sad that it's died out. A WhatsApp selfie is just not the same.

'Maybe it's not going to be travel, maybe it'll be sword-swallowing or skydiving,' says Patty.

I shrug, unable to imagine Mum doing either of them but equally unable to think of anything else.

'One thing it won't be is a military fitness session,' I say. 'I really can't believe I agreed to join that.'

'You were supporting Charlie,' Patty says. 'He obviously wants to get in shape for Peter — that man has a seriously good body.'

'I wouldn't have thought you'd notice another man's body, as smitten as you are.'

'One can still admire a Porsche while driving a Rolls Royce,' replies Patty. 'Talking of which, any word from your Mini Cooper?'

I frown at her, puzzled.

'Michael — the mystery man,' she says. 'I couldn't think what car he'd be but Michael the Mini works until we know otherwise.'

She winks at me and I shake my head in despair.

'Call him now,' says Patty. 'Just say hello and see if he fancies coffee one day.'

'Well, there is a new place I've heard of recently, but I don't know — surely if he wanted to meet up wouldn't he have called me, to say he had a nice time at the party or ask how I've settled in? There are loads of reasons he could have called, but he hasn't.'

'So, call him and tell him he's rude for not calling.'

I promise that I will call but tell Patty that I'll give it another few days. She sighs at me and gets up, heading into the kitchen. When she returns she has a phone attached to her ear — my phone.

'It's ringing,' she says, handing it to me. Patty knows all my PIN numbers so breaking through security and finding Michael's number was as hard as accessing my mum's phone. My heart is pounding as I hear the ringtone and I'm mentally whizzing through tones of voice to use when it's answered. To my relief it's not picked up and I have to leave a message. I tell him that I've settled in at Patty's and if he fancies it, I'd love to meet for coffee one day. I'm about to hang up when I feel I have to say, 'Oh, it's Angie by the way — your old neighbour. The one you left gnomes for.'

I end the call and look up at Patty, who gives me a satisfied nod.

Within five minutes my phone rings and I see Michael's name light up. I show Patty before answering and she gives me the thumbs up then leaves the room as I say hello.

'I was so glad you called,' Michael says, and I hear genuine happiness in his voice. 'I didn't have your number. You had mine from the visit to the vet but you called me from there and so I had no record of yours.'

I rummage through my memory for the details of that day and realise that's all true — thank goodness Patty forced me to do this. Our conversation is very chirpy and we arrange to meet for coffee next weekend. I'm on a high as the call ends and dance up the stairs to Patty's room to tell her the news. Her door is shut but I think nothing of opening it and looking in. She's on the bed video-calling Jack, and as I walk in she jerks up as if she's been caught dirty-talking — which she probably has.

'Bit of privacy, if you don't mind,' she says to me, waving me out of the room.

I retreat, slightly wounded. I won't have my best friend here for much longer and, truth be told, I'm not really ready to share her yet.

CHAPTER SIX: THE BUCKET LIST

I've barely opened my eyes when I hear someone pressing the front door bell and calling out our names as if they're a contender in the annual town crier competition. I roll onto my back and lie for a moment in the vain hope that Patty will get up to answer the door. Not a sound. I might have guessed — she'll sleep through the last days of earth. Although, given how traumatic that would be, managing to dream your way through the apocalypse is probably a good option.

I fling my legs out of bed, push my feet into slippers and my arms into a robe then plod downstairs. Last night wasn't a particularly drunken one but we were late back and after such a busy start to the year, I could have done with a lie in. Maybe it's just a delivery and I can go back to bed soon. Reaching the door, I peer through the spyhole and groan. It's my mother looking rather too animated for this time of day — no lie-in today then.

'You took your time,' she says when I open the door. 'I was about to call the fire brigade in case you'd caught that monoxide thing and fallen into a coma.'

I sigh in despair but step aside and let her in.

'A more sensible possibility is that we were both having a lie-in on a Sunday morning as it's not even eight,' I reply grumpily.

She checks her watch and shrugs.

'I'm a bit fast, it's a minute past on my watch.'

We head to the kitchen and I get some fresh coffee beans out — a day that starts like this really does need an extra caffeine boost. I hold a cup up to her and she nods; the act of grinding the beans and inhaling the delicious aromas helps to wake me. I fill the cafetière and place it with cups and milk on the table.

'No breakfast?' says Mum.

'No,' I reply sternly. I do not want her to take up residency. 'Now, what is so urgent that you've disturbed my beauty sleep?'

'Sorry,' she says with a hint of mischief. 'And I know how much you need it.'

I give her a little punch on the arm and ask her again what's up.

'I've done my bucket list and wanted you to be the first to hear it,' she says.

At that moment a bleary-eyed Patty walks through the door.

'Good Lord, was that you? How can someone so small make so much noise?'

'You can talk,' replies my mother. 'About the noise bit, not the . . . small . . . bit.'

Her voice drifts off towards the end as Patty puts her hand on her hip and purses her lips at Mum.

'An early wake-up and insults — this had better be good,' says Patty.

'She's written her bucket list.' I can see that I've immediately got Patty's attention.

'Now this I have to see,' she says, going via the cupboard and pulling out a packet of croissants and a jar of jam. 'But it needs sustenance.'

'You said there wasn't anything,' Mum protests, looking accusingly at me.

'I was hoping to go back to bed if I didn't feed you,' I confess. I'm really not awake enough to make something up. Mercifully, she accepts that without comment.

We all help ourselves to breakfast and Mum lays out a fairly short written list on the table, smoothing out the folds. She begins eating so I pick it up and start reading the first item on it out loud.

'Number one, "Do that *10 Years Younger* thing".' I look to Mum for an explanation.

'You know, that TV programme where they take someone who looks a bit of a mess and transform them,' she muffles through some shreds of croissant. 'They've usually had a hard life or something and their family don't even recognise them when they're done.'

I know the programme well; Patty and I often indulge guessing how old the contestants are and speculating whether they'll keep up any of the grooming after the show ends. After all, if you look old because you've twenty children, you'll still have them when the cameras stop rolling.

'I like that one,' says Patty. 'I might do it with you — not that I need to look ten years younger, but a couple knocked off might be handy.'

'There's usually surgery involved — new teeth implants and sometimes even facelifts,' I say with a little trepidation. 'Surely you don't want that, Mum.'

'Oh no, nothing that might hurt,' she replies, much to my relief. 'Just the other bits — the hair, the clothes, make-up and maybe that Botox stuff.'

'Botox stops the wrinkles forming.' Patty laughs. 'I think that ship has sailed, Mrs S.'

'Pots and black kettles,' murmurs my mum, reaching for the final croissant. Patty slaps her hand and takes it for herself. I rap the table with a teaspoon and call everyone to order.

'Okay, Mum,' I say. 'This would be a really nice thing to do with Zoe too and I think I can start to organise it, if you like.'

Mum is delighted with that and I'm cheering up after my rude awakening, imagining all three generations enjoying a bit of a pamper and makeover. I look at the next item on the list.

'"Ride a motorbike,"' I read out. 'Really?'

'Yes. I've never been on one and it used to look so exciting when I was a teenager — all those rockers in their leather jackets taking off down the highway. I always fancied James Dean and Marlon Brando. Your dad could never be persuaded to give it a go but this is *my* list and I want to try it.'

She's emphatic and I can completely understand her point. How many times did I give up on doing something just because my ex-husband didn't want to do it? Not necessarily something huge, but films I never saw, holiday destinations I didn't get to visit or food I didn't try because it was a dish for two and he didn't fancy it. Since the divorce I've gone for it, but if he hadn't run off with another woman, I'd still be dancing to someone else's tune.

'Your friend Ed might be able to help with that,' says Patty. 'Didn't you go out with his bike gang once?'

I did and it was exhilarating. I also discovered that his Harley Davidson chapter is comprised of mainly older gentlemen who've returned to biking as empty nesters. They were charming, and despite the leather-clad image, totally harmless. Again, I tell Mum I'll ask him about it; I seem to be getting rather a lot of action points from Mum's list.

'Number three.' Patty has taken the list from me and reads out the next one. '"Learn to waltz."'

'Like they do on *Strictly*,' says Mum. 'It's always the most beautiful dance with lovely flowing dresses.'

'Will Dad do this one with you?' I ask, wondering whether we also have to find a partner for her. She replies that he might do but she's going to learn with or without him.

I remember the customer who came into our shop to book the Flamenco trip and my thoughts instantly turn to whether this bucket list item could actually be an opportunity for the Mercury Travel Club. Learning to waltz in Vienna — what could be more magical? Despite not really wanting any more action points from Mum's list, I tell her to leave that one with me and I'll see what I can do.

'I knew you two would be able to help.' Mum is beaming. I can see now that this list means a lot to her and I have to do what I can to make it happen. Well, most of it.

As I'm getting warm and fuzzy feelings about supporting my aged parent satisfy her deepest desires, Patty looks at the next item on the list and gives a little gasp.

'Wow, you saved the best till last, didn't you?' she says. 'Lulling us into a false sense of security with the waltzing and the makeover — now I know why.'

'What is it, Patty?'

'Do you want to tell her or should I?' Patty continues.

'You do it,' Mum says sheepishly.

Patty sits up straight and clears her throat.

'Okay, here we go.' She looks directly at me. 'The final item on your mother's bucket list is . . . "Have an affair".'

My jaw drops now, so Patty reaches over and closes it for me. It's just as well we're that familiar with each other or there'd be drool all over the table. I can't speak so just spread my hands out in question.

'Are you and Mr S not getting on?' asks Patty.

'Oh, we're fine,' Mum says. 'And it's not as if I want to leave him. We're in for the long haul — till death do us part — but it can get a bit . . . samey.'

'Have you tried date nights?' I ask, remembering the advice she once gave me. Mum dismisses my suggestion with a wave of the hand.

'They work for so long but you always know who's turning up and the conversation always ends up being about the garden or the shopping. I want to be swept off my feet.'

She says this last sentence flicking her hair back.

'I cannot help you have an affair, Mum,' I protest. 'He's my dad and I'd never do anything to hurt him.'

'He needn't know — this is my list,' replies Mum. 'And as I've just said, I don't want to leave him, just have a bit of excitement. Like in that TV series, *Apple Tree Yard*.'

I know the one she's talking about and it's really quite steamy. A woman meets a man in a bar and he seduces her without her even knowing his name. It's quite erotic and not at all how I picture my mother.

'Blimey,' says Patty. 'I think I can safely say, on behalf of your dear daughter and myself, that we're relieved you haven't seen *Fifty Shades of Grey*.'

She laughs, trying to make light of the moment, but I'm still suffering a melee of emotions. Shock and horror that this is on her list but also anger and outrage that my mum thought she could bring something to me that would involve me betraying my dad. I love them both dearly, and while I'll help Mum, I won't hurt Dad in the process.

'It sounds like you're not going to help with this one,' says Mum, taking the list from Patty and folding it up again.

'Of course I'm not!' I exclaim, but Patty puts her hand calmly on top of mine.

'I'll see what I can do,' she says, giving my hand a discreet squeeze.

'And I'd rather not take too long over all of these,' adds Mum. 'None of us are getting any younger.'

I think I'm still dumbfounded when she eventually leaves the house — it's barely nine o'clock and my best friend has promised to help my mother have an affair. I have to pinch myself to check that this all really happened and I'm not simply having a nightmare.

CHAPTER SEVEN: GRANNY-OKIES ARE GO!

My nightmare will become a bizarre yet entertaining dream later this afternoon when Patty has Sheila and Kath round to discuss the cruise setlists.

Before then I try to question her about what she's promised my mother but she simply puts her hands on my shoulders and tells me to trust her.

'If you focus on the items you've said you will and I do mine,' she says, 'we should be able to do them all by the time I head off, and I promise I'll let neither of you down.'

I can't see how that's achievable, not if she helps Mum tick off adultery. I start to make this point but she gives me a very firm squeeze and mouths, *'Trust me.'* I swallow hard and nod reluctantly. I'll try and persuade my mother she doesn't really want to do this.

I have to have a cold shower before starting the rest of the day and, believe me, I am not a fan of these things. I just need the shock to shake me from — well, the shock. It refreshes my body but my mind is still full of Mum's list. I wonder whether I should tell Dad, but doing that or not doing it feels like a betrayal to one or the other. I look at myself in the mirror as I'm drying my hair and take a few deep breaths.

'Trust Patty,' I say out loud, and the woman herself appears behind me.

'And all will be well,' she says, planting a friendly kiss on my wet head. 'When have I ever let you down?'

She heads off and I know what she's just said is true; she may have done some truly crazy things but she's always been there for me and I just hope that continues now Jack is on the scene.

High-pitched screams downstairs let me know that the rest of the Granny-Okies have arrived, so I hurry myself up and get dressed. It really doesn't matter what I wear today as none of them will notice — all focus will be on the band, the songs and their costumes. As I walk down the stairs to greet them, I can't help but smile at the excited chatter taking place.

'I can't believe we got the gig,' Sheila is saying. 'It might only be a month but we'll be on their radar for other times, won't we?'

'My family are a bit cross I won't be here for Easter,' adds Kath. 'But they've watched me cook a Sunday roast for them for nigh on thirty years — they should know how to do it by now.'

The cruise company asked Patty to be a last-minute replacement for a band that can't do Easter because one of them is scheduled for an operation. She agreed instantly, wanting to show them that she could be relied upon and hoping that it would lead to bigger things. I hate to admit it but I'm quite relieved she didn't get a longer booking; I just have to pretend that I'm really happy for them all. I yell out a hello and step into a scrum of hugs and kisses. They are truly living their magic-wand lives.

After the divorce, I didn't know what I wanted from life and I was being pulled in all different directions. Caroline from the book club offered to help me with her life coaching, to find out what I truly wanted for myself. She gave me a magic wand and I had to wave it while imagining my perfect life. I chose to focus on becoming a businesswoman and I achieved that, but I also said that I'd love to have someone to share my life with and on that score I haven't really made much progress. Perhaps next weekend's meetup with Michael will start to change that. Anyway, it's time to stop living in my mind so much today; there's a lot going on in the real world and it's happening in Patty's garage.

I'd probably get a slapped wrist from my best friend if she heard me calling it a garage — it was re-christened a *rehearsal studio* some time ago. I walk in there now and have to stop myself from giggling as I watch all three Granny-Okies limbering up and stretching like prima ballerinas. Patty reaches above her head and tilts from one side to the next before folding forwards and attempting to touch her toes. Her hands reach as far as her calves before she's helped back upright by her band members.

'I think that's enough of a warm-up for now,' she declares. 'Maybe vocal exercises would be more useful.'

They run through the tongue-twisters and scales that I've heard them do many a time, stretching their mouths and getting their throats warmed up. I know that they have a serious gig coming up but it's still highly entertaining to listen to them getting 'Peter Piper Picked a Peck of Pickled Peppers' all muddled up and bursting out laughing at their attempts.

Finally it's time to look at the setlist and they've all brought suggestions in. Sheila shares her ideas and they're pretty much the songs the girls started with when they first got together — a classic eighties set featuring lots of Cyndi Lauper and Madonna.

'We should include a few of those,' says Patty. 'After all, we're word perfect in them and Cyndi is my alter ego, but this is a through-the-decades trip so we have to include seventies, nineties and noughties.'

'Is there anyone from the seventies who hasn't been arrested?' asks Kath, making a point which is rather cruel but not far from the truth.

'Well, put it this way,' says Sheila. 'We won't be asking anyone if they want to be in *our gang*.'

We all snort guiltily at that.

'The wonderful Kate Bush is still a paragon of virtue,' I tell them. 'I can see you all doing "Wuthering Heights".'

'Wow,' says Patty, looking up the song on her phone. 'With all the recent covers of her songs I can't believe that came out in the seventies. Just shows that the classics stand the test of time.'

'We certainly do,' adds Sheila with a Marilyn-esque little wiggle.

The majority of their set is sung straight but the opening song is always comedic as they pretend to be old grannies walking onto the stage. One of their classic entrances was to Bon Jovi's 'Livin' on a Prayer', where they played their fake Zimmer frames like air guitars. The audience loved that.

'How about a medley?' suggests Patty as she scrolls through lists of songs, frowning while deep in thought. She suggests three songs which I've never, ever heard suggested in the same breath.

The ladies listen to her ideas and pull up lyric sheets, and after some practice moves they turn to me and ask if I can help. I jump into action, getting what's needed and get into position.

I switch the garage (sorry, *rehearsal studio*) lights off, hearing the shuffling of feet as they get into position. I pick up the torch and sit down below them, lighting their faces from the floor. They're all wearing shower caps with a couple of hair curlers in. It's as far from the opening sequence of 'Bohemian Rhapsody' as you could get but that's what they're going with.

'*I killed a man,*' sings Patty.

'You did what?' exclaims Sheila. 'I'll have you over my knee for that.'

And so the song continues with Patty confessing her crime while the others counter every line by threatening to tell her father when he comes home and put her on the naughty step.

The medley switches quickly to a very cheesy eighties pop song. Now the lighting is fully up, the shower caps are gone and the audience can see that they've been in wraparound aprons throughout. They begin singing the Eurovision Song Contest winning entry 'Making Your Mind Up' and making the little dance routine that went with it completely comical. Of course, at the end there's the big reveal where they throw off the aprons and underneath they're in normal clothes — but if this routine works then they'll be in Spice Girls costumes. They launch into 'Wannabe' and I can imagine that when they're performing this there'll be a lot of audience participation.

'What do you think?' Patty asks when they've run through things a couple of times. She's panting heavily between sips of water, as are the others.

'It's complicated,' I reply truthfully, 'but if you get it right then it is really funny.'

Patty nods.

'We'll run through it a few times to see if it can work,' she says. 'We can always just start with something simpler but I think that "Bohemian Rhapsody" piece will surprise people.'

'Putting it mildly,' I add.

'What are we going to do about the other two Spice Girls?' asks Kath.

'We should be Posh, Ginger and Baby as they're the easiest costumes to have under aprons,' says Sheila.

'And we'll get facemasks of Scary and Sporty to put on microphone stands,' adds Patty.

The others nod in earnest agreement and continue to discuss how to seamlessly transition from one song to the other and which solos they'll have, to give the others some rest time. I reckon the King's Coronation had less planning than this.

As well as lighting, I'm in charge of refreshments, which means water during the rehearsal and Pinot Grigio as it comes to a close. When Patty gives me the signal, I head out to the kitchen and return with glasses, chilled wine and a tub of olives. The girls unfold some garden chairs and pull out a storage box to use as a table. It would be far easier for the three of them to come into the house but they seem to love this space. Patty puts on one of her favourite playlists and the post-practice drink turns into an out-and-out party.

They play to their individual strengths with Kath belting out Bonnie Tyler numbers and Patty showing the girls her Cher interpretation. Sheila is the rock fan and she flicks down the playlist, selecting Aerosmith and Run-D.M.C. doing 'Walk This Way'.

'Do you think we could cover this one?' she asks. 'It could be quite funny to walk on to the chorus all bent over on the sticks and frames rubbing our sore backs.'

The others agree and they listen to the track, but no matter how hard they try, none of the women can keep up with the rapped lyrics. It's hilarious to hear them even attempt it.

'How does anyone learn to speak that quickly?' asks Kath.

'And how do they find time to breathe?' adds Patty, taking a gulp of wine, which to her is as crucial as oxygen. 'Sorry, Sheila, but I think that's out, though we should definitely have a rock track in it. What else was big in the eighties?'

'Guns N' Roses.' Sheila presses play on the unmistakeable opening riff of 'Sweet Child o' Mine'.

'Oh, bagsy me being Slash,' yells Patty, jumping up and putting an upturned plant pot on her head in place of a top hat.

I know Patty loves this as we were both dancing around the living room when we watched the band play it at Glastonbury '23. We sat glued to the TV for the weekend, sitting on cushions on the floor to pretend we were there. We watched Billy Idol, the Pretenders and Blondie, then Elton John came on to do his headline set. Patty turned to me with glitter on her face and wine in a picnic glass (for the full festival effect) and said, 'You know, they're all older than me. There's still every chance that one day you'll be sitting here watching me on that stage.'

CHAPTER EIGHT: MOTORCYCLE MAMA

'It was the silence that I wasn't ready for.' Josie is telling a customer about her trip to Finland. She was completely overwhelmed by the time she spent in Levi and, for the week that she's been back, has not stopped gushing about it, which is absolutely fantastic as there are still people looking for a winter break. When Josie shows them the photographs she's taken then tells them about the dogsledding, the Ice Hotel and the possibility of seeing the Northern lights, we get a few more bookings.

'So, my little antipodean friend,' says Charlie, 'are you a convert to ice and snow now?'

'Not the slushy grey stuff you get in this country, but honestly — you and Pete should go. I can picture you in matching Sámi outfits herding your reindeer.'

She holds up a picture of the indigenous Sámi in traditional dress and Charlie scowls at her.

'Not sure I could possibly be seen in that amount of embroidery, but I like the boots.'

'Plus, I don't think they do a flat white in the Arctic Circle,' I add. 'So that might be a deciding factor.'

'Oh, I'm definitely out,' Charlie says. 'Talking of which, coffee anyone?'

I say no; I usually work all day Saturday but I've taken a half day today as we're doing one of mum's bucket list items. I wanted to show her we were taking it seriously — and at the back of my mind, I'm hoping that by giving her a bit of excitement with the easy things on the list, she'll decide she doesn't really want to go as far as having an affair. I still can't believe my mother actually wants to do this but everyone else seems to find it hilarious.

'You're joking,' exclaimed Josie when I told them both during one of our coffee breaks.

'Good on the old girl,' adds Charlie. 'I hope I'm still being scandalous when I'm her age.'

'It's not good,' I say earnestly. 'It's awful. And the worst part is she expects me to facilitate it.'

'Are you gonna put her onto a dating app?' Josie asks. My eyes widen. 'I can't think of any other way of doing it and there must be one for oldies.'

'Really?' I swallow hard.

'Yeah,' quips Charlie. 'It's called Carbon Dating.'

He gets a high five from Josie as I try to ignore them both. I'd like to ask Patty how she intends to make this happen but she's told me to keep my nose out of it as it's her item to sort and she knows I'll just try to stop it happening.

I tidy my desk, pick up my things and ask the guys to wish me luck. Charlie starts singing 'Born to Be Wild' as he heads out to the break room.

* * *

I start with Mum's desire to ride a motorbike, as at least I know she'll be safe with Ed. He finds it as amusing as everyone else but agrees to help and to rally some of his biker friends to make it happen. I can't have Mum going out alone so Patty and I plan to be with her. Ed's chapter are having a ride-out this afternoon and will end up at a pub in the countryside where there'll be a rock band playing. So Mum will get the whole experience of being out with a biker gang. And even though it's been a very mild January, I'm hoping it will be cold enough to put her off going out again. I've never known my mum to abandon her creature comforts, so today should be interesting.

We're all meeting at Patty's to get dressed for the occasion. In my mind this means ensuring my elderly mother is wearing several layers of thermals but it doesn't seem to be what she or Patty are planning. I hear them up in the bathroom when I open the front door and go up to investigate.

'What are you doing?' I ask as I walk in.

'Making your mum look a bit more rock and roll,' replies Patty, pausing to look up at me with a can of coloured hairspray in her hand. I peer behind her and my eyes almost pop out of my head when I see my mother with green, red and purple streaks across her head.

'Does that come out?' I ask in horror.

'You don't half sound like an old woman,' chortles my mum. 'I used to say that to you when you dyed your hair.'

This is true. Whenever I experimented with hair dye kits as a teenager, Dad would simply say, 'That looks nice, love,' whereas Mum would say, 'I hope you can get your money back,' or if it was really bad, 'That had better be temporary, young lady.' It has finally happened — I sound like my mother.

'Do you want some?' asks Patty, turning the spray can onto her own hair. 'I thought I'd just do the fringe and the ends so the parts that stick out of the helmet look a bit grungy. Can you do the back for me, Mrs S?'

My mum obliges, giving my best friend bright red tips and doing such a good job of it that Patty actually suits her new look. They stand together admiring their rainbow tresses in the bathroom mirror and when I move next to them, I look so boring and sensible in comparison that I grab the green can and give myself a money piece — a couple of highlights that frame my face. Not too adventurous, but I feel like one of the gang. Next stop, Patty's bedroom.

She has managed to get hold of some pleather trousers for Mum and a flying jacket with a sheepskin lining. I'm so relieved; at least Mum will be warm.

'Where did you get all of this?' I ask.

'Vinted,' Patty says. 'I'll just sell it all again later.'

Mum is admiring herself in the new get-up, and I have to admit that if she really needed to feel that she was breaking free of the stereotypes that surround older women, this is a pretty good way of doing it.

Patty gives her sturdy boots and big gloves but Mum rejects them, preferring her own wool-lined winter gloves.

'At least these fit,' she explains.

I can't help but smile at the dinky little gloves with silver buttons peeping out of the enormous jacket, and I begin to lose my sense of dread. I'm actually looking forward to this.

The roar of engines coming down the street has us squealing with excitement and rushing to the window to watch Ed and his friends approaching the house. Mum's eyes light up and I can tell from the flush in her cheeks that she is utterly delighted with what is going on and the fact that Patty's neighbours have come to their windows to see what all the noise is. As Mum and Patty go out to greet the bikers, I make a discreet call to Dad and tell him we're on our way out. After getting Mum's bucket list, I had to call and ask him if he knew about it. He told me that she'd kept the contents private but mentioned that she was doing it. I ventured to tell him about the list but he stopped me and said he respected Mum's wish and that after fifty-five years together he doubted anything she'd written would surprise him. I didn't like to add that I thought at least one of the items would. I just promised to keep her safe.

And I think the safety of my practically octogenarian mother was also on Ed's mind when he selected the friends to take part in this. The bike they've selected for Mum isn't a bike — it's a trike and it is magnificent. With its gleaming electric-blue body and shiny chrome pipes, it is simply stunning. It's painted with some Nordic pattern and the man who stands beside it looks every inch a Viking. He's tall, with long blond hair and a braided beard, and when he holds out his bear-sized hand to shake my mother's, I notice he has runic symbols tattooed on each finger. He tells her that he loves her hair and Mum quietly thanks him. She's dwarfed by him, and I think the excitement she was showing earlier has been replaced by a little trepidation.

'You're going to be in good hands with Eric, Mrs Shepherd,' Ed tells her as he helps her up onto the pillion seat.

I feel quite at ease now; the pillion seat is like a big armchair and I imagine the trike itself can't take corners at any scary angle, so I think Mum will be perfectly safe.

'Eric will look after her,' Ed says quietly. 'He volunteers for the Make a Wish charity — lots of people want to go out on a Harley, so he's used to it.'

I could hug this man. Despite our not making it to second base (do I really still say things like that? Apparently so), I can't deny he's a nice guy.

Patty and I mount the back of the bikes allocated to us — and she cannot resist a line about getting her leg over — then we're off.

It is cold when we get going, no matter how many layers we're sporting, so I'm glad when we get to our destination. I check that Mum is warm enough and she tells me that she's completely toasty as her seat was actually heated. I might just wrestle her for it on the way back.

Inside the pub are a crowd of leather-clad men and women as well as some civvies. I can't be certain but by the look of some of the other civilians, I think there might be a couple from that charity here. A man my age catches my eye as I'm surveying the crowd then nods at me so I return the greeting and walk over to him.

'Do you have someone here?' he asks and I tell him it's my mum. He tells me he's with his brother and points him out. From the lack of hair and eyebrows I guess he's had cancer, which the man confirms.

'Not sure how long he has but this is what he wanted to do; they're an amazing bunch of people,' the man says, and as I watch the brother cheering to the band who've just walked on stage, I realise just how true that statement is.

Grateful that my mum is only suffering from late-onset boredom, I head back to her and Eric. They start at the front near the stage and after a few very loud chords move to the back of the room and sit down, much to my relief. This biker music really isn't my scene at all and I'm wondering whether I'll be able to hear anything in the morning after this. Patty appears with a G&T in her hand.

'The problem with biking is that if you're at the front driving you can't drink at all, and if you're on the back you can only have one just in case you go sliding off when you go round a roundabout,' she says, as if it's a newly discovered scientific phenomenon. 'They're not really bad boys, are they?'

'We can be,' growls a passer-by with a wink.

The band starts playing a song that I actually know and I can feel the Numskulls flicking through the filing cabinet in my head to try and establish where I know it from.

'Oh, we had this record,' declares Mum and instantly I recall Dad playing it on our record player.

'Your dad rushed out when it was first released and bought it from the record shop,' she continues with a wistful smile on her face. 'It had one of those big holes in the middle.'

'Credence Clearwater Revival? You had an original copy of this song?' asks Eric, looking impressed.

'Oh, I don't know who it is, but it was this song and he must have bought it around nineteen sixty-eight?'

'Sixty-nine,' Eric says. 'That's when it came out. Do you still have it?'

'Oh, I never get rid of anything,' replies Mum truthfully. 'It'll be in the attic somewhere with all of his other records. You can come and have a look if you like.'

Eric says that he'd love to, so Mum gives this Viking her phone number, which is something I never thought I'd see. I was just thinking that I'd better warn Dad what has happened when Mum rubs my arm and says, 'Thank you, this has been lovely. I really must bring your dad here one day.'

And although I know she won't set foot in this bar ever again, I'm mightily relieved to hear that the person she wants to share it with is Dad.

CHAPTER NINE: ALL BY MYSELF

'They were a great bunch of people, weren't they?' says Patty over breakfast the Sunday morning after Mum's bike ride.

I nod through a mouthful of toast. I've often suspected that my best friend only asks questions when I have my mouth full so I won't answer and therefore interrupt her flow.

'It's such a worthwhile charity too,' she continues. 'The chapter raises money for that charity as well as taking people out on the bikes, so I was wondering about offering to do a fundraising concert for them — what do you think?'

My mouth is still full but I note that she's actually paused and is looking directly at me, waiting for an answer. I gulp down my slice of granary as quickly as possible and have a swig of tea to moisten my throat afterwards.

'I think that would be a great idea,' I say truthfully. 'It would give you the chance to rehearse your new numbers too.'

'Hmm, that's what I was thinking; but we'd need a venue. I can't see our usual crowd being happy in a biker bar.'

'And I can't see the chapter singing along to "Material Girl" either,' I add, laughing.

Patty starts singing the lyrics as she tops up our coffee cups.

'I could ask Michael,' I suggest. 'He must have information about all sorts of buildings and venues mustn't he?'

At New Year, one of the things I found out about Michael is that he runs a property maintenance company. He and his team have contracts with many of the halls, social clubs and theatres in the area.

'Oh yes,' says Patty, 'I'd forgotten — today's the day you two actually get together. Do you want me to make myself scarce when you get back? I suppose you don't have to bring him back here at all, do you? He has his own love nest.'

She stands up and does that ridiculous thing that schoolboys do — with her back to me she wraps her arms around herself and makes smooching noises.

'How were you ever in charge of a team of people?' I ask, tutting at her and putting my used crockery in the dishwasher. I leave her in the kitchen while I go upstairs to get dressed and clean my teeth, checking for any wayward seeds that might still be stuck. When I get back downstairs Patty has fortunately stopped snogging herself.

'Just jesting,' she says. 'So what's the plan for today?'

'I'm keeping it simple,' I tell her. 'We're meeting at a tea shop and we'll go for a walk before coming back for cake.'

'Sounds very chaste. I'm picturing you with your chaperone, early nineteenth century — you in a long dress and him looking like Mr Darcy.'

'I could certainly go for that — the Darcy part anyway.'

'Well, I hope he emerges from the lake wearing a wet see-through shirt for you,' says Patty. 'Although he'd probably catch his death during January in Cheshire and that's not a great start to a relationship.'

'I just didn't want there to be any pressure on us,' I continue, ignoring her. 'The way we met wasn't exactly conventional and for all I know, he may have decided he just wants to be friends. A walk means we can simply chat and there's no awkward staring across a dinner table at each other.'

'I hope it works out for you, Bo, I really do.'

'It's either this or I find a nunnery with a vacancy.' I smile, although as I say the words I wonder if there are any nearby.

* * *

I'm trying not to worry too much about today. We've just met and he's just a friend. A very new friend. Okay — a handsome, friendly, funny new friend but just a friend nonetheless. Have I built him up too much in my mind? After all, we had one afternoon at the vets and one New Year party — is that enough time to decide how you feel about someone? I've read somewhere that you know within six seconds or something ridiculous like that. True, I looked into his eyes when he opened his front door to me for the first time and wondered why on earth we hadn't met earlier, but wasn't that just the dopamine talking?

'You're overthinking it again, aren't you?'

Patty's voice stirs me from my thoughts and I realise that I'm still standing in the kitchen with one boot on and the other in my hand, poised to be placed on my foot. I shake myself back to reality and put on the second boot then my coat and scarf. I'm dressed for a walk but the scarf is a bright paisley design, which I hope says I've made a bit of an effort.

'You're going to be very early.' Patty is looking at the clock on the wall.

'I'm popping in to see Zoe first,' I tell her. 'I want to ask her about her gran's list to see if she knows any stylists who might help with the *10 Years Younger* part.'

'And ask her if she needs any acts for events,' adds Patty with a hopeful note. 'They do weddings and celebrations, don't they? Tell her we're happy to perform at short notice.'

I promise that I will while also envisaging the bride's face when she learns that the Granny-Okies are performing at her wedding. Horror is the first expression I can imagine.

* * *

My daughter Zoe is the manager of a big hotel and doing extremely well in her chosen profession. She works all hours, which is why she's probably doing so well, and she's dating a lovely man called James, who is older than her and who works just as hard. The time they do have free is quite precious and I don't like to intrude on it, but when I rang to tell her about her gran's bucket list, she said she wanted to help out. I've been invited over today to see how she can be involved.

'Hello, Mum.' She opens her front door wearing a beaming smile. 'Come on in, we've bought pastries.'

This is going to be one of those days where I eat too much of the wrong stuff and end the day still feeling famished — toast for breakfast, pastries for brunch and cake for tea. I can already feel the sugar crash lining itself up for tonight. Of course I could say no, but that would mean being impolite to Zoe and then to Michael — so, as Patty would say, I have to take one for the team.

James is in the kitchen dressed in running kit and he tells me that he's going for a jog to keep out of our way. He gives Zoe a peck on the cheek as he heads out.

'You're both looking well,' I tell my daughter, then ask for a herbal tea because I might have to eat pastry but I can't face more coffee.

'We're happy.' The smile on her face reaches right up to her eyes, which are gleaming.

I begin by showing Zoe some of the photos from Mum's biker evening, including one of her straddled across the huge Harley trike, throwing the horns sign with her hands. An apple-cheeked lady attempting to look rebellious is as funny looking as it sounds.

'You have to send that to me,' says Zoe. 'I'm having it as my screensaver. So, being a biker and looking ten years younger, is there anything else on her list?'

'Everything seems to have come from something she's seen on TV but we're tackling one thing at a time.' I wasn't lying. Neither was I revealing what I'd rather not think about let alone discuss.

'Okay, well, I've had some thoughts,' says Zoe.

The hotel hosts weddings most weeks of the year; as a result, Zoe knows many of the hair and make-up artists who operate locally.

'I'm thinking that we could perhaps have a spa day so Gran gets spoiled rotten,' she says. 'I'll book her and Grandad into a suite for the evening and treat them to dinner. I'll get James to take Grandad out while we work miracles on Gran — when he gets back, his wife will look simply amazing. How does that sound?'

'It sounds wonderful. Although I'm not sure one afternoon will get Mum looking a decade younger.'

'Trust me, these make-up artists can work miracles.' She laughs.

Zoe gets out a large diary and flicks through the pages, looking for a free date.

'I'm surprised you don't have everything stored electronically,' I say.

'I have both. On a weekend off I don't like to go online or I'll look at my emails and then the time vanishes. Plus, this one has lots of the business cards I collect.'

There's a Perspex wallet clipped to the back of the book with lots of cards, on which I can see a list of cake specialists, stylists, florists and beauticians. It's a paper Wikipedia of exactly what we need.

'Ohhh,' Zoe says, looking up with an excited look on her face. 'There is another option — it would be even better than a spa day.'

She swizzles the diary around so that I can read the entry; I check that I've correctly guessed what the idea is and she nods.

'I think that would be incredible,' I tell her, and my daughter and I high-five in excited anticipation.

Zoe will check that the idea is possible and get back to me. If not, she'll contact some beauticians to action Plan B.

'I'm really looking forward to this,' says my daughter. 'It'll be such fun conspiring together.'

I feel lifted by her words and am delighted that having this task to do together means that I'll get to spend more time with Zoe. Perhaps Mum is a genius after all.

James gets back from his jog just as it's time for me to leave. I explain where I'm going and Zoe tells me that she hopes it goes well, that I deserve to meet someone nice. It's quite ironic because only a year or so ago, I was telling her that she needed to meet someone. They have their arms around each other as they stand in the doorway waving me goodbye; Zoe has most definitely met someone more than nice.

* * *

I reach the park a little bit early, so rather than bide time outside I go into the tea shop and see that Sarah from the book club is working today. After waiting for the queue to die down, I head to the counter to say hello.

'You came,' she says with a smile. 'I'm so glad — are you on your own?'

'I'm meeting someone shortly,' I tell her. 'So keep back some slices of your best cakes.'

Sarah is about to take her break so suggests we sit down and have a cuppa while I'm waiting. To be polite I do just that, take off my coat and sit down close to the door where I'll be able to see Michael. I'm trying not to but I can't help checking the time on my phone.

'I'm sure he'll be here soon,' says Sarah. 'We've a bathroom out the back if you want to freshen up. I'll look after your things.'

I take up her suggestion rather than sit nervously waiting. I check that I don't have pastry crumbs in my teeth now and splash water on my face. When I head back out Sarah gets up from the table saying she has to mind the counter but that I'm welcome to wait for as long as I like.

I sit until the tea shop looks to be filling up and I get glances from families who need a table to sit at. It isn't fair for me to be taking up the space, so I tell Sarah that I'll wait outside.

And I do. I wait and wait. He's ten minutes late, then quarter of an hour then twenty minutes. I should call him, I know I should, and Patty will give me such a dressing down when I tell her about this. But he has my number, and if you're the one running late then surely you're the one who should call?

At the forty-minute mark it starts to rain and I know it's the sign I was waiting for. I have to stop pretending that he's coming — I've been stood up.

CHAPTER TEN: GONNA WASH THAT GIRL RIGHT OUTTA MY HAIR

When I got home, I'd hoped for a relaxing bath to ease the hurt but it wasn't to be.

'Patty, have you seen my face cloth?' I bellow from the bathroom. Rather than a sarcastic reply there's a silence, which usually means trouble, so I march down the stairs and into the living room where she's sitting with a butter-wouldn't-melt expression.

'Which face cloth?' she asks, as if it's normal to have hundreds of the things.

'The one I use for my face. The pale-blue one with a little duck embroidered in the corner.'

'Oh.'

'What's that supposed to mean?' My emotions move from annoyance to fear.

'I put it in the laundry basket after I'd used it,' she says.

'What did you use it for?' I ask.

'What do you think I used it for? Washing myself, obviously.'

'Washing your whole body with my face cloth?' I'm horrified.

'What's the problem?' Patty says with a cheeky grin. 'I went back to front.'

'AARRRGGGHHHH,' I scream, trying to get that image out of my head. 'It's a face cloth. The one I used to soak in warm water then place across my forehead and eyes to smooth out the wrinkles while enjoying a deep relaxing bath. I'll never be able to do that again! Every face cloth will remind me of you and your fandango!'

Patty finds my horror highly amusing and I can see she's bursting to laugh out loud.

'And besides,' I add, 'it's *front to back*!'

That does it — she roars with laughter and gets up and starts swiping an imaginary towel between her legs.

'Back to front, front to back,' she says while miming the actions. 'I guess I shouldn't tell you the rest.'

'Could it get worse?' I know that it's just about to.

'I did my legs too and had to wipe the hair removal cream off. Giving it a wipe rather than just washing it off gets all the stray hairs that hang on for dear life.'

I stand with my mouth agape. 'Wiping depilatory cream off your legs with my face cloth?' I repeat, to which she nods.

'It was the first thing to hand.'

Then a thought strikes me.

'Please tell me it was only your legs,' I beg. Patty simply shrugs and I retch.

I pick up a cushion and throw it at her then head back up for a shower. I certainly can't face the bath, not now.

* * *

Next morning I'm up early with a fire in my belly. I haven't had much sleep as I lay thinking about Michael and why he might have stood me up without so much as a text message. I haven't told Patty about it. I pretended that our date went well enough but I wasn't sure it would go anywhere. I cannot face telling her that once again my love life is a disaster, especially when hers is flourishing. The plan I decided on in the middle of the night was to give Michael twenty-four hours to tell me why he didn't turn up and after that, I just forget about him. I know that I could call him and ask — that's what Patty would suggest — but he knew the time and place and he definitely has my number now, so I really cannot think of a reasonable explanation for the no-show.

Fake it 'til you make it. I sigh as I fill the kettle. I'm wearing a full face of make-up and am dressed to kill. I might feel sad but I'm not going to show it. I make myself a coffee and put some bread in the toaster thinking about that feeling. I don't know Michael well so it's not really about him as a person, although I did think that we got on well at the New Year party and I liked him. And maybe it isn't sadness that's sitting like a heavy lump right in the middle of my rib cage; I feel as if I've failed. And I seem to keep failing — at this aspect of my life anyway. Husband, Ed and now Michael, all completely different people with different reasons for not working out but still the same end result — I'm standing here on my own. The toaster pops rather loudly in the silence of the kitchen so it jolts me out of my contemplation. I sit down with my breakfast and inhale deeply; the warm bready smell is very comforting and with the creamy butter half melted in, it's like a little hug. No wonder people turn to food in times of crisis — it rarely lets you down. When I've finished I get ready to leave and before I open the door, I inhale deeply and mentally recite an affirmation three times: *You are strong, you are wonderful and today will be great.*

* * *

Throughout the journey to work, I think back to the life coaching session I had with Caroline last year. It helped me to see what I really wanted in life after the divorce and kind of gave me permission to go after it. Back then, my priority was the business and getting a love life was something I knew I would want in the future but was in no hurry. Perhaps a year is too short a timeframe for both me and Michael? Just because my ex-husband, best friend and daughter have all found someone doesn't mean to say that I need to do the same. Patty was single for several years after her husband died so perhaps I'm trying too hard. It's just that I seem to be watching all my close friends and family setting sail with new partners while I'm left alone on my little desert island. Would that be so bad?

'Wow, someone means business today,' says Charlie as I walk through the door of the shop and shake the image of me talking to a coconut out of my head (even Tom Hanks had Wilson).

I give him a twirl and tell him that we are going to knock the sales targets out of the park today.

'Go, Angie,' he replies as we both sit at our desks and fire up the computers. 'So how did the date go?'

He had to make small talk, didn't he?

'Jury's still out,' I say without looking up from my screen. Again, I'm not lying just not telling the whole story. Charlie takes the hint and changes the subject.

'So, if you want to make us lots of money, you could focus on the Seville trip — it wouldn't hurt to have it sold out early,' he says. 'Find us some people who want to learn Flamenco — or at least watch it.'

'That's exactly what I was thinking,' I say. 'And as my mother wants to learn to waltz, I was wondering whether a dance holiday programme might have legs.'

Josie crashes an imaginary cymbal at my pun.

'Jiving, jitterbugging, jumping legs,' adds Charlie and I smile in response.

Focus, that's what I need today and that's what Mercury Travel gives me. There are always events which impact on the travel industry — events that are completely out of our control and in many cases can destroy businesses — but it's also true that you get out what you put in and I'm about to give this all I have.

The Seville trip is set up and we've taken a number of bookings, so I need to find some groups that might want to take up the rest of the spots. Vienna is the natural place to go to learn to waltz and although both places are very grand and elegant, they're different in character so there's a chance that people might want to book both. I'd like to arrange the Vienna trip for the spring — as much to help Mum's bucket list as see the city when it's just waking up. I wonder to myself whether a round-the-year programme of dance holidays would work? Our customers could learn beautiful dances in beautiful cities. I don't know much about the origins of dances so need to do some research. The obvious place to start is watching reruns of *Strictly* on YouTube, so I plug my earphones in and pull up some of the dances that have the highest viewing figures.

I should have known this would be a rabbit hole that I'd fall down and not emerge from for a very long time. It was simply magical watching the dances and costumes while listening to that wonderful music; I could have been distracted for the whole day if it weren't for Charlie pulling out one of my earplugs to tell me I was humming 'The Blue Danube'. I look up and see the customers he and Josie are serving smiling at me; I give them a little wave and say that I'm organising a very beautiful trip so they'd better keep an eye on our website.

Then I get back to work. I think I've got it; I don't want these to be long-haul trips, just short breaks, so that excludes North and South America, which is a real shame because so many of the popular dances were created there: samba, tango, cha-cha, swing and jive. All in the most viewed videos but all invented too far away. However, I've thought laterally about this and have come up with a way of including one of them without the long journey. When Charlie's customer leaves I print off some notes and ask him to join me in the break room.

'We plan a trip per quarter and we already have Seville planned. It's advertised as a Flamenco trip but we could see if we can find a tango instructor too as it's huge there,' I tell him. 'Vienna in spring for the waltz, Italy in summer for jive . . .'

'Italy?'

'Yes, there's a huge jive and lindy hop festival there every year,' I tell him, showing him the details. 'There are workshops and beginner lessons bringing together dance teachers from the UK, Amsterdam and Italy. It looks fabulous and all we have to do is get people there.'

'The lesson will be in English, won't it?' Charlie asks the question all of our customers will.

I nod and tell him they will, but the food, company and culture will be truly international.

'Then,' I continue, 'come Christmas, we take our guests to the one place everyone who watches *Strictly Come Dancing* really wants to go.'

'Blackpool Tower Ballroom,' he says with a big smile on his face.

'Precisely.'

We both like the sound of it but I have to check it out with a few people to see if it's likely to be commercially successful. I get back to my desk and look up some local ballroom dancing schools. They're likely to know if a schedule like this already exists and they may have ideas on marketing it. Filling the Tower Ballroom would be a huge undertaking so I'll need some partners for that, but pulling it off would be incredible.

I call the dancing schools and schedule some meetings after explaining why I need their expert opinion. Everyone agrees to meet up and some sound quite enthusiastic about the initial idea. I'll have to meet them all in the evenings either after or prior to the classes starting and I'm even invited to join in a taster class. Having something to do after work is certainly a better option than hanging around waiting for Michael to call, so I take them up on their kind offer.

Satisfied that I've done as much as I can on the trip, I get up, stretch and head to the break room, where I make us all a coffee. When I get back into the shop, Patty is standing there with her hands in front of her holding what looks like a box of cupcakes. I put the coffees down on Charlie and Josie's desks then turn to my friend, who hasn't moved.

'Are they for us?' asks Charlie. 'I could do with some afternoon sustenance.'

'They're for no one but my bestie Bo-Peep and no one else can *ever* use them,' she replies, holding the box towards me.

'Use them?' repeats Josie. 'How the heck do you use a cupcake?'

I walk towards Patty and peer more closely at the box, wary that there may be some trick involved here.

'Ha-ha, very funny,' I say as I realise what they are. They're not cakes but face cloths folded up into the shape of cakes. They're done really well and look delicious. I have to say as gifts go, I'd be devastated thinking I was about to tuck into one of these only to find it's terry towelling and am actually pretty disappointed right now.

Patty picks one up and presents it to me.

'Thought you'd like this one in particular,' she says through a snort of laughter. 'It has a cherry on top just to remind you of me.'

Obviously I throw it straight back at her, hitting her on the nose. She launches one at me and a towelling cupcake barrage starts. We're breathless in minutes and collapse into chairs laughing and gasping for air. When I was doing my affirmations this morning, never did I think that the day would end as it began — with the most ludicrous facecloth showdowns imaginable.

CHAPTER ELEVEN: OUR SURVEY SAYS...

Zoe has invited Mum, Dad and me to go out with James's parents tonight. It's an extremely brave move on her part because although my mum has met them and says she gets along famously with them, that is only her opinion. As James is older than Zoe by nearly twenty years, his parents are closer in age to my parents than they are to me. This excites Mum, who is determined to have a new best friend after tonight.

'Just think, we can go shopping together and have afternoon tea,' she tells me when I pick her and Dad up. 'Your father will have someone to talk with about cars and men stuff so he needn't bore the pants off me.'

'I am standing here, you know,' he says as he pushes her out of the door and double-checks the locks in front of her to prove he's done it. It's their ritual and if they don't do it, I'll be turning the car around in under five minutes to come back and make sure. Their neighbourhood watch has been on full alert recently because a teenager was seen skulking around wearing a black hoodie. I did remind her that all teenagers skulk and they all wear black hoodies, but she wasn't convinced until it turned out that the would-be prowler was in fact a neighbour's grandchild.

'It might have been a burglar disguised as a grandchild,' she protested when the truth was revealed. 'They don't come wearing striped jerseys carrying swag bags these days, you know.'

I could have responded by saying that they never did outside of comics but honestly, I just wanted the conversation to end. It's always been impossible to win an argument with her.

Happily, Zoe and James haven't chosen to introduce everyone over a meal. Instead, they've invited us all to a quiz where there'll be a buffet served halfway through. It's in aid of a charity her hotel chain is supporting and is being held in their events suite. It's a modern hotel, so I'm surprised when we walk in and see that it's quite a grand room.

'It has to be for the weddings,' says Zoe when I express this. 'You really cannot have a venue that isn't Instagrammable these days, and when we dress it up, it does look stunning. You could be in a palace.'

She takes us to a table, where James and his parents get up to shake hands and say hello, introducing themselves as Yvonne and Bob. Mum ignores the outstretched hands and goes for full-on hugs, declaring that she knows they're going to be such good friends. She then moves the seats so she's between James's mum and dad. In fairness, this is probably the best way to mingle, so I sit both dads together and take a place next to James.

'I know you love quizzes,' Yvonne says to my mum.

'Well, I don't like to brag but I could be your lethal weapon,' she replies modestly. 'As long as they have the right questions.'

Bob and Yvonne think this is a joke and laugh politely but I know she's deadly serious, and if we don't win or she doesn't shine then Zoe will be criticised for hiring the wrong quizmaster.

'Gran needs a soap star picture round and dingbats,' Zoe explains to them. 'Neither of which I can guarantee as I have no influence over this — I'm a contestant like everyone else.'

'Hmmm,' says Mum. 'I think I would have taken a quick peek at the questions if I were you. It won't look good if the manager loses, will it?'

'That's called cheating, Gran. And I don't think it will look good if I win.'

'Well, you'd better not sabotage us.' Mum links arms with Bob and Yvonne as she speaks. 'We're here for the big prizes. What are they, by the way?'

'Top prize is a weekend stay here with free treatments and full use of the spa, second prize is a champagne afternoon tea for two and the third has been donated by one of our suppliers, so it's a case of six wines.'

'If I'd have known that I'd have said we should split up,' Mum says enthusiastically. 'You could go for the afternoon tea, Yvonne, the boys can aim for the wine and I'll nab us the weekend stay. That would keep us going on excursions, wouldn't it?'

James's parents are looking at each other and the rest of the table for a clue on how to respond, but we all just shake our heads and smile so they begin to relax.

The quiz begins and is going fairly well thanks to the men; despite Mum's assertion that she's good at quizzes, it's actually Dad who's a master of trivia and general knowledge. Mum's contribution is declaring, 'Yes, I thought that was right,' whenever the quizmaster reads out the answer that we've written down.

There is a soap star section but to Mum's dismay it's filled with modern characters rather than the ones she remembers. Her reaction here is to tell Zoe that the questions are discriminatory on the grounds of age.

The music round kicks off with sounds of the sixties, and while both sets of parents seem to know both the artists and the song titles, I can see that many of the younger teams around the room are really struggling.

'So is this round discriminatory too?' asks Zoe when we score a perfect ten.

'Just re-balancing things,' Mum says haughtily.

Mum actually comes into her own when an anagram round is put in front of us.

'Wheat Odour Fizz,' I read out, completely baffled.

'*The Wizard of Oz*.' Mum's voice strains between a whisper and a yell.

'Good one,' says Bob, leaving Mum beaming.

'Rum Pet Frogs,' Zoe reads out, looking up at her gran.

'*Forrest Gump*,' Mum says with a wise nod after thinking about it for only a few seconds.

And so it goes until she's guessed them all. Okay, so even I could see 'In Attic' was *Titanic* but said nothing so as not to take this moment away from her.

After that round — where we got another perfect ten — the quizmaster announces half-time and declares the buffet open. Mum moves faster than a cheetah — which I discovered in round two, general knowledge, is the fastest land animal. I'd thought it was a puma. She gets to the front, fills a plate and is back to the table before the announcement is actually over.

'If you want the good stuff like prawns, you've got to be quick,' she tells Yvonne. 'But don't worry, I'll teach you all my tricks.'

'I hope you're going to teach me them too.' Bob seems far less scared of my mother than his wife.

As we eat, conversation turns to how well we're doing and how Mum was outstanding at the anagrams.

'I think I'm just very visual,' she tells everyone with such self-assurance that for a moment I wonder if she's been taking lessons from Patty. 'I always get the answers on *Catchphrase* — you know, that "say what you see" quiz.'

She takes a bite of quiche then turns to me mid-mouthful; her eyes are wide open and I know from her expression she's just had one of her ideas but can't speak until she's finished eating. I pause, waiting for her just in case this good idea causes me to choke.

'I've had an idea,' she declares after swallowing. 'I need to add something else to my bucket list.'

Given what's already on it, I'm dreading this and really wish she weren't telling me with everyone else hanging on her words, dying to hear what it is.

'I need to be on a quiz show,' she says. 'On telly, if you can swing it. Preferably *Catchphrase* but anything that works with my skills.'

'Oh, I'd love to see you on TV,' says Yvonne, getting a look of horror from Zoe, Dad and me. She hasn't learned yet that Mum needs no encouragement.

'How about *Pointless*?' says Bob, getting a grimace from Mum.

'No thanks,' she says, 'the clue's in the name.'

I explain that there are usually long waiting lists and auditions to get on quiz shows but say that I will look into it; there's no way of stopping this conversation if I don't.

'So what else is on your bucket list?' asks Yvonne.

Another topic I'd really rather avoid right now; I look up at Dad to see if there's any indication that he knows what's on the list.

'Well, she's already been out with a group of Hell's Angels,' he tells the table with an affectionate look over at Mum. 'Leathers, biker bar and all.'

He gets out his phone and shows them the picture I took of Mum with her Viking companion. James and his parents are quite in awe so I explain the circumstances.

'And I'm going to learn to waltz,' says Mum.

'Oh, that sounds beautiful,' Yvonne says. 'I'd love to do that.'

Never missing an opportunity to sell the Mercury Travel Club, I leap in and tell them I'm trying to organise a trip to Vienna for the full dance experience. I'm delighted when James's parents ask for the details when they're available and mentally clock up two more places sold.

'This sounds a great list,' continues Bob. 'What else is on it?'

I have no idea whether she'll tell everyone about the affair but I really can't risk it in front of Dad.

'Why don't you just leave it as a surprise, Mum?' I suggest with more than a hint of desperation in my voice. 'That way you can astound people when they happen.'

She thinks about it and decides I'm right so moves the conversation on to where you can get the best pensioner special meals, and by the sounds of it, Yvonne and Bob have a lot of knowledge to share.

I ask Dad to help me get some drinks from the bar, and as we're standing waiting to be served, I ask him if Mum has now told him what's on her list.

'She hasn't,' he replies, 'but knowing her it'll be something a bit different.'

I feel guilty betraying Mum's secret but really think my father should know. I open my mouth to tell him but he quickly puts his finger to his lips.

'It's your mum's list and I don't mind if it's a bit crazy,' he says. 'Relax and enjoy the ride — I'm going to.'

He winks at me, picks up the round of drinks and starts walking back to the table. As I watch him go, I'm coming to the conclusion that I really am the most conservative member of my family and an awful thought flits across my brain — did Michael stand me up because I'm actually really boring?

CHAPTER TWELVE: BOOMERS ON TOUR

'Do you think I'm boring?' I ask Patty the following evening.

I'm sitting on her bed while she finishes her make-up then gathers together some stage clothes; the Granny-Okies have an audition later and I'm going with them so I don't sit in the house fretting about why Michael didn't turn up. I'll fret in some draughty theatre instead.

'Would I have boring friends?' she replies, sweeping her hand down her body as if to say, *Look at who you're talking to.*

'Sometimes the lively one in the gang has a quiet friend just so they won't outshine them.' An insight I have gained from many a coming-of-age film. However, the dull one usually ends up discarding her glasses, having her hair curled and being the belle of the ball, which doesn't look as if it's going to happen this time.

'There's a difference between quiet and boring,' says Patty, sitting down on the bed beside me. 'What's brought this on?'

I sigh and confess that Michael didn't turn up and hasn't bothered calling me. Then I tell her about Dad being very laissez-faire about whatever was on Mum's list.

'I seem to be the only one who's shocked by what she wants to do.' I throw myself down on the duvet. She lies down next to me and takes my hand.

'It could be worse,' she says. 'What if she'd said that she wanted to smoke pot? Would that be worse than having an affair?'

'I don't think so,' I reply after a moment's contemplation. 'I think I'd be surprised and bemused because she's never wanted to do it before, but it wouldn't hurt Dad.'

'So that's what's worrying you?'

Again I take my time in considering this.

'I think so,' I reply. 'I would never do anything to hurt either of them, and yet here I am promising to do something that might split them up.'

'I understand that. Your folks are one of the constants in my life too. Maybe we should get your mum to try marijuana instead of having an affair; at least your dad could join in with that.'

Patty laughs and I join in as I picture the scene.

'I can just picture her having a wild time and loving it. She'll get a later-life spurt and will go off into the sunset to ride motorbikes and smoke pot in some commune. Dad will go with her to relive his youth and I'll be left here like some lemon.'

Patty starts laughing.

'I'm picturing your folks on easy-rider Harleys with big reefers hanging out their mouths, turning up at the garden centre kicking over the gnomes.'

'But still wanting their free pensioner cups of tea,' I add, smiling through my angst.

She stands and pulls me up, telling me that it'll work out and I'm to go with the flow for now. It's easy for her to say.

The doorbell chimes and we peek out the window to see that Sheila and Kath have arrived. I go downstairs to let them in while Patty finishes getting ready. They bustle into the living room, full of excited chatter.

'I'm thinking about putting a few Miley Cyrus moves in,' Sheila is saying.

'You could pretend you're having trouble with your haemorrhoids — call them your Piley Cyruses.' Kath gets a grimace from both of us.

'Gross,' says Patty, coming down the stairs like a grande dame greeting her people. 'I'm not sure we can base a whole song on your Anusol requirements.'

'We've based them on less,' Kath says, making a good point. 'And it's supposed to be good for eye wrinkles, so there are lots of angles.'

I'm part grimacing again and part checking out the hall mirror as we leave the house, looking at my wrinkles and wondering whether it's actually worth a try.

Frankie has set up this evening's audition with the organisers of a party festival which tours the country. It's held in local parks and is free to attend, so they need fairly cheap acts to open the line-up. Although it probably goes without saying that Patty is envisaging herself somewhere near the top of the poster rather than the bottom. She's also particularly offended that she has to audition, having genuinely believed that their YouTube footage should have been enough. I imagine the organiser will wish they'd settled for that by the time their set is over as Patty plans to give them both barrels.

When we reach the theatre, the organisers are surprised that the girls want a changing room as everyone else is just playing their set in jeans and T-shirts, but they point them in the direction of a tiny room. It's just as well they're all in their make-up as there'd be a Granny-Okie Grapple if they all had to use the one mirror in there. The stage hand comes to tell them they're up next.

'Break a leg,' I tell them and take my space in the seating area behind the organisers, hoping to hear what they say.

The lighting technician has his instructions and the stage goes dark while I hear the girls tiptoe on. Suddenly their torches go on and they're set for the new opening medley they've now perfected. 'Bohemian Rhapsody' morphs into 'Making Your Mind Up' and finishes with 'Wannabe'. Patty is in the Ginger Spice Union Jack dress with big granny pants underneath. She comes down from the stage licking her lips seductively, and as she gets closer to the organiser it turns into more of a cartoon lick, like a dog with a juicy bone would do. She presses her finger on his nose and starts grinding seductively as she shakes her hips — and the granny pants start to fall down until she can step out of them and drape them across the organiser's head.

They're sitting open-mouthed and I'm not sure how it's going, but the girls are good, and as soon as they start the Madonna medley the organisers are nodding along and even doing the vogue moves with them. They finish with their usual last song — 'Should I Stay or Should I Go?' — which has a lot of audience participation, with half the audience (in this case two people) being urged to shout 'stay' and the other half (me) telling them to 'go'. Sheila has changed into a nightdress and is egging on the go crowd because she's already taken her teeth out. She holds up a glass with a pair of dentures in it as proof.

The organisers applaud as they finish and ask to meet in the office for a conversation when they're changed. This doesn't take long and the girls head to the office and take seats. I stand at the back as there aren't enough seats and I'm an interloper anyway.

'We loved it,' says the lead organiser, who introduces himself as Zach and his assistant as Khai. 'I have to say I didn't know where you were going to begin with but I could see the boomer humour . . .'

He looks at Khai and they fist-bump his joke.

'Your key demographic will obviously totally get you,' he continues. 'And we're expecting them to make up potentially a quarter of the audience.'

'It's critical to us that our festival embraces all minorities and as diverse a demographic as possible,' Khai adds. 'And for us, diverse *means* diverse.'

I'm guessing neither Zach nor Khai have noticed that the Granny-Okies are looking completely bemused.

'Could you elaborate on that?' I ask as openly as I can. It's taken me a while to think of a way of getting an explanation without looking completely stupid. The organisers explain how gender, sexuality and race have been balanced across the programme.

'But age is a demographic that often gets ignored and we're determined to correct that,' says Khai, getting a 'too right' in response from Zach.

'Menopause is huge right now,' Zach continues. 'And we're looking to represent that. Our festival will be "change" friendly; we'll be selling portable hand-fans to keep those hot flushes at bay, lyrics up on stage for when you forget them and experts handing out information to break down the barriers. We know that many women your age will be coming along with their grandchildren so we want them to see themselves reflected on stage.'

'They'll also be coming just for some fun,' says Patty.

'Amen to that.' Khai holds his palm out to high-five her.

I can't tell from Patty's expression what she's thinking but they get the gig, and after the organisers say they'll be in touch with Frankie to sign contracts, we head out into the street rather bemused.

'I'm a demographic,' says Sheila, the first to speak.

'There I was thinking you were just a crazy old woman with good legs,' Patty says.

'I'll have you know I'm a diverse old woman with good legs,' says Sheila, laughing.

We head towards a bar and order some wine. Looking around, we see there are tables of women our age all chatting and having a giggle. I'm still struggling with the idea that we've all just been called a minority that needs to be represented in a diversity programme.

'We're not a minority in the population,' says Patty, getting serious on us. 'But we are when it comes to the entertainment business. There are always a few big stars that the media likes to point to and say — "look how wonderful she is for seventy" — but most of the time they're trying to shame us into hiding away or getting facelifts.'

Sheila and Kath nod wisely.

'I'm not sure whether to be offended or not,' I tell the girls after the drinks have arrived and we've toasted a successful audition. 'I'm barely at menopause.'

I get expressions of sympathy from them.

'It won't be long,' Patty says. 'And don't be offended, they're right — menopause is huge now, it's worth billions. Every celebrity and their ageing pooch have a view on it. They're always sharing their "journey" or selling their collagen supplements.'

'I take them,' Kath interjects, patting her cheeks. 'Not sure if they work but I'm frightened to stop.'

'There are even musicals and comedies about it.' Patty is getting that glint in her eyes I know all too well. 'It's big business and we should have a slice of it.'

She stands up, picks up the menu and moves a few steps away from the table. Then she selects something on her phone and turns her back to us. She presses play and the introduction to a song we all recognise starts playing. Patty swirls around, strutting towards us, puffing out her cheeks and fanning herself with the menu. She starts singing along, ad-libbing the lyrics as she gets to the chorus, '*I've had a hot flush, baby, this evening,*' to the tune of Donna Summer's 'Hot Stuff'.

Even in this raw state I can see it will go down a storm as everyone can join in so easily. In fact, that's what Sheila, Kath and half the restaurant start to do before Patty is even through the second verse. When she's finished she gets a round of applause and, of course, takes a bow. I think the Granny-Okies have a new string to their already bizarre bow.

CHAPTER THIRTEEN: SHALL WE DANCE?

'Sometimes I think January is like a fox trot,' says Marianne the dance school owner and instructor. 'Slow-slow-quick-quick. It starts off gently and then, before you know it, it's over and we're facing February.'

I reply that I know exactly how she feels. Although I'm trying to get on with life and not think about Michael, my thoughts inevitably return to him. It seems like only a minute ago that we were giving each other a friendly peck on the cheek at the New Year's party and yet the days that have passed since he stood me up feel like a lifetime ago. This morning I told Patty that I was no longer bothered that he hadn't turned up as he was likely only going to be a casual friend, and although I don't think she believes me, she hasn't pestered me to call him. As it happens, I've plenty of work on to keep me busy and this weekend we're off on our first book club weekend of the year, so I won't be twiddling my thumbs when the travel agency is closed. I also have Mum's bucket list to attend to and I'm here hoping to kill two birds with one stone by getting some customers for a trip to Vienna for waltz classes.

Marianne is everything you'd expect from a dance instructor: tall, strong and elegant — just being in her presence makes you want to stand up straight. At that moment, a drop-dead gorgeous man walks in and Marianne introduces him as Felipe, her lead ballroom instructor. I can't take my eyes off his loose curly hair, smooth dark skin and milk chocolate eyes as I hold out my hand. I practically buckle when he takes it and kisses it. Boy, I'd pay just to have this guy look at me, never mind the actual dancing. I close my mouth and swallow, wondering if every woman he meets approaches him like a goldfish.

'Lovely to meet you,' I croak, getting my voice back.

We sit down and I drink all of the glass of water I'm offered in one gulp.

'As I mentioned on the phone,' I say, addressing Marianne so that I can concentrate, 'the Mercury Travel Club is all about building friendships and community through journeys with like-minded people. I know there's a deep passion for dance and a real interest in both learning Latin and ballroom as well as watching the experts perform.'

Marianne and Felipe nod as I talk.

'The industry has been saved by the television shows,' says Marianne. 'At one time my studio would have mainly catered to children learning stage or tap, but now it's every age and we're full most of the time. We also host parties and weddings here.'

'And I didn't have to take up escort work for rich ladies when I hit forty,' adds Felipe with a gorgeous deep laugh.

I amaze myself by doing two things at once: firstly, wondering what his hourly rate would be (I'd pay it), and secondly, processing the fact that he is over forty. By my calculations, the age difference between us probably isn't that shocking after all. Considering I was never that good at mental arithmetic, this astounds me. Perhaps the school teachers just picked the wrong examples to use.

If a sugar mummy is fifty-four and her target is forty-three, how many years will it take him to lick every inch of her body? And for how long will her twenty-four-year-old daughter be mortified?

Anyway, back to the sales pitch.

'I just adore watching them all,' I say, 'as does everyone at Mercury and my family — hence my mother's desire to learn to waltz.'

'It's a beautiful dance,' says Felipe. 'So timeless and elegant. I will teach her myself.'

My immediate emotional response is jealousy — she's not having my Felipe! If he has his hands around anyone's waist, it will be mine!

And then he stands and says, 'Would you like to try it?'

He holds out his hand, and while spluttering that I'm far more of a spectator than a dancer, I'm drawn hypnotically to follow his lead.

He starts by teaching me the basic step of the dance, which involves us standing side by side doing a box step. I'm quite relieved that it's not straight into a hold position with the giddiness this man is inspiring in me.

'Forward left, side right, close left foot to right foot,' he tells me in a gentle, clear voice. 'Back with the left, side with the left, close right to left.'

His voice is like music, and although I probably look as clumsy as ever, I feel as if I'm gliding.

After a few practices he takes my hand and positions my arm on his shoulder with my elbow out wide. I can see how this would tone anyone up as just by holding myself in this position I can feel my muscles working. Marianne puts on some music and Felipe counts me in. Unfortunately, during our box step practice, we both moved forward first, so that's what I do and step on his toes. I feel rather embarrassed.

'My bad,' says Felipe, as if I haven't just given him a professional injury. 'I didn't point out that the lady steps backward first.'

He gives me a smile that could probably end all world wars and we try again. After a few rounds of stepping, rising and falling as instructed, I feel that I'm starting to get into the swing of it and can imagine Mum loving every minute of this too. Marianne has videoed this successful attempt and now asks us to pose while she takes a photograph. I ask her to send everything to me to help publicise the trips. It will probably go with a slogan like, *If I can dance, anyone can.*

I'm out of breath more quickly than I'd like to admit, so Marianne takes over as I sit on the sidelines and watch it danced properly. I have a private giggle as I realise that Marianne isn't even counting one, two, three — I can't see her lips move at all!

It is fun dancing but it's also fun watching the graceful moves of the professionals, so while I watch Marianne and Felipe, I mentally compose the promotional campaign to attract both would-be dancers and spectators. I know that Charlie will be all over this. He adores the glitz and glamour of *Strictly*, *Dancing with the Stars* — any show that involves handsome men in tuxedos twirling under a mirrorball. As I often tell him: there are occasions when he's a bit of a gay cliché. And I know I'm rich to call anyone a cliché, sitting here like a cougar with my tongue hanging out.

My fantasies come to a screeching halt as a lithe and beautiful woman walks into the studio, heads towards the couple and pecks Marianne on the cheek. She then embraces Felipe in such a way as to leave no doubt of their relationship. I'm actually warmed to see them together and relieved that he's with someone his own age (in the back of my mind I've decided that this means I stand a chance should they ever split up — although I doubt she stands on his toes). When they leave, Marianne and I get back down to business; she gives me tips on venues to approach and offers dance instruction both before and after the trip. This is what Mercury Travel is all about and I happily take her up on the offer.

'Give my regards to Felipe and his friend,' I say as I'm getting up to leave.

'His wife,' clarifies Marianne. 'They've been together since partnering in competitions when they were teenagers.'

'How romantic.' I imagine a lifetime of swirls and swoops.

'Yes, but sometimes I want to gag.' Marianne laughs. 'Although maybe I'm just jealous that I never found that type of love.'

'Me neither,' I tell her with a shrug.

* * *

Back at the house I tell Patty about my evening, sparing none of the details about my gorgeous dance partner.

'When are you planning to go on the trip?' she asks.

'I thought about early March. There'll be fewer crowds, the spring flowers will be out and there may still be a dusting of snow on the hills around the city. It will probably be very pretty then. I think you'll still be here — are you thinking of coming?'

'I doubt it,' Patty says. 'I'll probably be rehearsing too much. It's a shame it's not when Jack is on leave. I can just see us floating around the ballroom, him in his uniform, me looking ravishing.'

'How could you ever look anything else?' I say with a smile.

'Precisely. Right, off to get ready for my nightly Zoom call — don't wait up.'

With a saucy wink, Patty leaves me alone on the sofa with my memories of the evening. I felt as if I'd been transported to a magical world while I was dancing. Even now I'm picturing Disney's *Cinderella* — that huge blue dress and the handsome prince. Do we ever grow out of that? Being swept off my feet would be terrifying for a control freak like me, but that's not how it happened for Felipe and his wife by the sounds of it — they were friends and dance partners before it blossomed. Upstairs, Patty and Jack will be having a great laugh in between the virtual seductions, and I bet, knowing my best friend all too well, even they are rather funny.

I truly believe that long-term love is about being friends with your partner above all. You don't have to be in each other's pockets or even share that many hobbies, you just have to be there for each other. Last year when Michael was secretly tidying up my garden in return for me looking after his cat, I thought I'd found a friend. He was kind and considerate, and we never stopped talking during that party. I scroll through my phone to a picture of us both that New Year — we looked good together, natural. At the moment the photo was taken I remember feeling that my life was finally piecing itself back together again.

'Why didn't you turn up?' I ask the photo.

I could walk away and, after a while, forget about him, but I don't think I can do that. I've told myself that he could be lying in a hospital somewhere with concussion, and if he is then I'll look very petulant for not having called. I'll sleep on it, and perhaps after the Lake District weekend, when I'm out of my Disney dream state, I'll either pop round to his house or make the call and just ask. It's better that I know now — after all, who knows how long Felipe's marriage will last now he's gazed into my eyes!

CHAPTER FOURTEEN: BINGO!

It begins to rain on the way up to the Lake District, which seems entirely appropriate; on one of our family holidays here when Zoe was young she insightfully pointed out that there probably wouldn't be as many lakes if it didn't rain so much. The book that we're here to discuss, *Grave Tattoo* by one of Ed's favourite authors, Val McDermid, also begins on a rainy day, so the setting and the weather will be perfect.

'Did you get the chance to read it?' I ask Sarah. When she decided she would come along after all, I offered to give her a lift although I knew I was taking a risk with Patty also being in the car — her journey pastime is making up vulgar words from the number plates that pass by. Fortunately she's been focussed on the potential Granny-Okie playlist she's downloaded and hasn't started playing yet.

'Yes,' Sarah says. 'It was a bit of a rush because the tea shop's been really busy.'

'Is it always busy in January?' I ask.

'Yes, if the weather is as mild as it has been then there are always joggers and dog walkers along the canal. I think people like to get out in the fresh air after food and TV bingeing over Christmas.'

'I can certainly understand that,' I say. 'The fresh air part, not the jogging bit.'

We both laugh.

'Me neither,' says Sarah. 'But I read the book and enjoyed it.'

'Doesn't matter if you haven't,' Patty interjects. 'Just nod along and add in a few stock phrases.'

'I apologise for my best friend,' I say to Sarah. 'She doesn't actually read any of the books, she simply comes to the weekends away.'

'There's no need,' says Patty. 'Okay, tell me each type of book I'm talking about with these phrases: *I really thought I knew who'd done it but the ending was a complete shock.*'

'Murder mystery,' say Sarah and I in unison.

'Ten points each,' continues Patty. 'Okay, what about this one: *The author must have spent months researching the detail; it was fascinating to find out about that era.*'

'Historical,' we both say again with a smile.

'Okay, let me have a go,' says Sarah. '*I so wanted her to end up with the bad boy but they never do.*'

'Romance,' I call out.

'See?' says Patty. 'So, this weekend let's play book review bingo. These are the rules: I'll give each of you a list of clichés that I think you'll hear from the others and the first to tick them all off gets a G&T from me.'

I can't help but think it sounds rather cruel, as if we're mocking our book-loving friends, but Patty reassures me that they'll love it when they realise what we're doing.

'And of course it challenges you two to actually say something that isn't a cliché,' my friend points out.

That has me thinking, as I genuinely didn't guess the ending but I now have to find a way of expressing that without risking losing the bingo game. Damn it, I'm already feeling competitive about Patty's silly idea.

'Tell me about the Granny-Okies,' says Sarah and I don't even need to look at Patty to know that her chest has risen and fallen as she prepares to talk for the rest of the journey.

* * *

'A gingerbread shop?' asks Patty as we drive past. 'Is that all it sells?'

'Grasmere is famous for it,' I tell her. 'It would be a travesty not to try some.'

'And that's the churchyard, isn't it?' asks Sarah, pointing at the church next to the gingerbread shop. 'The one where Wordsworth is buried?'

'It is,' I reply. 'And again, it would be a travesty not to visit it, given that he features in the book.'

As I pull up to our hotel, the rain has stopped and the air has that smell of being freshly washed. We're in the centre of the village with its twisty lanes and slate-built houses.

'Hmm,' says Patty, scribbling away. 'I need to add that to the bingo — "should visit grave". You're excused for saying it this time.'

I protest that it's not a clichéd expression and therefore can't go on the card but she's not listening. She finishes scribbling then hands Sarah and I separate pieces of paper containing the phrases that we have to listen out for. 'Just as with bingo, you've each got different ones to look out for,' she says with a smirk.

Peter, Ed and Caroline have already arrived when we go to check in. They wave at us from the bar, where they look very cosy around a real fire with a bottle of delicious-looking red. We girls quickly head to our rooms, freshen up and then join them, ordering another bottle to ease us into the weekend.

'So what's the plan for these next two days?' asks Ed after we've toasted our book club. 'I guess we should really go and see Wordsworth's grave at some point.'

Patty purses her lips trying to hold back the laughter and I notice Sarah taking a discreet look at her piece of paper and giving me a barely noticeable shake of the head. That means she doesn't have that phrase on her card and it's one–nil to me.

I explain that my idea is to relax after our drive and discuss the book after dinner; that leaves tomorrow for exploring the village and the surrounding countryside. The hotel has a library room which I've reserved so we have a snug place filled with the smell of paperbacks and leather chairs to settle down in and discuss the story. This book actually combines both Ed's and Peter's literary loves. It's a crime story but with a historical twist involving a lost Wordsworth poem. So I hope that being here, where Wordsworth lived and died, brings the book to life.

'Have you been doing these weekend jaunts for long?' Sarah is asking the group.

'It's nearly a year since our very first,' replies Peter. 'We went to a haunted castle not far from here to discuss a ghost story.'

'And Peter met his partner, who was skulking in the dungeons wearing a tattered wedding dress,' adds Ed.

'I should have guessed then that was his thing,' said Peter with a smile. 'It was a lovely break anyway, so we kept them going.'

'It sounds very special,' says Sarah. 'I'm really looking forward to this.'

After drinks we head to our rooms to change for dinner. Mine is a small suite with a king-sized bed which seems a waste; if things had gone differently I might be sharing that bed. Although I still can't imagine doing anything more than lying in someone's arms; it's romance rather than sex I think I need — which is not the case for Patty.

'The bed in my room could certainly withstand some action,' she declares as she bursts through the door. 'I've just videoed it for Jack. This isn't bad either, shame Michael didn't work out.'

'Never say never,' I say. 'I've decided I'll call him when we get back. After all, he might have a good reason for not showing up.'

'You're right, he could have died for all we know — at least that would be excusable,' says Patty, getting a pillow thrown at her.

'Are you ready for dinner?' I ask, refusing to dignify her comment with any further discussion.

'Born ready,' is her reply.

* * *

We descend the stairs side by side, looking as if we've coordinated our outfits. We're both wearing thigh-length dresses in rich winter colours with high-heeled boots. Of course Peter notices it.

'You two look like you're about to do some catalogue modelling,' he says. 'Or appearing on daytime TV showcasing the fashions for this season.'

'Makes a change from me always modelling last season's clothes,' I reply, smiling.

Sarah looks stunning. She has thick auburn hair which I've only ever seen tied up, but now that it's down, it's gorgeous. With the deep plum tunic she's wearing, the effect is so glamorous.

'You look like a classic movie star,' I tell her, getting a shy smile in response.

The hotel does us proud with a dinner full of local produce including Lakeland lamb and sticky toffee pudding. We're almost ready for a nap by the end of the meal but Caroline wakes us up by clinking her glass with her knife and telling us it's time to adjourn to the library. We carry our full tums through the hotel lobby and take our seats with the book on our laps. Most of us have little post-its inserted to talk about paragraphs and pieces we have particularly enjoyed.

'I don't mind kicking off the discussion,' says Ed. 'And you may find this surprising but I was most fascinated by the historical element. Every time the narrative veered towards modern day, I just wanted to be back in Wordsworth's time or hearing more about Fletcher Christian.'

'I feel the same,' added Caroline. 'If this is true, the author must have spent months researching it — there were details I would never have known.'

My ears prick up and I take a quick glance at my bingo sheet, which I've hidden at the back of the book. I don't have that phrase but a look up at Sarah tells me she has and she gives me a tiny smile.

'Well, I'm going to surprise you too,' says Peter. 'I loved the crime-solving aspect, and I really thought I knew who'd done it but the ending was a complete shock.'

I can't actually concentrate on the discussion now as I'm so obsessed with winning this bingo game. I catch a glance of Patty out of the corner of my eye and she has a hand clamped over her mouth trying to hold back her laughter.

'Angie, what did you think?' asks Sarah.

Immediately, I wonder if this is a trick question and she's simply trying to get me to say one of the expressions on her list. I try desperately to think of something that Patty won't have. I ponder some possibilities:

'*I loved the characters and felt I really knew them.*'

'*I thought she really brought the landscape to life through her descriptions.*'

'*The segue between the two timelines really worked for me.*'

I doubt Patty would have thought of using the word segue, but I also know that she hasn't read any of it so decide to read out a section that I thought was beautifully written. I do just that and see Sarah gleefully ticking something off her sheet. How could that have happened? Wanting revenge, I ask her how she found the book. She hesitates, knowing the stakes are high at this stage then says, 'I'm not sure I'm qualified to critique really, being so new to the group. I'd rather just listen to your views.'

Aha! She thinks she's been clever but the newbie at book clubs often professes their inadequacy — it's as big a cliché as any other and I have it on my list. I cross it off and know we're neck and neck.

'The other thing I thought,' says Peter in a slow contemplative manner as Sarah and I have pens poised, 'is that the lead character was completely believable.'

'BINGO!' I shout, as does Sarah and everyone else in the room. It's followed by howls of laughter.

'You've been playing us,' I say, realising what has happened.

'Patty told us what we had to say.' Caroline is wiping the tears from her eyes. 'Watching you two getting more and more competitive was hilarious.'

I hit Patty with the book this time and claim a G&T for both Sarah and myself. We regroup and discuss the book properly, after which we retire to the bar. I quickly become engrossed in a conversation about Mum's bucket list with Peter and Ed while Patty, Caroline and Sarah chat together.

We all head to bed shortly after midnight and as I get to my room, Patty tells me she has something to tell me. I invite her in and sit on the bed, taking off my boots as she clears her throat and then begins.

'I was talking to Sarah about the day you got stood up.'

My shoulders drop.

'I really wish you hadn't,' I tell her. 'It's private.'

'It's probably a good job that I did.' Patty sits down beside me and takes hold of my hand.

I hold my breath, saying nothing. Patty gets out her phone and brings up pictures of the New Year party.

'I was telling Sarah about Jack and showed her this photo of the four of us together. She instantly pointed at Michael and asked whether he was the man you'd been waiting for. I told her it was and she said she recognised him. He came into the café a couple of times later that week with a woman, someone he looked very close to.'

CHAPTER FIFTEEN: THE HILLS ARE ALIVE

After very little sleep, I sneak out of the hotel to watch the sun rise above the mountains that surround this beautiful village. A watercolour sky of pinks and golds contrasts against grey-green fells, and in the distance I see a sprinkling of frost on the higher fells. It's certainly chilly and I hug myself, although in doing so I'm glad to be feeling something other than despair. I consider that word and decide it's probably too harsh but I don't know how to describe it. Disappointment? Defeat? Whatever it is, I should be grateful to Sarah for telling me about Michael and stopping me making a fool of myself by calling him.

'How are you not freezing to death?' says the voice of Patty behind me. I turn round to see her swathed in a woollen blanket that I last saw on one of the library chairs. She steps beside me, holds it open then enfolds me in it too. I'm instantly warmed by her body and the blanket — it's lovely.

'What are you thinking about, Bo?' she asks.

I sigh and snuggle into her. 'I was just wondering how many of these mountains we have time to climb before we head home.'

'Well, I know the answer to that one. Gingerbread shop v. mountain — not a hard choice to make. Now come on inside, there's a full English waiting.'

She bundles me back into the hotel, where the aromas of breakfast contrast with the fresh air outside. Both are wonderful in their own way.

My friends are already around our table, where coffee is being poured and toast being buttered. Sarah gives me a sheepish glance, so I walk towards her with confidence and sit down beside her. I squeeze her hand and whisper, 'Thank you for telling me. I needed to know.'

I then look up at the table and declare, 'Well, I'm off to the buffet before Ed the food monster gets there.'

I stand and the others follow me to fill plates with more than any one of us would ever normally eat in the morning.

I hadn't thought I'd actually be hungry but I've returned to the table with a little of everything and I eat it all without pausing.

'Blimey, girl,' says Patty. 'You're going to need to do all those mountains to work that lot off.'

'Pot calling kettle,' I say, looking at the empty plate sitting in front of her. 'And you're planning gingerbread later.'

'I was built for comfort not speed,' is all she says.

From the groans and moans of pleasure, there is agreement around the table that the breakfast is exceptional. When Ed is finished he looks longingly over at the buffet table.

'I'm at that junction where I've loved what I've eaten and I want more but I know it would be too much.'

'Always leave 'em wanting more,' Patty tells him. 'That's my motto.'

'You're a fountain of wisdom this morning, Patience,' I say as we all leave the table. 'If the Dalai Lama needs an assistant, I'll put a good word in for you.'

* * *

We load our suitcases into our cars and begin our walk through the village up towards Dove Cottage, which was Wordsworth's home. It's an exceptionally pretty place which you could imagine being recreated on a film set as a perfect setting for a city-girl-comes-home romance or a cosy mystery. The dark-slate shops with their bright-white window frames host mainly cafés, artworks and outdoor gear. I pause at one of the art shops and browse the paintings, thinking it would be fairly difficult to create anything that wasn't beautiful living here. I select one that reminds me of the colours I saw this morning and the assistant puts it behind the counter for me to collect on my way back.

Dove Cottage is a whitewashed building like many others around here. We're booked in for a tour and our guide tells us that the poet lived here with his sister Dorothy for eight years when he was twenty-nine and that he composed many of his famous works in the house. I'm surprised by how simple it is and express this.

'It was a time of plain living and high thinking,' our guide is saying. 'Wordsworth's words, not mine. He wrote them in 1802 and pretty much predicted how the world would unfold.'

He has been carrying a well-thumbed book of poetry and opens it now, clearing his throat before he begins to read.

> *The wealthiest man among us is the best:*
> *No grandeur now in nature or in book*
> *Delights us. Rapine, avarice, expense,*
> *This is idolatry; and these we adore:*
> *Plain living and high thinking are no more . . .'*

'He was lamenting the world's love of material things over nature, of show over substance, and I think he got it spot on,' says the guide. 'So the house is simple but the garden was the place he really loved. He called it "the loveliest spot man hath ever found" — let's go outside.'

From the spontaneous look of horror on Patty's face I know she would far rather stay in the warm, but I give her a shove to walk in front of me. As it's January, the guide has to try and describe how it would look in full bloom and although I nod along, I've never been a gardener so can barely relate to what he's saying and don't know many of the plants he mentions, although obviously even I know what a rose bed looks like. The guide then directs us to what was Wordsworth's favourite spot, a small hut at the top of some steps, which the poet apparently wanted to resemble a wren's nest filled with moss and surrounded by heather.

'So, men had sheds even back then,' whispers Patty.

We're told that it can't be fully appreciated from this angle and that we have to climb the steps to see it from Wordsworth's perspective. With all the huffing and puffing you'd have thought the guide had asked our book group to conquer Scafell, not a few stone steps. It's worth it as we all look out over the fells from Wordsworth's favourite spot. Peter certainly speaks for me when he says, 'I can see how he was inspired here.'

The guide recites 'I Wandered Lonely as a Cloud' while we stand taking in the landscape and give him a round of applause at the end. We walk back down the steps to end our tour and as we do Ed asks the guide whether it's true that Wordsworth went to school with Fletcher Christian.

'Yes,' he replies. 'They both went to Cockermouth Free School but William was six years younger than Fletcher, so I don't know about you, but I never knew anyone six years either side of me when I was at school. Been reading *Grave Tattoo*?'

We explain that we're a book group and we're in Grasmere because that's exactly what we've been doing.

'It's a lovely thought that they knew each other and certainly quite remarkable that such a small place could produce two such important historical figures, but I think it's probably a fantasy held by the author, as is the notion that Wordsworth met Fletcher in later life,' he says as he's shaking our hands goodbye.

'Did you get the impression that he didn't want his beloved poet sullied by the imagination of a crime writer?' asks Peter.

'It could be that he does his best to bring the poet and his poetry to life and all he gets asked about is a spurious connection with a mutineer,' Caroline says.

'So, lovely people,' Patty asks loudly in an obvious effort to change the subject. 'On more important matters — are we all ready for gingerbread?'

The group cheers and Patty tells us to follow her.

* * *

The shop is tiny but the aroma drifts around the twisty streets, drawing us in. It's right beside St Oswald's church where Wordsworth and his family are buried, so Patty hasn't escaped the literary tour just yet. But for now, she has some difficult decisions to make.

'Should I get the gingerbread, the rum sauce or the gingerbread fudge?' she asks, lusting after the products on the shelves.

I mentally count to three and by the time I get to two the inevitable decision has been made.

'All of them,' she says to the shop assistant, replying to her question with the inevitable answer, 'the large size, please.'

We all buy something and like Patty I take all three products, but unlike her, mine are to give away to Zoe, Mum and Dad. I'll be helping my best friend demolish her supply anyway.

It's mid-afternoon when we walk around the church and the graveyard to make our final visit of the day. Many other tourists are traipsing along the small footpath which leads to the very simple tombstone that tells us Wordsworth died when he was eighty.

'Not a bad innings back then,' says Ed. 'A life of fresh air and literary enlightenment must be good for you.'

'That's reassuring to know,' says Sarah, who has been quiet all day. 'Especially for book club members.'

'The fresh air part didn't help him much,' continues Patty, reading from a leaflet. 'He died after he caught a cold when out walking. I told you it was dangerous.'

The lead guide of some Japanese tourists seems to be rapidly translating Patty's words as I can see the concern and then smiles on the faces of her group.

'Walk-ing dan-ge-rous,' says an elderly man. He finger-walks to make his point.

'Hai,' replies Patty, nodding at him.

As we leave the graveyard, Caroline asks her what she said.

'It's yes in Japanese,' she replies, getting eyebrows raised in surprise from everyone.

'Cruises are international affairs, you know,' she says to our shocked faces. 'I tried to learn six words in as many languages as possible — yes, no, please, thank you and the most important of all . . .'

She has her audience as we're gripped to hear the rest.

'*Voulez-vous coucher avec moi?*'

This time it's Peter who throws something at her and Ed who tells her that's ten words anyway.

After collecting my painting from the art shop we head back to the cars for our journey home. The valley is dark now with the promise of a clear cold night in the air. I can't help but wonder what the stars look like from Wordsworth's little hut and wonder if he wrote any poems about them. I'll have to look it up when I get back.

'Thank you for inviting me,' says Sarah from the back seat as we drive down the motorway. 'It's been a lovely weekend and you have a great bunch of friends.'

'My pleasure. I'm glad you enjoyed it.'

Sarah pauses then says, 'I hope I didn't ruin anything for you.'

It's my turn to pause because the weekend wasn't ruined, but in a way, my hopes were dashed. In the end I decide to maintain the sense of bonhomie that has surrounded today and settle for a platitude.

'You didn't ruin a thing,' I say. 'I've had the most wonderful weekend too and I really hope that you come along again.'

'Oh, I'd love to,' she says. 'And I'd like to invite you both to the tea shop for a free cream tea when you have time.'

'There's always time for a cream tea,' Patty says.

I reach down and flick the radio onto an eighties channel.

'Now, Patty, let's hear what you'll be doing for your first gig,' I say.

'With pleasure,' she says. 'I like nothing better than a captive audience.'

She begins to sing loudly and out of tune just to keep the mood light, but as we wind our way through the Howgills and the road ahead turns very dark, I feel her hand reach over to me and give my arm a rub. There's just no fooling my best friend.

CHAPTER SIXTEEN: FAMILY FORTUNES

'Does your mum know the difference between YouTube and a TV channel?' asks Josie one day when the travel agency is quiet.

'I know she's watched YouTube,' I say. 'So I'm sure she knows it's not the BBC, but having it on the smart TV confuses her. Why?'

'I was just thinking about her bucket list item to get on TV and wondered if she'd be happy with us creating a quiz show of our own and filming it. I got a board game of that show *Family Fortunes* and it includes the buzzer thing.'

'She loves that show. But I don't think she'll be satisfied with a bargain-basement version.'

'Oooh,' exclaims Charlie, swirling his computer screen around. Josie and I get up to see what has excited him so much. He's on a website about applying for quiz shows.

'Look at this,' he says. 'By happy coincidence, *Family Fortunes* are recruiting contestants at this very moment.'

My heart sinks at the thought of Mum dragging all of us into her fantasy. I can't imagine Dad or Zoe being delighted at the prospect either. Charlie notes the look on my face and adds, 'I'll do it with her — maybe I could say I'm her nephew.'

'And I could be her niece,' adds Josie excitedly.

It seems that Mum's list has hit on a few things that other people want to get on board with and it took her to mention them before we all came out of the woodwork. It makes me wonder how many desires lie latent and possibly never indulged because we don't make time for them.

We huddle around Charlie's PC to see which other shows are listed as needing contestants. Unfortunately, *Catchphrase* isn't one of them, but there is an article about how to apply for these shows. I skim it now but will read it properly when I'm at home; the writer says there's about a one in ten chance of getting on a show, which seems like incredibly good odds to me. I realise as I'm reading this that I'm disappointed; I had hoped there'd be no chance of my mother getting selected and showing us up to the whole nation. I do know that's incredibly unfair of me considering my post-divorce meltdown went viral online and caused the type of embarrassment I'm imagining for my own daughter.

'I think we would stand a good chance,' says Charlie. 'A gay man, an Aussie and a pensioner — we've covered most of the bases and your mum would be hilarious as the matriarch.'

The problem is that I know she would.

'I've got a brilliant idea for our application,' says Josie.

'And if we get it, we might be able to get audience tickets for the Mercury Travel Club members,' adds Charlie. 'Maybe to use in a prize draw.'

So it looks like the quiz train is rolling and it's not going to stop.

'Can I leave this bucket list item up to you two?' I ask, getting only a nod because they're both totally engrossed in how to make this happen. The little bell on our door chimes and a couple walks in.

'I'll, err, serve these customers, shall I?'

Charlie looks up and gives the couple a beaming smile and offers to get them a coffee. Once they're settled opposite me with their drinks, he heads straight back to the PC and into a deep conspiratorial conversation with Josie.

Throughout the day I make good progress with the dance holidays and think I should be able to tie up the loose ends and announce the full details by the end of the week. Charlie and Josie stay in close cahoots, although their plotting is occasionally interrupted by the inconvenience of customers. However, I can see by the smiles on their faces as we close up that they believe they have this bucket list item nailed.

'Do you think your dad would want to be on the show?' asks Charlie. 'There's always a sensible one to balance the others — they can't all be wacky.'

'Of course, your mum would still be team captain,' adds Josie.

As if it were ever in doubt. Sometimes, when I consider the personalities of those around me, I wonder whether Patty and I weren't accidentally swapped at birth. She's far more like my mother than I will ever be.

'I honestly don't know, but he loves a quiz and if you're really going to do this, you may as well ask him,' I tell them.

They clap their hands together in excitement.

'We need five members and we have your mum, dad, me and Josie — so there's a space for you, Angie, and you are actually family,' says Charlie, tentatively clutching his hands together in front of him with his head tilted coyly like some naughty schoolgirl.

I know instantly which role I would play — the one who's the butt of all the jokes. I can just picture my mother berating me on live TV because I can't name five things you do in a tent or whatever ridiculous question would be asked. I tell them that I'm going nowhere near the stage but I will accompany the Mercury Travel Club members if they get accepted and we get audience tickets.

'Will you at least make up the team for our rehearsal?' asks Josie. 'We're going to do a little video to accompany the application.'

'Is there really no one else you can ask?' I plead. 'It can't be Patty because she might be away on the cruise when it's filmed, but what about Peter?'

'He's going to be our quiz master,' Charlie says. 'Go on, Angie — what happened to the go-getter that took this business by the horns and made us award-winning? The one that got up on stage, got propositioned in Nice and was a complete inspiration? What would Richard say?'

As he's speaking I'm thinking about everything I did post-divorce, and as he lists the highlights of the year, I realise that I'm still letting one person dictate my mood. And Charlie is also right — my hero Richard Branson would not be happy to see me like this. I wonder whether he gives relationship as well as business advice? I must look that up later. For now, I take a deep breath and channel the pre-Michael Angie, the one that gave it all a go. After all, nothing ventured, nothing gained. And I kind of think I have very little to lose right now.

'Okay,' I say, pulling myself up tall. 'You've got your fifth team member.'

Charlie and Josie cheer then hug me as we bounce up and down as if we've won already. We haven't even been accepted onto the show yet.

They insist on driving straight round to my parents' house to tell Mum that we're applying to be on *Family Fortunes*. I'm happy when Dad says he thinks it will be a great laugh and that we'll need to practise. Seeing the smiling faces all around and hearing the gentle mocking of each other's likely efforts has me grinning like that old Cheshire cat. My friends and I are lucky to have the chance to share my mum's crazy list and we're going to have fun doing it — or at least most of it. The application has to be in within the fortnight so our team decides that the first rehearsal will be tonight at Charlie's house. To make it more realistic (did I really think that?) we hurriedly make some phone calls, and within the hour we have two teams: us, the actual entrants, and our competition — Josie's boyfriend Matt, Zoe, James and his parents. Although this is only supposed to be a friendly rehearsal, I know that my mother will be raging if she loses to Yvonne and Bob.

'I'm sorry I'm going to be missing this,' says Patty when I get home to change. 'It sounds hilarious.'

'Can't you cancel the rehearsal and come along?' I ask.

'Not really, Sheila has already changed her plans to make it tonight and I want to be sure we're ready if Zach and Khai come up with any gigs.'

'Well, it's being recorded, so we can open a bottle and have a giggle later,' I tell her, heading up the stairs.

'Bo,' says Patty as I'm mid-step. I turn to look at her quizzically.

'It's good to see you with a spring in your step again,' she adds.

I just give her a big smile then take each step two at a time to prove how springy I am. Of course, when I reach the landing out of breath, I vow never to do that again.

Charlie has given us instructions on our outfits; if we ever get to be on TV then there's a host of things we can't wear, including stripes and blue, so we're not allowed to wear them now. My heart often goes out to people I see on television who've made a real effort to wear something nice but the way that the microphone is lying or perhaps the seating position they're forced into makes the clothes all bunch up and give them a spare tyre whether they have one or not. Underwear is also an issue. Being able to see bra straps or lines isn't flattering either. Weather girls seem to get it right. They all seem to go for those very structured dresses that don't look comfortable but don't bunch up either. I've got quite an elegant shift dress with sleeves that would probably be perfect. I flick through my wardrobe and pull it out; it has a bit of stretch in it so won't be uncomfy and should work well on screen. It might be too formal but I'll give it a go and let the team decide; my mum will certainly have an opinion on what everyone is wearing and won't want to be outshone by any of us.

And she certainly won't be in the shocking pink mother-of-the-bride type outfit — complete with feather boa — that she's wearing now.

'Wow,' I can't help but say as soon as I walk into Charlie's kitchen, where our competition is being held. 'I've never seen you in this before.'

'It's new,' she tells me with a twirl. 'I want them to see I've made an effort.'

Everyone around the room has raised eyebrows and is standing staring at her . . . and shaking their heads in disbelief.

'I feel I should have made more of an effort,' says Yvonne, looking down at her jumper and jeans.

'Oh, what you're wearing isn't important,' my mum tells her. 'It's me the cameras will be on.'

Peter assembles each team and makes us stand either side of the kitchen island. Josie pulls out the board game she has and the crucial piece of equipment — the *Family Fortunes* buzzer. If we want to answer the question we have to buzz in first.

'You'll be disqualified if you just shout out.' He says this to us all but is looking directly at Mum. 'Now, are we all ready?'

We all cry 'yes' and Peter acts out the role of host by introducing us and getting onto the first question.

'Name something in a lady's handbag,' he says in a cheesy TV quizmaster voice.

'Fluff,' shouts Mum, getting a snort of laughter from everyone. She looks at us all indignantly and tells us that there's always fluff in everyone's bag.

Peter scolds her for not using the buzzer and tells her that if she does it again she'll be disqualified. I'm glad it's him holding Mum to account and not me. She promises not to do it again so we once again prepare for the question. Honestly, the tension around this kitchen island is probably on par with an England penalty shoot-out.

'Name something that makes a man look distinguished,' Peter reads from a card he's written.

'A beautiful woman on his arm.' This time it's Bob in trouble for shouting out, but as his answer is accompanied by a chorus of 'ahhhs' and a cuddle from Yvonne, he doesn't seem too bothered.

'Okay, teams, properly this time. You do have to use the buzzer on the show so you have to get used to it now,' Peter says firmly but gently. We all promise to behave and he clears his throat.

'Name something you do on a second date.' I press the buzzer quickly, getting a nod of approval from him.

'Angie, give us your answer,' he continues.

'Go for a nice walk.' I get disappointed murmurs from my team mates.

'Sorry, Angie,' says Peter, 'that's not in the top answers.'

'It's not her fault,' my mum pipes up, giving me a big hug and pulling me down towards her so she can plant a kiss on the top of my head. 'She never gets past the first.'

I cannot fault her timing and simply burst out laughing. I can't stop, and soon the others join in. If we ever do get on this show then the Great British public will probably learn more about me than they ever wanted to.

CHAPTER SEVENTEEN: WHO'S THAT MAN?

'Do you think you have a chance of being selected?' Patty asks as we stroll arm in arm along the canal on the way to Sarah's tea shop, come Sunday morning. It's my birthday and I've insisted on a very low-key affair, but Patty is equally insistent that we have cake.

It's lovely and brisk out and the setting is serene; the water is still, cyclists, joggers and dog walkers seem filled with the morning promise, and they all nod their heads or say good morning as we pass. Even the ducks bobbing gently look as if they're out for a pleasant perambulation. In the verges beside the path, small shoots are starting to appear alongside the snowdrops. With the blue sky and small white clouds it would be easy to assume that we're past the worst of winter, but from experience, it always seems that as soon as the crocuses start to flower, they're flattened by a blanket of snow. I always want to tell them to hide away for a little longer to be safe. I realise as I'm thinking this it's a little like my own life so wave the thought away.

'I guess we have as much chance as anyone else,' I reply, forgetting about the crocuses and taking Patty's arm. 'Mum was very funny even when she was inadvertently insulting me.'

Patty snorts and replies that somehow my mother always manages to pull off that combination.

'Anyway,' I continue, 'do you have the set finalised?'

'We do and you'll see it soon,' she says. 'We have a warm-up gig coming up on the fourteenth.'

'I'll rally the troops,' I tell her.

* * *

We reach a small metal bridge where three children wrapped up in big coats and scarves are playing Pooh sticks, so we stop and watch for a moment. The older ones seem to be indulging their younger sister but soon get competitive when her stick catches a current or slipstream or whatever canals have and wins the race. We all cheer and then laugh. It's amazing how the very simple things in life can bring the most pleasure. Patty reaches into her pocket and, after checking with their parents, offers the children a packet of fruit pastilles as their prize. They're delighted and we walk away happy with the world.

'I take it back,' says Patty as we approach the tea shop.

'Take what back?' I ask.

'My Mr Darcy comment. This is a lovely place to come for a date. I might even bring Jack for the stroll we've just had and then bring him here — if the cake is any good.'

'Great love stories can't all start on a cruise liner,' I tell her, feeling vindicated.

* * *

I remember last time I visited the tea shop, thinking how it was warm and cosy without being twee. That's still the sense I get now. The walls are a pale sage colour, which works well to complement the landscape outside. The furniture is light Scandinavian brushed wood, which makes the whole place say 'come in and relax'. So we do. Sarah is serving a customer when we arrive but she smiles at us. While we're waiting for her I peruse the small selection of gifts she has on sale — cards, candles, little dog biscuits and potpourri sachets, all of which look beautifully handmade. I pick up one card. The design is a little gnome couple hand in hand. For a moment, it makes me pine for the time last year when my own gnomes — Gnorman and Gnora — were mysteriously left on the doorstep. They're in storage at the moment waiting for me to find my own home. Their appearance made me think that someone was looking out for me and it turned out they were. Or Michael was, at least; how could he have gone to so much effort then and suddenly stop now? *Oh well*, I sigh to myself, *onwards and upwards*.

Sarah finishes serving her customer, tells her assistant that she's taking a short break, shows us to a table marked *Reserved* then disappears into the back kitchen.

'I've made something special as I heard it was someone's birthday,' she says when she emerges with a tray bearing the weight of a cafetière and an enormous sponge.

'Red velvet?' I ask in hope on seeing the frosting. She nods.

'I *adore* red velvet,' I say with added emphasis to ensure a large slice. There was probably no need for it as Sarah is cutting builder-size portions for both of us. I can feel the glare of her other customers on the back of my neck.

Having served us and a tiny piece for herself, her assistant comes over to take the cake back to the counter. Almost instantly, chairs start scraping back while customers are drawn towards it.

Sarah pours us coffees and tells us she's delighted that we could come.

'You've made me so welcome in the book club, it's good to be able to return the favour,' she says.

'Well, I don't think you'll be welcomed by Caroline again when I tell her what she's missed out on,' I mumble while nibbling a little bit of frosting stuck on the fork.

'Oh, she's the one who advised me what to bake and I've invited her here too,' says Sarah. 'Her and Ed are coming on Thursday to see if it's big enough to host the club one night.'

I look around and know it is but think we'll probably have to wait until summer so we're not walking along the canal path in the dark. I say this and Sarah nods in agreement.

'It's lovely here in the summer,' she adds. 'You should come when the swans and their cygnets are out. Their graceful movement adds serenity to anywhere, I always think.'

'That's often said about me,' says Patty, wolfing down her final crumb of cake.

'I think the word you're looking for is *rarely* — it's *rarely* said about you,' I say, getting a prod with the fork.

We all laugh and I look at Sarah, wondering whether she'll become a close friend when Patty leaves for the cruise. There's always a vacuum when my best friend vacates any space, and although I could never replace her, it would be nice to think I'll have someone to go out with.

'Morning, everyone,' says a voice behind me.

'Oh, David, hello,' exclaims Sarah, getting up and giving the man a hug — so much for having someone to go out with. 'Please join us.'

The man pulls up a chair and we make space for him. Sarah jumps up to grab him a cup and a slice of cake then sits back down.

'This is David,' she says as we all shake hands. 'He's my cousin and wine connoisseur extraordinaire — what he doesn't know about wine isn't worth knowing.'

He shakes his head and replies that he simply enjoys a glass but the real expert in food or drink is Sarah — he can't hold a torch to her cakes.

'Although I can make toast,' he adds as a joke.

'That's impressive in my books. If you can make toast without burning it then you're already streets ahead of me.' I get a smile from everyone except Patty, who's nodding in agreement.

David isn't one of those men who dominates conversations; he says he's heard about the book club and the lovely weekend we've had and asks us what we're reading next. Then he politely joins in when Patty talks about the

Granny-Okies and their forthcoming gig. He seems like a very nice guy. He looks slightly older than me, has dark hair with greying temples and hazel eyes beneath metal-framed glasses. He's not amazingly handsome but, as Patty might say, is smart enough to take home to your mother. I wonder if anyone has ever said that about me.

After ten minutes or so, Sarah gets up and asks Patty if she wouldn't mind tasting a new recipe she's experimenting with. I offer to give an opinion too but am told that it's okay — Patty will be enough. The two of them disappear into the kitchen and for a moment I'm offended that the woman I thought might be my new best friend is actually going off with my old best friend. I'm staring after them when a new pot of coffee is delivered by the assistant and David tops up my cup.

'I'm sorry about Sarah,' he says. 'She's always trying to set me up.'

The penny drops and my first reaction is relief that Patty isn't running off with a woman who makes outstandingly good cakes. She once said she'd marry Mr Kipling, so that is a real concern.

'Ah, I see,' I reply. 'My apologies too — I didn't realise we were both being trapped in her lair.'

'Although a cake shop isn't a bad place to be held hostage,' says David, raising his cup to me. 'Here's to the ransom not being paid until we've worked our way through the scones at the very least.'

We clink cups and I try to think of something to say as we've been thrust into this situation. There's no need as David is an easy conversationalist.

'Tell me about the Mercury Travel Club,' he says. 'I've heard you started it.'

I could talk for hours about my beloved club and tell him the philosophy of bringing local people and businesses together to have fun and build loyalty.

'That sounds fabulous,' he says when I've finished talking. 'Though I'm not sure how you'd involve a small accountancy firm — which is where I worked until recently.'

'Taking you to the *Czech* Republic,' I say.

He laughs politely even though it's an awfully weak joke.

'So how do you fill your time now?' I ask.

'Well, I enjoy golf,' he says, 'and actually I can sort of cook. Even though it's just me most of the time, I do pretty well and every now and then friends will drop round and I'll rustle up a spag bol or something similar. It's nice sharing food with people — I guess that's where the love of wine comes from.'

'Hospitality must be in the genes.' I nod at the cake counter. 'I'm afraid to say that I truly can't cook for toffee and my ex-husband actually ran off with a chef.'

'I'm sorry to hear that.' David looks genuinely concerned. 'You'll have to get your revenge on him by letting me cook dinner for you one night.'

Having lived through a month where getting a date with the man I thought was interested in me has seemed nigh on impossible, this invitation takes me completely by surprise and I simply sit there stunned.

'Don't worry if you can't,' adds David hurriedly. 'I know this is sudden and quite awkward. Neither of us knew we were coming here today to be set up and that's not the reason I'm asking; I would appreciate having someone to eat with — bring your friend if you'd like.'

My throat has gone dry so I take a sip of cold coffee and look up at him, smiling.

'My apologies,' I say confidently. 'You're right, I wasn't expecting this, but it would be lovely — so thank you, I'd love to come to supper.'

I hand David my number and he puts it into his phone then immediately messages me so that I have his. There will be no months of silence — we have each other's contact details so if I don't hear from him, it'll be because he's not interested.

'Is there any day of the week that you can't do?' he asks. 'I imagine you work a six-day week so can't do a Friday night.'

'As long as I don't drink I can do any night, but Saturdays are better and I can't do the fourteenth as I have Patty's warm-up gig that night,' I say.

'Would it be too much if I came to see her?' He seems quite keen.

I tell him he's welcome but in the event of my mother or daughter also turning up, he must under no circumstance say he has come with me. I suggest he bring Sarah as his cover story and he agrees.

'Well, I'm due at the golf course in a couple of hours so I'll call you next week and hopefully we can get together before the fourteenth,' he says, standing to leave. 'It really was lovely meeting you. I'm going to have a smile on my face all day.'

He gives me a peck on the cheek, and as he turns to say goodbye to Sarah, I spot her and Patty peeking out from the kitchen, watching the two of us. I shake my head at Patty as she gives me a tiny round of applause with her fingertips.

'Cake and a date,' she exclaims, hugging me after David has left and she's emerged from her hiding place. 'A birthday can't get better than that.'

CHAPTER EIGHTEEN: DINNER FOR TWO

'I'll say one thing for him,' remarks Patty as I'm getting ready to go for an early doors supper with David. 'He's not slow on the invitations. How quickly did he call you after that tea shop date?'

'Within forty-eight hours.' I recall how relieved I was when he actually did.

'And he's going to cook for you?' Patty continues.

'That's what he tells me.'

'Is he good at proper cooking? You know, all that kneading and grinding stuff,' asks Patty.

'*Patty.*' I give her one of my looks. 'Stop it right now.'

'I was just thinking that I hope he turns those hands to more pleasurable pursuits before long.' She winks. 'If you know what I mean.'

'An alien who had never met an earthling would know what you mean. You're not exactly subtle.'

'As some of the Geordie crew members on the last cruise used to say, "Shy bairns get nowt." I loved that expression; it could actually be my motto,' says Patty.

'I'm going to get you a T-shirt with it printed on.' I give myself a final spray of perfume and usher her out of my room.

'Do you think it might go anywhere?' Patty continues as we walk downstairs.

'I've met him once,' I remind her. 'He was nice company and he got in touch quickly, so we'll see. I'll give you a full report tonight.'

With that, I give her a little wave and head out to my car.

David has given me an address in Cheshire and as I drive out of Manchester, the houses become more spacious. I'll be sticking to my one small glass of wine with whatever he has cooked and am happy about that — I don't want to rush any potential relationship ever again. Patty would call this a fairly chaste courtship (if that's what it is) but I'm not her. I probably would have been concerned about this if I hadn't read the wise words of Richard Branson. My guru has advised me well on business matters this past year and I wasn't sure whether he'd have anything to say on relationships but his blog does offer a little insight. He's been with the same woman for forty-odd years, and recounts how it was love at first sight for him but that his wife wasn't that keen initially. He persisted and little by little won her over. Richard said that relationships aren't about the fireworks but the ongoing friendship and respect people have for each other. He advised being the best version of yourself to lift up your partner and this is what I'm trying to do. I figure that if David and I can become easy in each other's company and with each other's friends and family, then the romance will follow. That's the theory anyway.

David takes my coat and leads the way into the kitchen; it is large and open plan with bi-fold doors that open out onto his garden. He's not a gardener, so the space is laid to lawn with a small patio area bearing covered-up garden furniture at the end where it will catch the evening sun. It looks a lovely spot and I can't help but wonder whether I'll be coming here long enough to enjoy a glass of wine while embracing the final warm rays of a sunset. I'll have to have progressed to staying over by then.

'I thought we'd try a full-bodied *Zut Alors, La Plume de Ma Tante*,' David says to me, taking a bottle of wine from the rack. Or at least that's what it sounded like to me. I didn't actually recognise the name David reeled off rapidly so can't even begin to tell you —I smile as if I have a clue what he means. It's not important anyway as he's opened the oven door and this whole room smells instantly delicious.

'I've made a bourguignon,' he says, opening a casserole dish and taking out a spoonful which he lays to one side to let cool before putting the rest of the dish back in the oven and turning the heat down. 'And I hope you don't mind but I've invited over a friend and his wife — they're golf buddies and dying to meet you.'

I'm not sure how I feel about this as I thought it was supposed to be a first date, but maybe he's nervous too. Anyway, I'm quickly distracted as he blows on the spoon then holds it out towards me; I take a tiny piece of beef and my eyes roll in delight.

'Gorgeous,' I tell him honestly. 'The meat is so tender — just wonderful.'

I've lived with Patty for so long that I know I won't be able to go back and tell her his meat was tender without getting the most obscene roar of laughter in response. I must be picturing the scene as David asks why I'm smiling to myself. I reply that I'm simply looking forward to the evening, and indeed I am.

His friends are very amiable and chatty. They're both golfers but when they discover that I'm not, they veer the conversation away from birdies, eagles and albatrosses onto holidays and travel. It's just as well as I'd started to think I was at an ornithologist convention.

'I could organise trips to the very best courses in the world,' I tell them, trying to combine our great loves. 'And if there are a few people then I'll get better rates than you'd find yourself.'

'That's not a bad idea,' says David. 'If Angie can find us a deal, surely we can muster enough interest in heading to the sun to tee off.'

'And I'd find a resort where there's enough to do for non-golfing partners,' I add.

There's interest and my dinner companions agree to try and get a group together. David pulls a cheesecake out of the fridge which he tells us was baked by Sarah, and despite feeling very full, I take a small slither.

The conversation between the men moves onto other forms of sport and when David takes his friend out to the utility room, his friend's wife simply shakes her head in amusement.

'I always think it's useful that they have something to keep them occupied,' she says to me. 'Nothing worse than a man who hangs around the house needing you to keep them entertained.'

I say that I agree but thoughts flick back to my ex-husband, who was often out of my hair and certainly didn't need me to keep him entertained. I thought he was out with his friends from the local chamber of commerce and I suppose he was — well, one particular female friend anyway. But that's long over and I've achieved so much in the time since our separation and divorce.

'Why don't you come to the golf club one day?' she says. 'We have a ladies-only morning and, if you like, I could give you a lesson. It's a good social scene and you might even be an undiscovered Jin Young Ko.'

She laughs and then seeing my blank expression explains that this person is the women's world champion. I tell her that I doubt it very much as I have no hand–eye co-ordination but that I'll think about it.

The men come back in and I tell David that I have to be going but I hope to see him at Patty's gig.

'Angie's friend has a tribute band; she's playing this week,' he tells them.

I dread them all saying that they'll come along, but happily they sigh their regret as they're off to the theatre.

* * *

When I get home, Patty is still up, sitting on the sofa with a glass of wine on the coffee table and her tablet lying beside her.

'Been videoing Jack?' I ask and she nods.

'But he had to cut the call short. One of the kitchen assistants got a bit too enthusiastic with the shredder. It was supposed to be plain coleslaw but now they've had to tell the guests it's beetroot.'

She watches my expression as I move from being horrified at what I've just heard to realising that she's joking.

'Honestly, Angie,' she says. 'I do believe I could tell you absolutely anything and you'd believe it.'

She gets up, heads into the kitchen and returns with another glass. She pours us both a small measure and we take up our positions — her outstretched on the sofa and me in the big armchair with my knees tucked under. If things don't work out with Jack and David we already have our old married couple positions sorted.

Patty asks me how the evening went and I tell her honestly that it was a nice night with good food and friendly banter.

'Do you think it'll progress beyond that?' she asks. 'Or do you even want it to?'

It's a question I ask myself privately all the time, not just about David but any man. I sometimes think I've forgotten how to have sex. I wouldn't tell Patty this and now I simply reply that I don't know but I'm happy to let this relationship run its natural course.

After finishing the wine, Patty gets up and stretches.

'Time for my beauty sleep,' she says. 'A big week coming up — the Granny-Okies comeback gig.'

'There should really have been an announcement on the news,' I reply.

'Talking of which,' says Patty, 'there was an item on the news that you'll be really interested in.'

'What's that?'

'Apparently, the compilers of the most recent Oxford English Dictionary have been adding all these new words like *hashtag*, but they were so preoccupied with that, they actually forgot to include the word *gullible*.'

'Oh, ha-ha,' I reply. 'As if I'm going to fall for that one.'

'Suit yourself.'

Patty heads up to bed. I fell for this trick when I was a teenager as I've always been easily taken in. However, despite knowing that it's a joke I cannot resist the urge just to check, so as silently as possible I pull the dictionary off the bookshelf.

'I can hear you,' yells Patty, making me jump and drop the damn thing. 'While you're there look up the word *nincompoop*.'

CHAPTER NINETEEN: LET ME ENTERTAIN YOU

Valentine's Day is always a major day for bookings. Yes, there are those couples who are already in their romantic hideaways but there are others who get engaged or give each other travel vouchers or simply decide on the spur of the moment to celebrate their lovey-doveyness with a hotel, a sandy beach or a hot tub. And we're here to make those dreams come true.

The weather is typical February, which also bodes well for bookings, so all in all, I'm looking forward to being distracted from the lack of any passionate entanglement. I'm not sure yet where things will go with David, although he has called to say he enjoyed Saturday, so today would be a good day for him to reveal his thinking.

I'm going into work early in preparation so arrive before the others, unlocking the door and pushing the mail across the mat as I open it. I pick it all up in one bundle and dump it on my desk before heading to make myself a cuppa. We still get post from suppliers who have probably worked out that it's easy for us to miss their sales incentives if it comes by email. I also quite like reading through real mail and tidying my desk while having a coffee. It's quite meditative.

Back at the desk with my hot drink, I flick through the bundle of mail and open a couple which seem to have interesting offers that might sell well today. There are a few targeted at the wedding and honeymoon markets, which are incredible nowadays. When I think back to the options I had getting married, it's almost embarrassing: church or registry office with a three-course sit down and a disco. Of course, at the time, I was delighted with that and had a fabulous day. Patty was chief bridesmaid — refusing to be branded with either of the words 'maid' or 'honour' — but she made a speech and it predictably stole the show. I put the wedding offers in my top drawer, ready to pull them out and delight any couples looking for their own private barefoot beach ceremonies, and go back to the pile of mail.

I stop at a card-shaped envelope with my name on it. I can feel my heart pick up a beat and all of a sudden I'm sixteen again hoping that when I open this it's from a secret admirer and someone somewhere has a crush on me. I tear it clumsily and can tell it's a card. Ripping further at the envelope, I steady my heartbeat in readiness for it just being another sales promotion. Pulling the card out, it's the one that I saw in Sarah's café — with the gnome couple. I open it and the sender has written simply, *Thinking of you x*. I guess it's from David and that he picked it up when he was visiting Sarah — perhaps she noticed me looking at it and told him. It's a very cute card but again gives me no clues as to *what* he's thinking. Is he always thinking of me in the moments we're apart and therefore wants to spend more time with me? And why only one kiss? Perhaps there'll be roses later and this is just a small gesture as he knew I'd be in early today. I tell myself that it's non-committal because he didn't want to embarrass me in front of my colleagues. He needn't have worried about that.

'Oh my word,' exclaims Charlie as he bursts through the door a few minutes later. 'You should see the glorious pressies Peter had delivered this morning. Exotic flowers, Belgian chocolates, champagne — I feel thoroughly spoiled. And we're going for a couple's massage too.'

'Wow, he really pushed the boat out.' I tuck my gnome card away in the bottom drawer. 'And what did you get him?'

'I've told him it's a big surprise which I need to give him after work.'

'So you've got the day to think of something.'

He nods nervously. 'I adore that man. I could never imagine being without him and I need something that reflects how I feel.'

In an instant, I know what to do. Last year, Charlie was about to propose to Peter but got cold feet. I open the top drawer, take out a honeymoon brochure that has just arrived and walk over to his desk. I slide it over to him without saying a word and then head back. I look over to him when I'm seated and after he's read it, his eyes light up and he smiles at me. He asks whether I can hold the fort for half an hour and when he returns he looks scared but gives me the thumbs-up.

* * *

The day passes as I knew it would, with record bookings and a shop full of happy couples. We've sent people to Paris, Rome, the Caribbean, Seychelles, Mauritius — every romantic destination you can think of. Their happiness is infectious and despite my own ambiguous start to the day, it rubs off and I'm in a wonderful mood as we close up for the evening. Before we've had the chance to lock the door, the little bell rings and I look up to see Sarah coming in.

'I just wanted to let you know that I can't make Patty's gig tonight,' she says. 'Sorry, I didn't want to call and it seems like a lame excuse but I've just been invited out.'

'Wow,' I say. 'A last-minute Valentine?'

'Possibly,' she says coyly. 'Did you get anything?'

I'm guessing she must know so I pull the card from the drawer and show it to her.

'It's from your café, I think. I'm guessing it's from David.'

She looks at it and reads the greeting then hands it back to me saying, 'Oh, yes — I think I saw him buying it.'

With that, Sarah tells me to wish Patty luck and says goodbye.

* * *

Patty, of course, doesn't need luck. When I get home she's on her way out, saying she's meeting Sheila and Kath for a soundcheck. I still can't get used to my friend having 'soundchecks'. I cook some fresh pasta as it only takes minutes and then get dressed in jeans and a cropped leather jacket. I set to work with my wrinkle-blurring stick beneath the make-up then tousle my hair to try and look young and carefree. Standing back from the mirror, I check out my handiwork and decide I've done a pretty good job. Then again, I often think this only to have my hopes dashed when I stand next to an *actual* young person. Maybe that's the key to a youthful appearance — only ever stand next to people older than you.

That shouldn't be a problem tonight as I doubt the twenty-year-olds of Chorlton will be queuing to get into the rugby club to watch the Granny-Okies on Valentine's night. The club tends to have an older clientele and I'm guessing Josie and Matt will be the youngest there. I don't know whether Matt would rather do something romantic with his girlfriend but Josie wouldn't miss this comeback for anything — she finds my best friend absolutely hilarious.

The venue is already busy when I arrive so I grab a table near the back and get a drink. We'll be up dancing for most of the night but will need a recovery spot after the exertions. The room starts buzzing and I spot Patty peering out from behind the stage curtain; she blows me a little kiss then retreats. Before long, Josie and Matt join me, closely followed by Charlie and Peter. They're hand in hand and both are beaming.

'He said yes!' yells Charlie, holding out Peter's hand towards me, where there is a slender gold band.

We leap up and kiss them both, ordering a bottle of prosecco because they don't have champagne. There isn't time to hear more about the proposal because the opening chords have started. Our little group heads to the front to encourage the dancing to start and sure enough, the rest of the audience starts to sway along.

They play their eighties classics, everything from soft rock to cheesy pop, and the rugby club quickly gets into the spirit, cheering each intro as soon as they recognise it. The Granny-Okies give it all they have and are called back for an encore when the set is finished. When I hear what they're about to do, I realise Patty was prepared for this. It's the song she started strutting to after the audition, 'Hot Stuff' by Donna Summer. They've changed their costumes — they're in miniskirts with very low-cut V-neck T-shirts in blue, pink and yellow. Patty strides across the stage, flirting with any men in the front row, shaking her cleavage at them, singing the chorus and telling them that she needs some loving tonight. She attempts a very clumsy slut-drop, revealing flesh-coloured surgical stockings and bloomers and getting a few wolf whistles.

Then Sheila flumps onto a chair at the back of the stage and starts waving a hand in front of her face. Kath and Patty go over to her and when they turn round, they've all got fake sweat stains under their armpits and breasts which the coloured T-shirts show up to great effect and their faces are bright red. It sounds disgusting but the effect is hilarious — even more so as they pick up oversized lace fans from the side of the stage and change the words to 'hot *flush*'.

> *'Can't remember why I went upstairs, baby,*
> *Thinking I might need HRT . . .'*

They're fanning themselves and it's so perfectly choreographed it turns into the most unerotic burlesque dance I've ever seen. By the end of the number the audience has turned from being men on the front row to a crowd of middle-aged women belting out the new lyrics. '*I've had a hot flush!*' they're yelling at the top of their voices. The cacophony must sound riotous outside the building and as the number ends, I spot a couple of younger guys standing on the edge of the cheering crowd sneering. They don't look like typical patrons but by this time, no one is checking tickets. One finishes his bottle of beer and I can absolutely tell he's going to throw it at the stage. He raises it behind his shoulder and I move quicker than I have ever done in my life. Before he's fully pulled back I'm in front of him and grabbing at it. He looks down at me in astonishment and tries to push me off, but by now a couple of staff have spotted him and they wrestle him and his group out of the door.

From the stage, Patty makes a heart sign with her hands and tells the audience that she has one more song and it's just for me. She calls me up on stage and puts her arm around me.

'Because you're the one I'd like to be a Golden Girl with,' she says before singing the title track, 'Thank You for Being a Friend'.

I lean my head into her and look out at my friends smiling along with us. Turns out I did spend Valentine's with the people I love.

CHAPTER TWENTY: ALL DRESSED UP

'You were incredibly brave at the gig, he was twice your size,' Patty says to me as we stroll arm in arm towards the pub come the weekend.

'Small but mighty,' I say in a low, gruff voice, holding my free arm out in a bodybuilding pose.

A group of joggers in glow-in-the-dark vests run past us clutching little water bottles. We move aside to let them pass — in my case, it's as much about not wanting to be covered in the sweat that's dripping from them as it is about politeness. It's a bright, brisk day, definitely one to be out in the fresh air but wrapped up and cosy rather than torturing yourself in Lycra.

'I don't think they're New Year's resolution runners, do you?' Patty asks me.

'No, they look as if they've been at it for quite some time. And I'm sure they're all very healthy, but from their faces they never really look as if they're enjoying themselves, do they?'

'Runner's face . . .' Patty pulls a pained grimace. 'Wine drinker's face . . .' She relaxes into an expression of bliss and sighs.

'You see, they've got it wrong — a little of what you fancy, that's the key to a youthful countenance,' she concludes.

'I've never known you to stop at a little.' I smile and hug her arm a little tighter.

The walk through Chorlton takes us down Beech Road, which is filled with trendy shops and cafés catering to a cosmopolitan crowd. Yummy-mummies with off-road baby buggies and middle-agers with empty-nest-filling puppies sit side by side eating avocado on sourdough and flat whites. The vibe is friendly and the street has a buzz that I love. Chorltonites know they've become a bit of a cliché but embrace it anyway. It's a great place to live — only a short tram ride to Manchester city centre yet just by the canal, so with a short walk you could almost feel as if you're in the country.

Patty stops at an independent clothes store and looks at the dress in the window. It's a deep-red shirt dress with a kind of abstract floral pattern so that it doesn't look like a nan dress or as if you're wearing a florist's window.

'Do you think I could get away with that?' asks Patty.

My best friend is a tall blonde who was probably a shield maiden leading Viking raids in a previous life. People notice Patty when she walks into a room; wearing this, their eyes would be on stalks.

'I think you'd look stunning,' I say.

'Not too young for me?' she asks.

I check my watch and tell her that we have time to go and try it on; we have a big day ahead of us but nothing to stop us clothes shopping.

The assistant looks over and says hello as we walk in and trigger the little door bell. It's a small space but very busy with customers browsing the clothes rails. It's nothing like a department store with identikit ranges — the shop owner has each piece in a couple of sizes but the range is broad and eclectic. At first glance it looks a fairly random selection but as you browse you can see a capsule wardrobe in the making. It all works together without looking manufactured. Patty asks to try on the red dress and takes it into a changing room which has been formed behind an old-fashioned wardrobe door.

'That looks very Narnia,' I say to the assistant, who thanks me and tells me it was one of her favourite books and the reason for the shop name — Pevensie. I nod but haven't a clue what that reference means.

'You walk into the wardrobe a normal person and come out a magical creature,' she adds, smiling.

And indeed my best friend does.

The wardrobe door opens and Patty walks out looking an absolute vision.

'Wow,' says the assistant. 'Can I take a picture for our Instagram?'

Patty agrees, doing a few poses, and the purchase is made. She decides she's not going to take it off.

'It's going to be perfect for the dance lessons,' I tell her. We're heading there later this afternoon with the customers who have already booked onto the Vienna trip.

'It makes me feel fabulous, and who knows, I might even dance better in this.' We leave the store with the clothes she put on this morning in the shop's brown paper bag. She hasn't even put her coat back on; it's slung over her arm for the remainder of the walk to the pub.

'It's amazing how great clothes can make you feel, isn't it? As if somehow a dress finds the real you hidden underneath the sensible knitwear.'

I'm reminiscing about my own post-divorce transformation last year. After realising the trauma had left me looking ancient, I had the whole makeover and vowed I'd never let myself go again. While I'm not right back at ground zero, I wouldn't exactly say that I'm feeling like the dynamic Bo-Peep who rose from the ashes.

'Is that why you're currently in a polyester mix when I know you have a fabulous cashmere back home?' asks Patty, raising her eyebrows at me.

'Busted,' I reply. 'It just doesn't feel like a cashmere day.'

Our first activity for the day is brunch. We reach the pub and are taken to our reserved table; the lighting is low, and against the matte grey walls, Patty and her dress certainly stand out. A few people look up as we pass and I catch some admiring glances in Patty's direction from both men and women. I'm happy to see the place is busy and I contemplate how the trend for brunches must have saved many a pub. The advantage of this place over a café is that we can accompany our eggs with a Buck's Fizz and that's what we plan to do. It was booked as a celebration of Patty's return to the stage, and as the gig went wonderfully well, the glass of bubbly seems very apt. It arrives shortly after we sit down and we toast last night's great performance.

'And here's to your coming adventures on the high seas,' I add.

'I know,' exclaims Patty with a little shudder. 'Not long now and I'll be back on that ship. I'm excited and nervous at the same time.'

'It's not like you to be nervous,' I say as I read the menu, even though I know what I'm ordering.

'I might not show it,' Patty says. 'But I get butterflies before I get on stage. Once I get going and we're into the first song it's okay, but I was talking more about seeing Jack again.'

I look up at her in surprise.

'It's one thing flirting remotely and another spending every day together in a floating bathtub,' she says.

'I'm sure the cruise operator would be delighted to hear his luxury vessel described like that.' I laugh then add, 'I thought you and Jack got on brilliantly?'

'We do and we did,' Patty replies. 'Honestly, when we got together I finally understood why they cut to a firework montage in all those romcoms — it was amazing, but he'll have been away from me for months and he might be thinking that I was great in small doses but maybe not for the long haul.'

'I'm sure he wouldn't have bothered calling you every day if that were the case.' We both order our Eggs Royale from the waitress. 'And I'm equally sure that you'll pick up where you left off, unless you're having doubts about him?'

'God no — I've finally met a man who tells me he can cope with all this.' She brushes her hands down either side of her body. 'I'm not letting that go in a hurry.'

I know it hasn't only been about finding someone who could cope with Patty's massive personality, it's also been about her being ready to date again. A feeling I know only too well.

'So, can this David cope with all of you?' Patty asks, interrupting my train of thought.

'I'm not sure there's as much of me to cope with,' I say light-heartedly.

'There was last year,' says Patty. 'You were flying by the end of the year, and if you don't mind me saying, you seem a little flat this year. Am I wrong?'

I shake my head as I can feel tiny tears prickling at the edge of my eyes. I take a deep breath and swallow them away. Happily, the food arrives and we both exclaim our delight a little too enthusiastically. It's as if we've never seen a poached egg before — although, as I cut into the firm whites and let the soft yolk ooze over the smoked salmon, I can see it is a perfectly cooked one.

'How come I can never get this just right,' I say, letting the flavour luxuriate in my mouth. 'It's either all undercooked or all rock solid.'

'We were made for loving not cooking,' replies Patty. 'Now, back to my question . . .'

'Yes,' I say, nodding but not looking up. 'It feels flat. I had this huge journey last year picking myself up from rock bottom, and when the year ended on such a high, I thought it would just keep climbing but it hasn't — not for me anyway.'

Those final four words come out more barbed than I'd intended and I'm aware how bitter I sound. I look up at Patty.

'Sorry,' I say. 'That sounded awful. It's just that it felt as if we were on that journey together and we both had a fabulous New Year, and then you've continued to soar while I flounder and I'm scared I might lose you. Even Mum has a second wind — she was a sample-snaffling old woman last year and now she's a biker who wants an affair!'

Patty snorts and has to grab a napkin quickly to stop the mouthful she's just consumed reappearing.

'Firstly, you will never lose me,' she says when she's recovered. 'And you've had some bad luck when it comes to love, but what about this David guy? You seemed to like him after that date at his house.'

'It was nice. He and his friends have a good social life and it's nice to be part of a group. It's good to meet new people and I'll need that when you're away. Then maybe when you and Jack are onshore, you can join us.'

'We'd love to,' says Patty. 'However, I'm sensing a "but".'

'But . . . I *really* need to know what happened with Michael before I can move on. I simply can't get him out of my head no matter how much I try.' I'm aware that the words are about to come out fast and furious. 'One minute he's pursuing me — albeit by doing the gardening, but still — and then he seemed so enthusiastic when I invited him out, we even had a kiss at midnight and I really quite liked him. I thought we'd be taking it from there.'

I stop briefly for air then continue.

'Then he doesn't call but I find out he doesn't have my number so I forgive him and, again, look forward to getting together — he sounded so keen when I called, so it makes no sense whatsoever that he stood me up. And why would he be happy to hear from me if he was seeing someone else?'

'Maybe he just doesn't have the courage to turn you down directly?' says Patty as I take a moment to inhale then exhale deeply. 'Some men are like that — they hate conflict.'

'I didn't think he was like that. He seemed gentlemanly.'

'You could always ring and ask,' says Patty. 'Get that closure and then it's more likely to work with David. Magic up some of the bravery you showed tackling that bottle-thrower and demand answers.'

'Maybe,' I sigh, ready to change the subject.

Fortunately, from the corner of my eye I'm aware that a young woman has started staring at us as she loiters a little distance from our table. I turn to look at her and she comes over.

'Sorry for stalking you,' she says to Patty with an embarrassed fluster. 'I've just seen you on Pevensie's Insta page — you look amazing in that dress.'

'Thank you.' Patty gets up and gives her a twirl. The woman takes a photo and says she'll post it on the pub's page.

'It's like your dress is having a day out,' she says before thanking us and promising to leave us in peace now.

'That's not a bad idea,' I tell Patty as she sits back down. I certainly don't want to continue our conversation or go back to the house. 'We didn't have anything planned before the dance class, did we? Let's take your dress on a grand tour.'

CHAPTER TWENTY-ONE: LADY IN RED

The red dress takes itself back to Patty's so we can dump the clothes she came out in this morning and I can change into something a little more glamorous. It then hops onto the tram and into the city centre. Neither Patty nor I sit down; instead we hold the overhead rails as if we're riding the subway in downtown New York. My slate-blue dress is nowhere near as eye-catching as Patty's, but I've borrowed some of her scarlet lipstick and I feel invincible. I guess that's why they call it warpaint.

'Where shall we take Poppy?' asks Patty, and I instantly realise that she's named her dress.

'As she's new in town, I think we need to do some culture first — perhaps the art gallery?' I reply. 'Then dance class and a cocktail — what does she think to that?'

'Oh, she's very keen on both those ideas,' says Patty, 'particularly the cocktail part.'

Bizarrely, taking 'Poppy' out for the day feels far more exciting than if Patty and I had just decided to head into town. It's as if we have a new friend and we're honour-bound to show her a good time. We disembark near the beautiful central library and walk the short distance to Manchester Art Gallery. An early afternoon chill is starting to embrace the city now that we're in the shadow of its splendid Victorian buildings but there's no way we're putting our coats on. We simply turn the walk into a stride and are soon through the glass doors of the entrance and back into warmth.

'So, what would Poppy like to see?' I ask as we look at the list of collections and exhibitions.

'I think she'd like to see the costumes,' Patty says. 'To see if anything is as fabulous as she is.'

We head to the lift and press the button for the first floor. After all, we can't walk the stairs and risk ruining our current levels of gorgeousness with underarm sweat stains, can we?

The collection is organised in chronological order, running from the Victorian to the modern age. Despite thinking ourselves the bee's knees, these dresses showcase the most incredible craftsmanship.

'I think even Poppy would have to admit we'd look fairly plain by these standards.' I nod to an elaborate velvet dress with a full skirt.

'She's just pleased we no longer have to wear those.' Patty points at a torturous-looking corset with an impossibly small waistline.

'How on earth did they ever fit into those? Did they make women smaller back then?'

'Smaller and often invisible,' Patty says.

Beside the dress is a walnut parlour table with a silver tray containing sherry glasses, alongside an explanation that the dress would have been worn at social gatherings.

'Although, if that's the size of glass they drank from during their girls' nights out, then maybe that explains things,' Patty adds. 'Compare that to a gin balloon.'

'You couldn't even fit an ice cube in that,' I say. 'They must have had the gin neat.'

We move through the timeline, past the impossibly small hips of the 1920s and the tiny bra-less bosoms of the 1960s, relieved to find a dress that we believe we could actually fit into.

'Finally,' says Patty, admiring the long, sequinned gown. 'It's a bit bling but at least it's normal woman sized.'

'Glad you think so — it's mine,' says a voice behind us.

We turn and our eyes are chest height to a person with impeccable eyebrows and cheekbones to die for.

'Poppy O'Cherry, at your service,' they say, holding out their hand as if they expect us to kiss it. I take it and give it a weak shake. 'I donated that after winning Drag Dance UK.'

'Sorry for calling it bling,' I say. 'It's spectacular.'

'Nothing wrong with a bit of bling,' they reply before looking Patty up and down. 'You're the red dress lady, I've seen you on Insta.'

Patty curtsies. 'And it's also called Poppy, so this is quite the coincidence.'

'Well, you are killing it,' declares the human Poppy. 'Get yourself in here — we need a selfie.'

They pull Patty into a cheek-to-cheek hug and, pouting, take a few photos. I check my watch and tell them that we have to head to the dance studio now.

They air-kiss and Poppy O'Cherry sashays away.

* * *

The studio is in a different part of the city away from the Victorian grandeur and surrounded by what would once have been squalor — the warehouses of yesteryear. Now they're fashionable offices, shops and clubs, including Marianne's dance school.

I've booked a waltz lesson for the Mercury Travel Club members and when we arrive, they're all there waiting, including my mum and dad, who are done up to the nines.

'You two look wonderful,' I tell them, scanning them from head to toe.

'I wouldn't want to let the *Strictly* judges down by being shabby,' says Mum. 'I made your dad polish his shoes twice.'

He holds up a foot to show me and I congratulate him on a job well done.

'You know the judges won't be here,' I say to Mum.

'In spirit, they're on every dance floor in the country.'

I can't argue with that.

Marianne claps her hands to get our attention and shows us the steps to the waltz. I'm hoping that with my prior knowledge I'll have a head start on this lot but as I look around the room, they seem rather more foot sure than I was. At least they're all going in the same direction.

Felipe and Marianne are going from couple to couple, so my other hope — that I'd be paired with the dark, handsome instructor — is also dashed. I'm with Patty and she's the lead. I scream as she throws me backwards into a tip and the whole room stops to look at us.

'That step isn't in it, is it?' asks Mum.

'Improvisation, Mrs S.' Patty pulls me back into a tight hold.

The dance restarts and I ask Patty to stick to the rules as I'm the one who has to do this in Vienna. She does as she's told, although she does count out loud the whole time.

'Why don't we all swap partners?' suggests Marianne. 'Patty, you dance with me.'

I'm delighted when Felipe approaches me and watch as Mum and Dad swap with another couple.

'You've improved since last time,' Felipe tells me.

'Well, I haven't stood on your foot yet.' I laugh.

It seems like no time at all before we're swapping again and I get Patty back. Dad is with Marianne and Mum with Felipe. I can see him having the same effect on her as she gazes up at him and a little blush rises to her cheeks when he takes her hand.

Patty adds a little swing to her moves but they're generally the right steps and it's fun. I catch a glimpse of us in the mirrored walls and tell her that we make quite a handsome couple.

'Maybe we should just ditch the men,' I say. 'After all, we already live together.'

'If this cruise doesn't work out, you've got a deal,' Patty says.

I watch my parents across the room and note that Mum is no longer gazing up at Felipe; she's staring daggers at Marianne, who is positively gliding across the floor with my dad. When the music stops, Marianne applauds Dad, who takes a bow. He has a huge smile on his face and is about to take the instructor's hand for the next piece of music when Mum barges over.

'Ladies, excuse me,' she says, elbowing Marianne and firmly grabbing Dad's arm, taking him to the opposite side of the room in a way that is the complete opposite of ladylike.

'How can she want an affair when she gets that jealous?' I murmur to Patty.

'Cake and eat it,' replies Patty as we start moving again.

I certainly wouldn't put that past Mum, but I'm quite encouraged by what's just happened. She chose Dad over Felipe.

* * *

'It must be time for cocktails now,' says Patty after we've said goodbye to everyone.

We head to a bar that is supposed to have the best espresso martinis in town and on the way there, my phone rings. It's Zoe.

'Mum, where are you heading now?' she asks. I tell her the name of the place and she replies that she's not far off so she'll meet us there.

The bar is relatively quiet so we have no trouble getting a good table. Patty orders their signature espresso but when she goes to order the same for me, I put a hand on her wrist to stop her. I'm suddenly exhausted and know that I don't want to risk being awake all night because of a shot of caffeine. I ask for a Virgin Mary and even saying the words makes me salivate at the thought of all that tomatoey vitamin C nourishing my body. When it arrives I suck a huge mouthful through the straw, giving me comically hollow cheeks in the process.

'Blimey,' says Patty when I've come up for air.

I spot Zoe coming in and wave her over. She bounds towards us with a smile on her face, gives us both a little kiss then sits down and signals to the waiter. She orders a virgin mojito and explains that she's just been at a conference in town and is driving home.

'I saw from social media that you've just been at the dance school so hoped you might be in town,' she says. 'I wanted to let you know I've sorted out Gran's makeover day and it's going to be amazing.'

Her eyes are gleaming as she explains her idea and it's fabulous — Mum will love it.

'I was wondering if you could get Poppy involved?' she asks.

'Patty's dress?' I'm as puzzled as my friend looks.

Zoe stares at us as if we're mad.

'It's lovely but I have no idea what you're talking about,' she replies. 'I mean Poppy O'Cherry — they seem to love you two.'

Zoe pulls out her phone and shows us the social media storm we've created today — or rather the #ladyinred has created, I'm just the sidekick. From the first picture in the boutique, through to our brunch date, the tram ride, the art gallery and the dance school, people have been 'spotting' us out and about and sharing it. On top of that, we discover that Poppy O'Cherry has hundreds of thousands of followers and has shared everything to their fanbase.

'That's brilliant publicity for all the places we visited today,' I say, genuinely delighted that they seem to have benefited from our little day out.

'I look pretty good, don't I?' says Patty, scrolling through the pictures with her usual modesty.

'Getting back to Gran.' Zoe takes her phone off us and regains our attention. 'Could you ask Poppy if they'll help?'

Patty promises to try but adds that as a performer, Poppy is probably already very busy.

'We have audiences waiting for us and we can't let them down,' she adds with a diva-ish flick of the hair. 'I should know.'

Zoe and I look at each other then, without a word, both of us dive in and tickle Patty relentlessly until she begs us to stop.

'My ribs hurt,' she yells through laughter. 'My feet, my ribs — is there no part of this body that has not been ravaged today? There's nothing left for Jack.'

At that moment, the bar owner comes over, tells us she's been following our day online and asks for a selfie with the bar sign in it. Patty readily agrees and stands up to have the picture taken. The owner offers us a free drink but I thank him and say no — I'd much rather pay my way with small businesses and anyway we have to head home.

Zoe drops us off and once back I instantly head for the bedroom to change into pyjamas then into the kitchen to make some camomile tea. I'm surprised to see that Patty has changed too.

'I thought you'd be keeping Poppy on for your call with Jack,' I say.

'You've got to be kidding,' she says. 'I can't keep up with her. I've locked her in the back of the wardrobe so she can't cast her silky spell on my man. He's getting the jammies and cocoa version of me tonight.'

'I like that version,' I tell her, then wish her goodnight. It's been a grand day out but even I'm glad to hear Poppy is back in captivity.

CHAPTER TWENTY-TWO: THE IN CROWD

'The Vienna holiday is selling itself,' says Charlie later the following week as he's checking our performance to date. I stand behind him as he looks at the booking summary; he's right, the trip is pretty full.

'I have a golf club dinner tonight and was hoping to drum up some interest there,' I tell him. 'Can you keep a couple of spaces open? I'm there primarily to talk about golfing holidays but I'd like to showcase the range of the Mercury Travel Club too.'

He agrees to keep a couple of the email enquiries on hold until the morning and to tell anyone coming in off the street that it's at capacity but we're creating a waiting list just in case of cancellations.

'I have to be honest and say that I wasn't sure a dance-based trip would have particularly wide appeal,' he tells me. 'But after watching all the social media coverage of your weekend, everyone wants to dance like the lady in red — me included if that Felipe is leading.'

'I'm going to tell Peter you said that,' I say, smiling. 'Your *fiancé*.'

'God, how I love hearing that word, but he won't mind. He loves me and both my left feet.'

'Which I bet haven't touched the ground all weekend,' Josie chips in. 'Did you make any decisions about the wedding?'

Charlie grins like a naughty schoolboy and tells us that he was trying to be professional but they've been talking about it non-stop.

'The brochure you gave me for the honeymoon was gorgeous — an island in the sun and a glorious sunset as the day ends,' he says dreamily. 'And I think we'd like to do something a bit different to the normal registry office affair for the ceremony. Perhaps something glamorous or exotic.'

'I wouldn't expect anything less. So is that what you'd like? A wedding on an island?'

'Maybe, but I'd like you both to be there so that might not be feasible.'

'We can close the shop for a long weekend,' I say. 'Think of all the business it could drum up.'

'Are you planning to pimp my wedding, Ms Shepherd?' exclaims Charlie in mock horror.

'Oh, you know me. I pimp my best friend, my mother's bucket list and my new boyfriend's golf buddies — I'm shameless.' I know the word Josie will pick up on.

'Boyfriend . . .' she repeats. 'So you've actually ditched Michael for David then?'

I tell her that you can't ditch something that you haven't actually started.

'But David's a go?' she persists.

I give a little 'maybe' shrug and get a whoop in response.

'Angie and David sitting in a tree — K.I.S.S.I.N.G.,' sings Josie childishly.

Happily, a customer walks in and stops any further interrogations, so Charlie and I leave Josie holding the fort while we head out to the staff room and continue our assessment of how the year is going. We're six weeks in and traditionally this period is peak booking time, so we should be doing well and happily we are. I write up our progress on the whiteboard.

'Long haul has done tremendously well, so I think we should try and capitalise on that to capture more of the market in autumn,' I say. 'Perhaps another focus on safaris?'

'Add in some culture and relaxation too,' suggests Charlie. 'Tigers and Taj Mahal, Zebras and Zanzibar — that kind of thing.'

I write that up without having any clue whether those animals live anywhere near to the places mentioned. We both know what he means.

'Cruises are still huge,' he adds. 'But I think we're so well known for them now we don't really need to focus on marketing them.'

'Nevertheless, I'll ask Patty if her company can offer any additional incentives but overall I think you're right. What else is big now? How about wellness? Any mileage there? We did all say we'd get fit this year and so far we've done absolutely nothing about it.'

'Only because the military fitness man was fully booked for January — he might have slots available now. We should ask.'

'I'll do that,' I say. 'And I'll take a look at the retreat market. Would you fancy going on one?'

'A holiday of denial? Doesn't appeal to me.'

'Enlightenment and spiritual awakening,' I tell him. 'Plus there's the chance to lose a few pounds and have glowing skin before a big day.'

He takes the hint and tells me he'll look into that one, and as we both leave our meeting to rejoin Josie, I catch him checking out his profile in the shop window and discreetly pulling his tummy in.

* * *

I find myself doing just the same a few hours later when I'm zipping up my dress for the golf club event. It's their AGM, where they do official things like review the accounts and make their annual list of refurbishments as well as decide on member events. David has managed to get me a slot to talk about the holiday opportunity, so I want to do a good job. Looking my best always boosts my confidence but this dress is just a bit too snug, so I change into something a little more accommodating and instant~~ly relax. I re~~ally must get on to that fitness trainer soon.

'Why don't you join us in the bar afterwards?' I say to Patty as she's helping me fasten a necklace. 'You can talk me up.'

'Isn't it only for members?' she asks and I tell her not to worry, the bar accepts any lowlife.

'Obviously,' is her retort but she adds that she'll try and get along later.

* * *

I sit outside the committee room feeling like I'm waiting for the headmaster to call me in. Which he does — well, David does — after twenty minutes or so. The whole committee is dressed formally in club ties and blazers. I feel and look like the outsider, but as Patty would say, flaunt your difference.

'A golf club is about community,' I begin my rehearsed opening. 'Like-minded people enjoying their hobby, respecting the traditions and having fun together. This is a place to build friendships that last, and I think a partnership with Mercury Travel could enhance those friendships and create even greater loyalty to your club.'

'Not that we have any problem with loyalty.' David laughs, addressing the committee. 'If anything, we can't get people to leave.'

He nods towards an elderly gentleman and the rest of the committee join in the obvious in-joke. I smile as if I understand and continue to talk about travel opportunities, visiting courses around the world with activities for non-golfers and, of course, discounts for members of the club. At the end I thank them for their time and get a polite round of applause. David stands to show me out, telling the committee, 'Angie has a great little business in Mercury and I'm sure we can help each other out.'

Once back in the corridor, David tells me they'll just finish up and he'll see me in the bar.

I'm mightily relieved to see Patty in the bar when I walk in, and tell her as much. 'It felt as if I were intruding into some secret sect.'

'I suppose it is a bit like that.' Patty points up at the walls, where rolls of honour and plaques commemorate the great and the good of this club going back to the pre-war days. 'How was David?'

'Oh, he was fabulous, supporting me and cracking a couple of jokes to break the ice. Saying I have a great little business and trying to get their support.'

'Hmm,' says Patty. 'Now, what are you having?'

She gets us both tonic waters as it's a work night and we both drove here. David comes in with a big smile on his face.

'They liked you,' he tells me. 'Are you free to talk to our chairman? He'd like to come and chat.' He nods at the drink in my hand. 'You haven't had too many of them, I hope.'

He says this with a little laugh and I reassure him it's completely non-alcoholic. He waves an elderly gentleman over and he shakes my hand, thanking me for the presentation. He looks over at Patty as if he's trying to work out who she is.

'You may have seen me on stage,' she tells him as she holds out her hand for him to shake. 'If you like things a bit saucy, that is.'

The chairman looks slightly bemused and David quickly pulls him and me to one side, leaving Patty standing alone.

'She's joking,' I tell the chairman. 'She's my best friend and is part of a wonderful tribute act — they'd go down a storm here.'

'I doubt that,' David adds quickly as in the background I hear Patty slurping the end of her drink and hiccoughing. David moves us even further away.

I catch her eye and give her a 'stop it' shake of the head. She simply shrugs her innocence in return.

'I was telling our chairman that you'd probably be able to secure a good deal at Monte Rei — it's his dream course and we felt it would be a good trip to take for his retirement.' David looks at me with eyes wide open, indicating that I have to say yes to this.

I nod and say that we can certainly look into it and we have taken golfers to Portugal before. I'm a bit fearful that the club are going to expect more of a discount than we'll be able to secure but don't say it.

'It's a good job David met you when he did,' says the chairman. 'The place needs a fresh set of ideas when I go.'

Patty chooses this moment to interrupt and tap David on the shoulder.

'If I wanted to play here, would I have to bring my own bat and can you start anywhere on the pitch?' she asks.

I snort but David looks horrified.

'Patty is teasing,' I tell him. 'She knows full well it's called a club and you play on a course.'

'Actually,' he replies, trying to sound light-hearted, 'you can't play at all unless you're a member — whether you bring your bat, racquet or club. I could put in an application for you, what's your handicap?'

'My devastating good looks are often too distracting for those around me,' says Patty without missing a beat. Even the chairman is amused now, but David looks flummoxed and I have to spare him any further embarrassment.

I take Patty by the arm and tell her I'll see her back home; happily, she does as I ask so I can get back to discussing some travel bookings.

* * *

When I get home later, Patty is still up, sitting on the sofa with her arms folded. I say nothing but pop upstairs to get changed and when I come back she's in the same position.

'I think you terrified poor David,' I tell her. 'He's not used to Patty in full flow. What did you think of him?'

'Honestly?' she asks, and my heart sinks a little.

'Always,' I reply.

'I may be wrong,' she says. Her tone is gentle so I know she's worried she's going to hurt me with her next words. 'But I think he needs you to impress that chairman. And if he's retiring then maybe David sees himself as the next one.'

'What's wrong with that?' I ask, picturing myself on the arm of the chairman and quite enjoying that image.

'Nothing if he wants the real you, who has friends like me and a mother who's barmy,' says Patty. 'He looked terrified that we would do something to embarrass him, so I hope he doesn't just want you for your discounts.'

'Of course he doesn't,' I tell her. 'It was my idea to present to the club and he'll get used to my family — I'll just have to introduce them slowly.'

'Very slowly. I'd suggest you start with Zoe — the normal one.' Patty stands, kisses me on the head and heads towards the stairs. 'Sweet dreams.'

CHAPTER TWENTY-THREE: FEEL LIKE A WOMAN

I have an important task to perform this morning and I call my mum to tell her what she has to do. As I expected, she's not happy.

'I don't want to come out without any make-up on,' she whines. 'I would never do that normally and I want to look ten years younger than I really am, not like some frumpy version of me.'

I understand completely and am always bemused by before and after photographs where the person is simply frowning with slumped shoulders in the first and smiling with a brightly coloured top on in the second. Perhaps a smile is all it really takes to make us look and feel younger. It's certainly cheaper than Botox.

She arrives at the travel agents in the early afternoon and, as expected, she's far too glammed up for the task in hand. Although she wouldn't take any notice of my instructions, Josie is not one to take no for an answer.

'Come on, Mrs S,' she says, taking off the beautiful blue scarf my mum wears to bring out her eyes. 'You gotta give these beautician people something to work with, can't have their job done for them by the time you get there.'

She leads Mum into the bathroom, where she stands like a petulant schoolgirl while Josie takes a cotton wool pad and cleanser to her make-up. I have to suppress a giggle as I remember all the times through the ages that Mum has stood wiping make-up off me, whether it was when I was five and had liberally applied her best lipstick to my lips, cheeks and eyelids or when I was fifteen and she was telling me that I looked like a floozy.

Once wiped clean of her make-up and stripped of her accessories, we take Mum out into the shop, where Charlie has gathered together some customers. With me taking the video on my phone and Josie doing the interviewing, we began that really awful section of *10 Years Younger* where members of the public have to guess the poor victim/participant's age. I always find this really cruel — those taking part have often gone through real trauma, and there we are bringing them down even further by telling them those events have taken their toll and they do indeed look ancient. That's why we're not going into the street and instead are using kind customers who understand what's going on and know what to say.

'Gorgeous cheekbones. I'd say she's seventy-four,' says the first, as instructed.

'I can see where Angie gets her looks. I'm calculating that you must be nearly eighty though you don't look it,' says the next, getting a smile from me for the impromptu compliment.

'Look at those ankles,' says another. 'You must have been a dancer. I'd say seventy-six.'

My mother is in fact seventy-seven and we've organised the answers so that they average out at this exact age. I know she'll be disappointed that they haven't arrived at a younger age but, as Josie said, we have to give the beauticians something to work with, and as my mum really doesn't look bad for her age, I can't see how they're going to knock ten years off her appearance. But that's their job, and after doing our video and emailing it to Zoe, we send Mum on her way to the first appointment — the dentist for a whitening — and get back to work.

'So the grand unveiling is tomorrow night at seven?' Charlie checks and I nod as he puts the details in his phone.

'Mum doesn't know yet but it's a fashion event at the hotel,' I tell him. 'Zoe's place hosts them for one of the big boutiques every year; they showcase the spring ranges and people buy tables so it raises money for breast cancer research. I've got us a table, so everyone is invited.'

'Including your new squeeze, David?' asks Josie.

'Alas no, he has a golf club thing going on, so I'll be with my usual partner-in-crime,' I say, although even if we had got to that stage, calling a man in his late fifties a squeeze seems a bit of a push. My new cuddle, maybe — one day.

'If there's a raffle, Mercury should donate a prize,' says Charlie. 'What do you think people would want?'

'If they can get Mrs S. looking sixty then I'd say a little of what she's had.' Josie laughs.

'Oh Lord,' I reply with a sudden sense of panic. 'What if they do even better and my mum is standing there looking younger than me?'

'You'd never hear the last of it, that's for sure.' Charlie is guffawing but I don't think it's particularly funny.

'I need to have my hair done before tomorrow.' I'm looking up the hairdresser's number in my contacts. 'It's not just Mum but everyone going is there to see spring fashions so they'll all be dressed to the nines.'

'Good point,' agrees Charlie. 'We'd all better look dapper. The Mercury Travel table should shine like a little mirrorball hangs permanently over us.'

He says this looking up to the ceiling and waving his hands airily. I know what he's thinking and he says it almost immediately.

'Why don't we have one in the shop? I'm going to buy one.'

He sits back down and gets straight onto the internet; a husband and wife come in asking about last-minute availability in Madeira so I leave Charlie to his search and take them to my desk.

* * *

'Angie, do you mind me using the footage of you dancing with Felipe to promote the Vienna trip?' Josie asks towards the end of the day. 'We've only got a couple of spaces left and it would be good to have it full by the end of the week.'

As it's already in the public domain on the dance school social media, I tell her to go ahead. In truth, I'm actually quite flattered by it as Felipe makes me look a far better dancer than I ever felt.

The dance trips are practically sold out and I know from talking to some of those who've booked that there's a mixture of dancers and non-dancers going. As Marianne said to me, some people simply love to watch dancing and they're going for the romance and spectacle of the city as much as anything. I'm extremely excited to be accompanying Mum and Dad on this trip as I've always wanted to go to Vienna but for some reason never have. My ex-husband used to like the sun and, of course, when Zoe was a child, she loved beach holidays too so that's where we tended to go. It's another aspect of life post-divorce or post-kids that you have to consider — what *you* actually enjoy doing with your free time. I only realise at this precise moment that I haven't been to a beach resort in two years and I don't miss it. I've stopped thieves on a cruise ship and sung karaoke in New York — two things I definitely wouldn't have done with the ex. I wonder what kind of holidays David prefers.

I'm snapped out of my contemplations by a call from my mother.

'They're amazing!' she screams down the line. 'I didn't know teeth could sparkle like this. I'm on my way back to Mercury — Charlie will want this treatment when he sees me. I look like that Rylan person on the telly.'

'Mum, no — you can't come back,' I reply quickly. 'We can't see you until the makeover is finished. I want to be as surprised as everyone else, but trust me — Charlie is going to want everything you're having done. I've already seen him holding up his jowls in the mirror.'

Mum gushes about needing to show someone and I smile with the whole of my face — it's wonderful to hear her so excited. She has a room at Zoe's hotel so that Dad doesn't see her until the grand reveal. I tell her to get booked in and relax for a couple of hours. I know the wardrobe people will be with her shortly, so she has a busy schedule ahead. Reluctantly, she agrees to stick with the plan.

'I don't have jowls,' says Charlie when I finish the call. 'It's simply a jawline in need of a little contouring.'

'Yeah, me too,' I say with a snort. 'And in my case it's a lot of contouring.'

* * *

I head home wondering how I'm going to fill the evening as every inch of me wants to head over to Zoe's hotel and see these amazing teeth Mum was enthusing about. I know I'm going to have to scour my wardrobe for something a little bit special. Despite the warning not to overshadow Mum, I am very worried that she's going to look like my younger sister after all this. However, when I put the key in the door, I very quickly learn that my time has already been commandeered.

'Angie, come into the studio,' calls Patty. 'We've been rehearsing something and I need to know what you think.'

Guessing that I'll enjoy whatever the Granny-Okies have cooked up, and now with a glass of wine, I open the door to the garage.

It's very dark in there. I can hear the three of them shuffling in the corner but can't quite make out what they're doing. There's a chair not far from the door and Patty tells me to sit down then close the door. I do as I'm told, plunging the room into further darkness as the only shard of light disappears.

'Are you ready?' Patty calls out.

My eyes are adjusting to the light and I can tell that they're all wearing something long and shiny. If it weren't for the giggling I would suspect a satanic ritual were about to take place with me being the victim. As it is, I'm merely being experimented on in the name of entertainment.

Suddenly, the opening chords of an eighties classic starts up and then that famous thrash of the cymbals and drums

— *dah, dah-dah-dah*. It's 'Eye of the Tiger' and I can't wait to see what they do to this.

A single light bulb goes on and I'm puzzled as Patty has strip lights in here usually. I realise she's rigged up the single work light that her hubby used to use to work on the car and thrown the cable over the garage beams so it hangs just above her head.

Sheila and Kath appear from the corner: the shiny outfits are boxing robes and underneath they're wearing silk boxing shorts and vests. They even have the little boxing boots on in matching colours. As the intro plays through, they pretend to skip and spar with each other, then the vocals begin and they stop fighting to sing the verse, but as the chorus begins Patty emerges from the darkness.

Oh my word, what is she wearing? Yes, the robe, the shorts and the boots, but she appears to be topless and then she reaches the light and I see it's an inflatable fancy-dress bodysuit that looks like a muscled six pack. It's very disconcerting to see my friend looking half naked and with a man's upper torso. I reach out to touch it but Patty flicks my hands away then licks her finger and sizzles it down her fake chest.

A boxing match ensues with Patty defeating first of all Sheila and then Kath, all while not missing a beat of the song. As it fades and she's doing her victory lap, the girls get up and pull the stoppers on Patty's outfit, making it deflate.

I stand and give a round of applause when it's over.

'Did it work?' asks Patty, breathless.

'If you lot can sustain all those little boxer skips every night then I think the audience will love it,' I tell her. 'Although it was very weird seeing you come on stage topless, even more so when you went all saggy.'

'It was even more weird looking at myself. I have to say, you see all of these articles for women about being "beach ready" but at least we have the option of wearing a one-piece and covering up. Men have to have their torso exposed all the time and it's not a comfortable thing to do — even when it's fake. No wonder most of them opt for baggy T-shirts.'

'Are you saying they have it harder than us?' I ask.

'Just reflecting that I've found another reason why I prefer being a woman.'

She then launches into Shania Twain's 'Man! I Feel Like a Woman!' and the four of us conga dance to it all the way back to the wine bottle in the fridge.

CHAPTER TWENTY-FOUR: YOUNG AT HEART

I spend *a lot* of time getting ready the following morning. Although I hate to admit that I am this shallow, I tossed and turned all night with terrified imaginings about today.

The audience were sitting at those little round tables they always have at award ceremonies. Everyone looked glamorous as they ate tiny portions of food and took tiny sips of wine from impossibly fine china and crystal. I've obviously been watching too much *Bridgerton* because they were all in Regency era dress with huge powdered wigs too. There's a catwalk running down the centre of the tables and suddenly the emcee from *Cabaret* appears and calls out, '*Mesdames and Messieurs, I give you la plus belle dame du monde.*'

The curtains part and my mother glides out looking like a supermodel as the audience gasps then erupts into cheers and applause. She reaches the end and holds out her hand for me to join her; the Regency ladies turn to look as I stand. Their faces become masks of horror as I walk to my mother. I'm like Fantine after she has to sell all her hair. And yes, I know I'm mixing up my musicals here but what can I say? I watch a lot of them. Inspector Javert intervenes and decides it's off to the gallows with me. His officers grab each arm and drag me along the catwalk as the audience yells, 'Off with that hideous head!'

And worst of all, my mother joins in — so all in all, one might conclude that I'm fairly nervous about today.

* * *

'You need to reframe this,' Patty shouts through the bathroom door after I've told her for the fifteenth time that I'm nearly ready. She'll know I'm lying as she'll still be able to hear the bath water splashing around.

'You need to be proud that you and your daughter have worked together to help your mother fulfil one of her biggest wishes.'

I hadn't thought of it like that, and when I do, suddenly my dream changes and there's no emcee leading my mother down the catwalk; instead it's me and I'm getting a round of applause for the makeover as people ask me to organise the same for them. I really am shallow.

I take the facecloth off my face (one of the new cupcake ones that Patty bought me) and pull the plug out of the bath. I must look as steamed and plumped up as I'm going to and indeed, when I look at myself in the mirror, I'm nowhere near as bad as the Fantine of my nightmares. I open the door and Patty is standing there, arms folded.

'I thought you might actually dissolve if you didn't come out soon,' she says. 'Now, what are you wearing? We don't have time for an existential wardrobe crisis too.'

'Did you take lessons in tough love or did it just come naturally?' I ask with a friendly jab.

I inform my friend that I have decided to act on her wise words and dress to ensure that my mother shines out. I call Zoe and ask if she knows what colour Mum will be wearing for the grand reveal and tell her that I'll choose something that doesn't clash or match. Zoe won't give me any clues, so I run through the colours I have in the wardrobe and she eventually says I can wear the midnight-blue dress she chose with me on a shopping trip last year. I put it on and accessorise minimally then look at myself in the mirror. It's smart but blends into the background, like something one of those hostesses at haute couture stores might wear, showcasing the new season to their high-end customers. And yes, I've only ever seen this in movies, so once again my references have no real-life substantiation.

I drive us to the event, which is luncheon rather than dinner. I get a little shiver of déjà vu walking into the events suite, which is set up with large round tables either side of a red-carpet catwalk. It's almost identical to my dream. I sigh with relief as the first group of ladies walk in and they're wearing jumpsuits and shift dresses with no sign of a powdered wig in sight.

'We're here, Mum,' says Zoe as she hurries towards me. She shows us our spaces then rushes off to greet some guests and shake some hands.

The room is bedecked in the charity's trademark pink colour, but rather than looking like a Barbie set, it manages to be tasteful yet fun. There are balloons rather than flower displays at the centre of each table and the pale-pink napkins are shaped in the breast cancer ribbon shape. Seeing them brings a shock of realisation and a little shame that I've been worrying about how I compare to my mother when so many people have lost theirs to this awful disease. I pull myself together and walk over to Zoe, asking her if she'll introduce me to the regional fundraiser who has put this event together. My daughter points the lady out and I head over to find out if there are any future efforts that I can help out with.

The room fills up and with the women comes chatter and laughter. By the time lunch is served, the atmosphere is joyful. On our table are Charlie, Peter, Patty, Josie, Matt, James and Zoe; looking round, we have the highest proportion of men in the room. The table next to ours jokes that they'll need to borrow one to carry the case of wine back to their car if they win it and James immediately stands and takes a bow, saying he'll be delighted to help. There's no space on our table for Mum and Dad so I ask Zoe where they'll be sitting.

'At the top table,' she replies, and I shrug an *of course* in reply.

The lights go down and there are a few whoops from the audience. A spotlight beams down onto the catwalk and to rapturous applause, out walks Poppy O'Cherry resplendent in a pink satin bodice, thigh-length boots with feather trim and a gigantic candy floss–coloured beehive on their head. They put their hands on their hips and sashay down the catwalk, pausing at the end and asking the audience, 'Too much?'

They all shout back 'Never!' To which Poppy replies, 'I didn't think so.'

The fashion show begins and a gorgeous range of outfits is paraded in front of us. We all have a mini catalogue, and as the models strut their stuff, we follow along, looking up the details of each piece of clothing, checking out the prices. We're told that we can, of course, order it in our own size and have it delivered to us within forty-eight hours, and that ten per cent of any sales made today will be donated to the charity.

'Which means they've jacked the price up by ten per cent,' whispers Patty, saying what others are probably thinking, but it still seems a bit unnecessary when we're at a charity event. She gets an elbow for that one. It strikes me that I must spend a good proportion of each day jabbing Patty for saying or doing something inappropriate. It's almost like having a husband again.

A model appears wearing a stunning black formal jumpsuit. The model herself has legs up to her ears, so that helps, but I'm a respectable height and I love this.

'Ooh, now this is a bit special, isn't it?' says Poppy O'Cherry as the model approaches.

Poppy reads from the card, 'A flattering wide leg, with a neat belt around the waist — well, where else would you have a belt? This has a round neck and mesh sleeves — that's so we can hide our bingo wings, girls. All in all, bloody gorgeous,' they conclude. 'Keira here has accessorised the jumpsuit with a clutch bag and gold jewellery, which are also available to buy today.'

I'm sold. I'm picturing myself at a beautiful restaurant on the banks of the Danube one evening in Vienna. I look as tasteful as the city itself as I glide between my Mercury Travel Club members, who are beaming from having fulfilled their waltzing dreams.

'Are you buying that?' Patty drags me back to reality, nodding at the pen I have poised over the order form.

'I was thinking about it. Why, did you want it?'

'Bit too understated for me,' she says, shaking her head.

That's a good sign for any outfit, so I immediately write down my order. The model wearing the jumpsuit has done her circuit of the stage and is now making her way back when Poppy says, 'Gorgeous, but a bit plain for me.' They wave their arms down their pink ensemble to make the point.

Patty gives me an *I told you so* look.

'It's not a compliment that you have the same taste in clothes as a drag artist,' I tell her.

'In your opinion. We both need to stand out.'

When the fashion show has finished and the orders collected, it's time for the event I've been waiting for. Zoe gets up and stands next to Poppy.

'So, we have something a bit special now, don't we?' says Poppy, cueing my daughter in.

Zoe explains Mum's bucket list and her desire to look ten years younger. She then thanks the people who've helped with the transformation that the audience is about to see and, yet again, we're told that if we book their services today then a contribution to the charity will be made. I'm glad Mum's list is making a difference to people but I just want Zoe to get on with it so I can see my mother.

It begins with the video we took; Mum looking dowdy while people guess her age. As planned, the average ends up being just slightly older than Mum is now. Not a depressing result but with room to play with for the beauticians.

'So, let's see what you've done with the old girl,' says Poppy. 'Come on out, Mrs Shepherd.'

Necks crane to see this transformation and there's an audible gasp when she appears. Mum looks fantastic. I look across at Dad, who is on his feet blowing wolf whistles in between wiping the tears from his eyes. He looks so proud of his beautiful wife.

When she smiles I can see the lovely white teeth she's so proud of and I can tell she's wearing very flattering clothes. Her make-up is stunningly perfect but it's the hair that does it. My family have all been blessed with the brunette hair she had as a young girl and now it's been restored with subtle balayage to soften the colour for my mum's age and skin tone. Her normal bob shape has been given layers and shaping which bring out her cheekbones. They really have done the most beautiful job, and once again I feel myself reaching for the pen and that hairdresser.

'So beautiful I want you off my stage as soon as possible,' says Poppy affectionately, giving my mum a hug. 'But now the real test, let's see how old the public think you look now.'

I feel myself tensing up as I don't want Mum to be disappointed and happily Zoe hasn't gone out to anonymous members of the public. Instead, Poppy takes the roving microphone into the audience and asks the ladies seated at the tables.

They each tell her how gorgeous she looks and then say an age which is generally younger than Mum is. And although I know they're being kind, Mum does look younger and it's not just about the makeover — she looks full of life. I'm bursting with happiness for her.

The final person Poppy tells us they will ask is James, and Zoe has obviously briefed her boyfriend well. He's been writing down the ages everyone has said and I can see him doing mental calculations as Poppy approaches. When they get to our table, they give James a little time to get the number right by asking Charlie and Peter what they think of her outfit. After a little light-hearted banter, they turn to James and ask him his honest opinion.

'Because this lady will know if you're lying,' Poppy says, wagging their finger at him.

He stands and leans into the microphone and I can tell the poor guy is nervous. He adds to the other comments saying how stunning Mum looks and, in all honesty, she looks so much younger. He says an age and there's a murmur around the room as everyone does the calculations. Poppy gets handed a piece of paper as James sits back down.

'So here's the result,' they say as, on stage, Zoe hugs her gran.

'Mrs S, the audience here think you look an amazing sixty-four years old. That's not ten years younger . . . that's an amazing *fourteen* years younger.'

Balloons are released from the ceiling as everyone cheers and I can see Mum wiping a tear from her eye as carefully as she can. Dad leaps onto the stage and kisses her tenderly on the cheek before holding her hand and then presenting her once again to the audience. Zoe's crying too and I realise I'm on the brink of it. I'm so happy for Mum and Dad — so happy.

The red carpet has been rolled away and the space is now a dance floor. 'Sisters Are Doin' It for Themselves' starts us off and I leap up to grab my mum and daughter from their respective partners and whirl them around to the music.

What a day.

CHAPTER TWENTY-FIVE: CLUB TROPICANA

Zoe managed to get a local lifestyle magazine to attend the event on Saturday and although they came to cover the fashion show and charity fundraiser, they were as captivated by Mum's transformation as everyone else. They posted their photographs in their weekend online addition, which added to Mum's elation as she now thinks she's as famous as the reality TV crowd.

'Though far more dignified than most of them,' she says to Charlie as they scroll through the pictures in the shop on Monday morning.

Mum arrived at around ten and looks as if she's taken up residence, so I ask if she has anywhere else she needs to be.

'Of course I do,' she declares. 'Your father is taking his young wife out to lunch, although I might wear sunglasses as I'm afraid of being pestered for all those shelfies.'

'I think you mean selfies,' I say, getting a shrug in response. 'But I imagine you'll be okay.'

I have to eat my words when the next customers enter the shop and give a wide-eyed gasp when they spot Mum.

'We saw you online,' they exclaim to her delight. 'You look amazing. We have to have a picture with you.'

They snap a few photos and Charlie quickly passes Mum a Mercury Travel mug to hold but she puts it on the table behind her, saying she doesn't do endorsements yet. I barely hold back a snort of laughter.

After Mum leaves we settle down to a full day of bookings and customer enquiries. The charity event has left us on a bit of a high and I always find that if we're all smiling when a potential client walks in, they're far more likely to walk out having booked a trip and so be smiling along with us. The lifestyle magazine also gets in touch and wants to write an article about Mum and bucket lists in general. It's a fabulous opportunity to promote some of the big destinations people tend to dream of going to but also to simply talk about retreats. Charlie and I instantly agree to be interviewed later in the week.

'I'm beginning to believe in karma,' I tell my business partner as we finish the call.

'There's never a downside to being kind to people.' Charlie sounds so wise that I might just find him a wizard's hat to wear whenever he wants to say such things. He asks me why I'm smiling at him but I decide against telling him that I'm picturing him in *Lord of the Rings* or *Harry Potter*. Instead I just say that I'm happy.

That changes quickly when, as we're about to close, Patty bursts through the door like a woman on a mission.

'You two,' she says, pointing at me and Charlie. 'Sports kit on and meet me in the leisure centre at six o'clock.'

She turns to leave.

'Whoa — hold on, cowboy,' says Charlie. 'Why?'

'Clubbercise,' she replies. 'They've had three cancellations for tonight and I've signed us up. They're booked up for weeks ahead so we're lucky to get them.'

I don't feel particularly lucky but keep my mouth shut. After all, we did all say that we wanted to get fit — but I think we meant it in the theoretical sense.

'And it won't be that long until I see Jack again. I need to get this magnificence into even better shape.' Patty gives us a little shimmy. Oh, to have only an ounce of this lady's confidence.

Charlie looks quite excited by the prospect and tells us that he's seen Clubbercise classes on YouTube and that it's just like dancing so he's up for it.

'They all have glow sticks and shake them around, don't they?' he adds.

Patty nods and tells him that's why she's meeting us there.

'Number one,' she says, 'I need a stronger sports bra to keep the girls in check, and number two, I need to get us all some glow sticks.'

Like a superhero she then disappears in a whirlwind off to complete her mission. Charlie locks the door behind her then claps his hands together in delight.

'What should I wear?' he says.

'Well, it's not actually a nightclub, so I'm guessing sportswear.' Is the answer not obvious?

'I mean what colour,' he replies. 'I might have a dayglow vest from when I was in Ibiza but not sure whether it'll be a bit snug now.'

'Maybe just white?' I suggest, guessing that any fashion advice I give will be dismissed as too dull.

I'm shocked when Charlie nods and tells me that would work as the lights might pick it up. When asked what colour I'm wearing, I can honestly reply black as I truly do *not* want the lights to pick me up at all.

I head home and rummage through a holdall of clothes that I just dumped in the bottom of the wardrobe when I moved in here. It contains all the things you buy because you might need them one day — scarves, belts and blouses in colours I wouldn't normally wear but was feeling adventurous on the day. It also contains a pair of leggings and a black sports vest that I bought last year. They're not well worn. As I dig, I realise that I'd forgotten I owned most of these things and the sensible thing to do would be to take the whole bag to the charity shop and leave it there. I know I wouldn't miss a single item. However, in the split second it would take to leave the bag out ready to be donated, I have second thoughts and ram it back into the wardrobe ready to be carted to another house when I eventually move.

I do have a good pair of trainers, and when I'm kitted out I think I look quite sporty. I put my hair into a ponytail and give it a little swish. I always think women who have big swishy ponytails look far more sporty than those who don't, so if my body doesn't look fit, at least my hair will. I zip a hoodie over the top to complete my outfit then head downstairs and check the address of the sports centre we're going to. I notice that it's not far from Cross Road and the rental house I first moved into after the divorce, the road that Michael still lives in.

I check my watch and know that I have time to make a diversion past his house. It's almost on the way and I'm obviously dressed for the gym so could honestly say that I was passing by and thought I'd see how he was. Patty would kill me for doing this but I need to know. I need to look him in the eye and ask why he stood me up and why he's been ghosting me. My best friend would tell me to simply move on. I have done and this is simply getting an answer. I'm not picking at the wound, I'm just checking to see that it's healing nicely. I won't get away with doing this after the class as Patty will probably follow me home, so I won't be able to make the detour. Nope, it has to be now.

I grab my water bottle and keys then rush out to the car with my heart racing. I guess it's good to build up to the class anyway.

I know my way to Cross Road so head straight there, practising my greeting as I go.

'Hi, there,' I say out loud to the empty car. 'I was just on my way to the gym and thought I'd check that you're okay?'

Or maybe I should be more direct and less enthusiastic.

'Michael, hello.' This time my voice is serious. 'As you haven't been in touch, I wondered whether you've been ill or had an accident?'

Hmm, if I'd been that concerned wouldn't I have called around earlier?

'What happened?' I yell into the rear-view mirror. 'One minute we're snogging at midnight and the next you've turned into a pumpkin.'

I'm turning into Cross Road before I've perfected any of them and decide the first option is the one to go with. I park outside his house and take a swig of water from my bottle as my throat is suddenly incredibly dry. His car is parked in the drive so I guess he's home, but so far I haven't seen him peering out any of the windows. I exhale, open the car door and walk assertively down the drive then ring his bell. There's no answer so I try again and, getting braver, I walk over to his living room window and peer in. No sign of life. I feel deflated as I walk back towards the car; I was ready for answers and I'm not getting them today. As I reach the car, his neighbour comes out of her house and asks if I'm looking for Michael. I reply that I am and ask if she knows when he'll be back.

'Oh, no idea,' she says. 'He might be out with his lady friend.'

My heart stops racing and skips a beat. I thank her and say I'll call some other time. I turn down her offer of leaving a message for him. I guess I have my answer after all; he really does have someone else. As indeed do I.

On the drive to the sports centre I'm filled with an emotion that I know only too well. It's that moment when you just have to accept that something is over or isn't going to happen. I think it's the acceptance part of grieving and I felt it last year when my ex-husband laughed at my idea that he might want to get back together with me. I'd been convinced that he was leaving little hints at reconciliation but it turned out that I was deluded. I recall now the moment it actually sunk in for real — it was over and Patty was there to pick me up. Of course, this is nothing like that and I barely know Michael, but I guess a part of me was hoping we could be friends. In the car I put on some music and sit up straight. *His loss*, I tell myself as I leave the street and head towards the sports centre.

Patty is already there in her leggings and black T-shirt. I'm surprised she isn't wearing a louder outfit and tell her this. She pulls out glow sticks and head boppers for all of us.

'I think we'll stand out in these,' she says.

However, as the centre fills with people obviously going to the class, I'm not sure that we will; everyone looks up for a party rather than an exercise class and the excitement is infectious. Charlie turns up in a bright white vest and a glow-in-the-dark necklace.

'Oh, where did you get that?' asks Patty enviously as she hands him the other accessories.

'The pet department,' he says proudly. 'They're for when you walk your dog in winter.'

Bedecked with our boppers, dog collar and glow sticks we look like Christmas trees but so does everyone else. The doors open to the class and loud dance music fills the corridor. Whooping, everyone piles into the dark room and the instructor on stage gets us moving almost instantly.

The beat is very fast and the choreography takes a lot of getting used to, but it's fun. I stand on Patty's toes at least once and get trodden on by Charlie in return but we're giving it all we have, and as I turn to my friends and see the smiles on their faces I can't help but smile broadly back. I really do have the best people in my life, so whoever this lady friend is, Michael can keep her.

CHAPTER TWENTY-SIX: EINE KLEINE NACHTMUSIK

'Where are you going?' asks Patty as I grab my coat and bag. 'No, wait, let me guess — the golf course?'

''Fraid so,' I tell her. 'They want help setting up a fashion show like we did for Mum. I'm taking them through the finer points of detail and the likely revenues they'll get.'

'Don't they have someone who can do all that?'

'David does it now, but if he can show that he's networking for the club, it improves his chances of becoming chairman,' I tell her. 'And before you say anything, that would be a good thing and I'm happy to support him.'

'If you say so. But it does seem like you've become very keen on golf all of a sudden — why the transformation?'

I repeat that I'm just being supportive and that is most of the reason, but having accepted that Michael is no longer an option, I do know that I'm putting all my eggs in the David basket. Of course, I can't tell Patty any of that.

'Besides which,' I say, 'you're focussed on getting ready for the cruise and you need me out of the way.'

'I am ready,' she replies. 'I've decided you can't really improve on perfection.'

I give a snort of laughter as I wave goodbye and tell her that's very true. She's perfect as she is.

When I walk into the golf course boardroom David gets up to greet me, giving me a peck on the cheek then directing me to sit beside him. Alongside the chairman is a woman I haven't met before and she's introduced as Kathryn, the events assistant. She shakes my hand firmly and without her even speaking a word, I can tell that the *assistant* title probably belittles her role in the club.

'The lady of the hour,' says David, looking at me with a big smile on his face. He pours me a glass of water then checks whether the chairman needs any, which he doesn't.

Zoe has given me the profit and loss results for the evening she hosted and I present these, noting that Kathryn is the one to ask questions and make suggestions.

'My daughter held this to raise funds for a charity, but I'm guessing that you could also raise funds for any repairs or refurbishment that's needed,' I tell her.

'That's what I was thinking,' she says. 'We're going to need work on the greens in the coming year, so I thought about hosting this and maybe getting a sponsor to cover the costs.'

I agree that would work as I take her though the list of contacts we've built up. The chairman stands and says he'll leave us to it, so I continue to work with Kathryn while David sees the chairman out.

'I think it's always useful to set a target for the fundraising,' I tell Kathryn, 'that way you can keep a tally and encourage more donations as you get close.'

She nods as she takes notes, then David re-enters the room and asks Kathryn if she can handle things from here. She says that she can and I give her my numbers, saying she can call any time.

David has a huge smile on his face, so I presume this is all building brownie points for him; he tells me that the ladies' team president is delighted with the event, and as she's the chairman's sister-in-law that makes everyone happy.

'I think we should celebrate,' David suggests. 'Shall we have a drink?'

'Or,' I counter, 'as you're going to be constantly disturbed by members if we stay here, why don't we grab a taxi and head into town?'

When I see a wave of reluctance furrow his brows, I tease him about being joined at the hip to the golf club.

'If it turns out to be necessary,' I say with a smile, 'my friend Patty knows a very good doctor and we might be able to persuade him to come ashore and surgically separate you from this place.'

David laughs and admits the golf club is his second home then gets out his phone and orders the cab.

When the car arrives, David opens the door for me and I slide into the seat while he goes around to the other side. The radio is playing a Cyndi Lauper classic that Patty always does in her sets and it makes me smile. I'm about to tell the driver that I love this song and the Absolute 80s station he's tuned into when David gets in, closes his door and tuts.

'How about something more relaxing?' he says to the driver. 'A bit of Classic FM, perhaps?'

He's managed to say the word 'perhaps' in such a way that it sounds like 'immediately'. I catch the driver giving me a glance but he does as he's been asked and violins replace Ms Lauper.

'"Time after Time" was far more relaxing than this,' I say to David as the horn section starts up.

'How on earth could anyone prefer that over Beethoven's Sixth?' he says with a smile before humming along and doing orchestra conductor moves with his hands. He takes hold of my hand and waves it in time with his so we're both conducting it now and I laugh along with him.

'You might like "November Rain" by Guns N' Roses,' I tell him. 'That has a full orchestra backing.'

I am saying this with my tongue firmly in my cheek, but both the taxi driver and David look at me as if I'm insane and I have to confess to them that I was joking.

We arrive before the end of the symphony and as we're climbing out of the car, the driver is already switching the radio back to the previous station. I quietly tell him that I don't blame him and he gives me a wink.

'I'll have you enjoying eighties music one day,' I tell David as we walk into the tapas restaurant that Patty and I love. I tell him that this place is a favourite of ours as the waiter directs us to our table.

'It's a bit dark, isn't it?' he says as we're seated and left with the menus.

'Cosy,' I tell him. 'Now, the wine we like is this Rioja.' I point at the one that Patty and I usually choose. 'Unless you prefer white?'

'No, I like red but I'm not fond of Rioja — do they serve Montepulciano d'Abruzzo?' he asks.

'I'd have thought you'd be annoyed if they did,' I say. 'After all, it is a Spanish restaurant.'

'I have Chenin Blanc with fish and chips,' he replies, making a valid point. I myself prefer prosecco with my takeaway, but that's not made in England either.

'True,' I say. 'It just feels quite rude not to be choosing Spanish while we're here.'

'But there is an Italian wine on the menu, so it must compliment the food.'

As the waiter has arrived and is ready to take our drinks order, I don't put up any more objections but let David order what he enjoys.

I'm horrified when he orders us a small-sized glass each.

'As it's only Wednesday and we're both up early tomorrow for work,' he says, probably noticing my mouth hanging open in shock.

It's only seven o'clock and we'll probably be home by ten, when I would usually ensure I drank several glasses of water and be perfectly okay in the morning. I say none of this but realise I have some serious behavioural training to do on this man. He'll never be able to come out on a night with my friends if I can't loosen him up a bit. That's my challenge for the next few weeks.

'What would you like to eat?' he asks.

Patty and I usually share some tapas or the charcuterie board, but I don't suggest this as I imagine David has already selected what he wants.

'I'm going for the lamb skewer,' he adds, confirming my thoughts. 'Not keen on too many spices and that looks quite simple.'

I shouldn't be disappointed because this isn't like a Patty and me night out — after all, he's not her, and just because my best friend has found her man doesn't mean that I can go out and replace her with one of my own. I need to accept David for who he is and respect the fact that he is his own man. I order the monkfish.

'Good choice,' says David, clinking his glass against mine. 'I almost chose that myself.'

Why do I feel as if I've passed an exam?

As we eat I can't help contemplating all of the couples I know, most of whom have come together in the past year. Peter and Charlie seem smitten, Josie and Matt share a wicked sense of humour, Zoe and James are workaholics who like to relax at home, while Patty and Jack just sound as if they fancy the pants off each other. They aren't identikit by any means; they just seem to share something. And I have to find the one thing we have in common — after all, many couples have different tastes in music.

'We have the Vienna trip coming up soon,' I say, fishing for that interest we might share. 'You probably would have enjoyed that, waltzing to Strauss in the city where he was born.'

'I probably would,' he replies and I inwardly sigh with relief. 'I'd love to see an orchestra play some of his music there; I think somehow musicians perform with greater emotional depth in their home city, if you know what I mean.'

'I do,' I say. 'I always wanted to see A-ha in Oslo — I thought that would be great fun, but it never happened. Maybe I should look out for a reunion.'

David smiles at me and says it would be a long way to go to hear their one hit song.

'So you do know your eighties hits,' I leap to reply. 'I knew you were hiding a misspent youth behind that sensible golfing exterior.'

'Guilty,' he says, holding his palms up.

I really hope that's true so turn the conversation to our childhoods and teenage years. I tell him about backcombing my hair and nearly choking on the amount of hairspray I had to use to make my locks as huge as possible.

'I remember girls doing that. Did you have the lacy gloves and big shoulder pads?'

'Of course,' I reply proudly. 'Wouldn't be seen dead without either. What about you? Were you a cuffed jeans and bomber jacket à la *Ferris Bueller's Day Off* or rolled-up sleeves and Ray-Bans like Don Johnson in *Miami Vice*? I'm guessing the latter.'

'Definitely more Don Johnson. I was always into my sport, so I think my wardrobe was mainly polo shirts in all sorts of colours with the obligatory sweater draped over my shoulders.'

'Such a Sloane!' I exclaim, laughing. 'And did you have the bouffant hair?'

'Oh yes. With the sunglasses pushed up on my head whether it was sunny or not.'

He tells me about realising that he was no good at either football or rugby from an early age and wanting to belong somewhere. He tried golf and finally found the sport that suited his temperament.

'I like to think about things,' he says. 'I'm better when the challenge is about improving my own score rather than beating someone else.'

I contemplate that this attitude probably makes David more of an introvert than anyone else I know and that's probably a good thing. Branson's advice, to respect a partner for who they are, comes to mind as we're heading home. The evening may have started with me doubting that we'd ever find anything we had in common but it's ended up being a perfectly nice evening.

The cab pulls up at my house and I'm wondering whether to invite David in for coffee when he leans over, gives me a peck on the cheek and wishes me a good night's sleep.

As I say, it was a perfectly nice evening.

CHAPTER TWENTY-SEVEN: BETWEEN THE LINES

'Perfectly nice?'

Patty is not at all impressed with my analysis of last night.

'It was,' I protest. 'We had a lovely meal, glass of wine and found out a bit more about each other. That's what normal people do — we can't all meet on a cruise ship.'

'I suppose so . . . Didn't you want to invite him in for coffee? You do know that I wouldn't mind — this is your house without any restrictions. I would have vanished into my room with just a nod of the head.'

I tell her that I do know that but I knew I'd have a big day at work so didn't want to risk it turning into a party. I didn't mention that I couldn't imagine David ever coming back to party. My reasoning seems to placate her and we move on to the book club meeting which I'm currently getting changed for.

'So it's about walking,' she says, picking up the book we're discussing tonight.

'Kind of. It's really about a couple who lost everything.'

'So it's a bit like that film with Reese Witherspoon? Exhaustion, adversity, some kind and some cruel people along the way?'

'I really wish you'd read some of the books we select instead of just trying to reduce them down to soundbites,' I scold her. 'This was incredibly moving.'

'I promise to try next time.'

'You always say that. Why don't you pick something for the group? Then you'll have to read it and can come along.'

She has that thoughtful look on her face and then suddenly smiles as if a light bulb has appeared over her head.

'I know exactly what I'll pick,' she declares with a glint in her eye that can only mean mischief.

* * *

Work today has been tiring with the final preparations for Vienna as well as the ongoing bookings, but I think we're ready. In an ideal world I think I'd be happy with the sofa and a cosy crime on TV tonight, but I know when I get to the book club I'll be glad I went and will probably sleep much better than if I'd been lazy for the whole night. Besides which, I really do enjoy seeing my friends.

We're the last to arrive because Patty became all secretive after agreeing to select our next book. She vanished for half an hour and when I shouted out that we had to leave the house, she appeared carrying a large holdall stuffed with something — presumably book related. The regulars are all here and I shuffle in between Sarah and Caroline as Patty gets us a drink.

'I'm really pleased you recommended this,' I tell Sarah. 'I found it very inspiring.'

'Me too,' adds Patty, handing me a glass of wine. 'Such an odyssey.'

I glare at her and get a little grin in return. This woman has more cheek than a blue-bottomed baboon.

The discussion gets underway with everyone having enjoyed the book in some way. It's the story of a couple, where the husband is diagnosed with an incurable brain disease and then they lose all their money and their home through a bad investment. They're literally left with nothing except a few hundred pounds, so they buy a tent and set out to walk the 630-mile-long Salt Path.

'I was lying in bed reading this,' Peter starts us off, 'and I realised how quickly life can turn from being perfect to horrific. I looked around me at my wonderful home and loving partner, knowing how safe and happy we are and simply couldn't contemplate losing it all. I'm not sure I would cope half as well.'

Although everyone is nodding in agreement, I think Peter would cope well. He's a strong individual and he would do anything it took to keep Charlie safe. I say all of this and he smiles.

'I love him,' he says, 'but 630 miles? That would be stretching it!'

We all laugh and continue the discussion, wondering whether we'd take in a sodden, muddy couple who needed somewhere for the night and being thoroughly ashamed to confess that we probably wouldn't.

After reviewing the book, we all grab another drink and the evening turns to general chatter.

'David tells me you had a lovely time last night,' says Sarah, and I'm a little surprised until I remember that she's his cousin.

'What did he say about it?' Patty barges into the conversation with her trademark subtlety.

'That you talked about eighties fashion and that you're off to listen to Strauss in Vienna,' replied Sarah. 'He's very envious of that.'

'What else?' Patty persists.

'Erm . . . I think he thought the food was nice, and of course he really likes you, Angie,' adds Sarah. 'Oh, and he mentioned the charity event you've helped with. He's really enthusiastic about that. He thinks it'll raise his profile. I imagine you're going to that, aren't you?'

I tell Sarah that I am and that I had a lovely evening too.

'Yes,' Patty says. 'I heard it was *perfectly* nice.'

I give Patty such a nudge that she almost spills the wine at her lips. I'm annoyed with her; just because my relationship doesn't fit her ideal for me is no reason for her to dismiss it.

Caroline clinks a pen against a glass and calls the book club to order.

'We need to decide on our next book. Now, we already have several suggestions on the list from last time, so rather than choose anyone's particular preference, shall I just close my eyes and pick one at random?'

There's a murmur of agreement, which is interrupted by Patty standing up and heaving the holdall onto the chair.

'If you don't mind, I would like to make a very different suggestion,' she says, getting raised eyebrows from the whole group.

'We're intrigued,' Ed says.

Patty slowly unzips the holdall and reaches her hand in.

'Thank you for allowing me to come to my first actual book club meeting. As you have all probably guessed, I'm not much of a reader and am occasionally known to scour the book reviews before I join you on the weekend trips just so I know what to say.'

'We would never have guessed,' says Peter sarcastically.

'She hides it well,' I say with equal sarcasm.

'*Anyway*,' continues Patty, drawing the attention back to her. 'I thought that if perhaps we all read something that I love, I might be able to take part properly. And so, if you're amenable, this is what I suggest as our next read.'

She pulls out a stack of 1980s *Jackie* annuals and there is such a gasp of delight that other people in the bar turn round to see what has happened.

'Oh, I loved this,' says Caroline, quickly skimming through it.

'Me too,' adds Peter. 'It beat the football mags all the other boys were reading.'

The annuals have everyone enthused, including me. I wouldn't mind spending my evenings re-reading the problem pages that absorbed my teenage years. Happily, the group are delighted to give this a go, so Patty hands us one each and we agree to read and pass round so that we've all seen each edition. What a joy — I can't wait to do this.

* * *

'I didn't know you still had these,' I say to Patty when we get home. 'They could be worth a fortune.'

'They are to me. I know people collect them but I don't think I could ever bear to part with them. I remember my mum coming into my room and telling me to turn the light out and go to sleep, so I used to do as I was told then switch on the torch from my bedside table and hide under the bedclothes to finish whatever feature I was reading.'

'The equivalent of being on your mobile all night.' I smile. 'I imagine the experts back then said reading by torchlight would ruin your eyes.'

'Probably. Every joy in life comes with a doom merchant telling you not to do it.'

I'm tired after my long day and am making myself a cuppa ready to take up to bed when Patty says, 'I'm sorry for asking all those questions about your night with David.'

I'd forgotten how annoyed I was with her earlier in the evening and sigh as I could do without all that whizzing around my head as I try to sleep. I decide confrontation is not what I want right now.

'That's okay. I know you're only looking out for me, but I am a big girl and you have to let me make my own mistakes.' I instantly regret my choice of word.

'Is it a mistake?' she asks. 'I mean, it's only a mistake if you end up buying a house together or giving him all of your money for a sure-fire investment — you'd never do that, would you?'

'Of course not. We've only known each other a few weeks. You're making him sound like a con artist. If he declares undying love and says we could be married but he needs ten thousand pounds for a visa then I'll let you know.'

'Good, and if Jack does that I'll let you know. Seriously though, how do you feel about him?'

I pause and think about it, trying to find the right word, but unfortunately only one comes to mind.

'He is *nice*,' I say. 'We only have a couple of things in common but he's easy to get on with.'

'What do you have in common?'

I tell her about the conversation we had in the tapas bar.

'So the thing you have in common was being young in the eighties?'

'That's not fair,' I say. 'Do you have something against him? You've only met him once and seem to have formed an instant opinion. I wouldn't dream of saying all this about anyone you dated. What do you and Jack have in common? He's a doctor and you were an air stewardess. He has kids and grandkids while you hate children.'

'It's a spark,' she says, looking quite annoyed. 'There's a spark between us and it's enough to light a flame — we laugh together and have had incredible chemistry from the start.'

'Love isn't always like that,' I tell her. 'Sometimes you have to nurture it and let it grow slowly. It's as much about companionship at our age.'

Patty looks at me as if I've grown two heads.

'It isn't, Bo,' she says. 'You're not old and you're as entitled to passion and excitement as you ever were. You're right in that I don't know David but please be honest with yourself, and if the spark isn't there then no amount of nurturing or blowing on it will ever create a fire. Don't settle for second best.'

I'm taken aback by her words — angry, hurt and shocked. It's all right for her, she'll be off on an adventure with the man she loves, leaving me here in a house that isn't mine. I dread her coming home and telling me he's moving in. She'll let me stay but I'll be the third wheel and I can picture us out with all our friends — all couples except me. They'll be kind and include me but will have those coupley conversations and always use *we* rather than *I*.

I can see it all happening. I'm about to be left behind by everyone.

She's wrong about David; I can bring him into our fold. Maybe Patty is too much for an introduction but perhaps he'd get on better with Peter and Charlie. Peter is a well-known local businessman so they may have things in common, although I doubt David ever read the *Jackie* annual. I'm going to show Patty that *nice* is a perfectly good launch point for any relationship.

'I haven't — goodnight,' I tell her, taking my tea and marching up to bed.

CHAPTER TWENTY-EIGHT: THIS MEANS NOTHING TO ME . . .

As we're waiting in the departure lounge, I call Kathryn and book a table for eight at the golf club fundraiser. She's delighted and asks whether I'd also like to offer a prize for the raffle. I laugh as this is exactly what I told her to do — always push a corporate booking for a little extra. Charlie and I had already decided that we would offer a prize, so I tell her we'll donate a discount voucher for bookings over autumn as that's really the only thing we can afford to give away. I know David will have to be seated with the rest of the committee, so I'll be taking Peter and Charlie, Caroline and Ed, Mum and Dad, and Josie, who will be partnering with me for the evening. Patty is rehearsing and it's been on the calendar for some time, so I know it's not simply an excuse. I actually think she'd have jumped at the opportunity to point out how unsuitable David is. Now all my other friends can enjoy an evening with him and tell Patty she's wrong.

Happy that it's sorted, I turn my attention to my fellow travellers, who are all extremely excited by the trip to Vienna. I approach the little group, who are currently hanging on every word Felipe says — perhaps it's not the lure of this beautiful Austrian city that has them excited after all.

'What's going on here?' I ask my mum, who is as enthralled as everyone else.

'Felipe was just showing us how posture and simply holding yourself up properly makes you look like a dancer even before you start moving.' She pulls her shoulders back and sticks her chest out.

'It's true,' says Felipe. 'Try it; imagine a piece of string on the top of your head pulling your whole body up tall.'

Of course, we're all doing this now as well as some others in the departure lounge who are just listening in.

'Now, hold this position and remember to breathe,' adds our dance instructor.

That's the part I'd forgotten, and when I exhale that imaginary piece of string seems to snap and my chest is facing the floor again. I'm told it just needs practise but I can't imagine ever being able to hold myself tall, breathe and move my feet in a co-ordinated way. Not all at once. Felipe walks among our group, pulling shoulders back and lifting chins upwards and I can see that they're already loving all of this. Well, who wouldn't?

We're called to board and Dad takes Mum on his arm and walks her towards the boarding bridge. She still looks absolutely amazing after the makeover and the look in their eyes is of a love sixty years in the making. I won't ever get there, but with a fair wind I might still have a thirty-year romance in me. I pull myself up tall as Felipe has shown us and make my way onto the plane with what I hope is a graceful glide. Of course, not watching my feet, I trip over as it slopes downwards and go flying into the man in front of me. Luckily, he's more sturdy than me, so we don't turn the passenger queue into a domino rally. I thank him for catching me and focus on walking properly rather than gliding.

After a smooth flight and an easy transfer, we start with a tour of Vienna city centre on a sunny spring morning. And it is beautiful.

'You see photographs of the main squares and palaces but you assume that it's not all like this,' says Dad, echoing my thoughts completely.

'I feel like I should be wearing a period costume,' I say.

We've come to visit the Schloss Schonbrunn, where the sheer grandeur of the buildings and gardens leaves you simply speechless.

'The predominant architectural styles in Vienna are baroque and gothic,' our guide tells us. 'This palace was once the home of the Emperor Franz Joseph and our beloved Empress Sisi.'

'I've watched the TV series,' says Mum. 'She had to get married when she was sixteen and was a bit bored with the life of a royal.'

'Indeed,' replies our guide. 'A little like your Meghan Markle, perhaps?'

This causes a debate among my group that has absolutely nothing to do with the magnificent surroundings of the palace, so I urge the guide to move everyone on.

'She was considered very beautiful,' the guide continues, 'and was so desperate to hold onto her looks, which she considered the reason for her popularity among Austrians, that she invented her own beauty creams. One of them was known as Crème Celeste — can anyone guess what it contained?'

There are a few random guesses, including goose fat from one lady and sea kelp from my mum.

'How would she get hold of that in a landlocked country?' asks my dad.

'She's an empress,' replies Mum as if it's obvious. 'She'd get a minion to ride out to the nearest rock pool.'

'Where would the nearest coastline be?' asks another of the guests. 'It must be hours away.'

'Italy, I imagine,' Dad says. 'Hours by train, so weeks by horse.'

'A few days with a fast horse and they could pick a bulk order,' says Mum.

The guide is clearly quite astounded at the debate that has ensued. He probably only gets an interested silence when he asks groups this question. He clears his throat to get our attention and we turn to face him.

'Actually, it was white wax, almond oil and rosewater,' he tells us.

'Oh, I use rosewater,' Mum says. 'Does that mean I can be an empress?'

'You'll always be my queen,' Dad says.

I gag and tell them to get a room.

* * *

After the morning tour, we're dropped off at the dance studio. Although the exterior is in keeping with the rest of the grand Viennese street it stands on, the interior is a modern air-conditioned dance studio where only the sparkling crystal chandelier hints at a more courtly history.

The studio owner comes out to greet us, shaking the hands of the men and kissing the hands of the women with extreme propriety. I wonder whether everyone coming here feels like royalty within moments of meeting this lovely man.

He begins by giving us a short history of the dance we're about to learn.

'This is one of the most romantic and graceful dances in the world,' he tells us. 'Much faster than the traditional waltz and it developed from some of our local folk dances where couples would dance in the round — as we do in the waltz. During the Hapsburg period, the dance became popular with the aristocracy as Johann Strauss created the beautiful music we will dance to today. I will warn you all that this dance was considered scandalous.'

He pauses as we giggle then grabs one of the ladies and pulls her close.

'The man,' he continues, staring into this woman's eyes, 'had to hold the lady close and put his hands on her hips.'

He does just this and although he's hamming it up, the atmosphere is electric.

'He must gaze deeply into her eyes as they twirl faster and faster.'

He takes the lady on a spin around the room that is dizzying to watch.

'You might just be able to see the lady's ankles as they peep out below the dress.'

Our instructor has us all dying to try it out, and after his demonstration he arranges us in pairs and puts on 'The Blue Danube' — a piece of music that we all recognise as much from advertisements as anything else. By the end of the first lesson we're at least all moving in the same direction and those who have a natural aptitude for dance seem to be following the steps without moving their lips. I'm not in that camp, in case there was any doubt, but Mum and Dad look as if they were born to dance this. I don't know whether it's the makeover or the adventures Mum is having through the bucket list, but they do look more in love than ever. I think ahead to the remaining items that I have to organise and really cannot imagine fulfilling Mum's wishes — it would break Dad's heart.

Just as I'm basking in the glow of parental love, Mum leaves Dad and taps Felipe on the shoulder, asking his partner to swap. As with most things Mum does, there's not a lot of choice in the matter, so my parents both end up in the arms of people much younger. Their new partners are dance instructors from Marianne's school, and although my folks looked good dancing together, the extra tuition they're now both getting leaves me breathless; I didn't know either of them could move so quickly. The music reaches its grand finale and my customers break out in spontaneous applause. Their cheeks are pink from the exercise and the smiles reach across the room. Mum has picked a wonderful activity to try and her dream has given all these people a fabulous day. Not for the first time, I wonder why people leave bucket lists until they're old. And why I don't have one.

Our four-day stay here follows a similar routine each day; we visit one of Vienna's stunning palaces or galleries in the morning and continue with our dance lessons in the afternoon. We take a cruise along the Danube, stroll through the parks with their colourful spring flowers and take in the Klimt exhibition at the amazing Upper Belvedere gallery. I also find some local micro-breweries where Dad can sample some Austrian beers and, of course, we make time to sample Vienna's other famous export — the Sachertorte. I'd done my homework before leaving and knew that there were always queues at the Hotel Sacher. I've booked out the tea room for our group, and as well as tasting this delight, we're treated to a glimpse into the kitchen, where chefs are preparing the famous glaze.

'Just a glimpse,' the maitre d'hôtel tells us. 'The original is a secret recipe known only to this hotel, where it was invented by sixteen-year-old chef Franz Sacher for an Austrian state banquet back in 1832.'

'Was everyone in Austria called Franz?' my mum whispers, getting a giggle from those nearby.

The maitre d' goes on to say that there are more showy 'vulgar' confections nowadays.

'Like that harlot of a cake, the Black Forest Gateau.' His look is one of humorous distaste. 'In Vienna we create only elegance.'

I think of the buildings, the music, the dancing, and decide that elegance is the word that best describes this city.

The cake arrives with a dollop of cream and I take a small forkful, savouring the deep chocolate perfection — oh yes, I could definitely live here. I wonder if there are any golf courses for David?

* * *

On our final evening we have a grand ball where everyone can show off their new skills. Rather than eat and then dance, the school has transformed its studio and we're having our final session together surrounded by glittering lights that bounce off the chandelier. Everyone is dressed up in evening wear, the women in long dresses and the men in tuxedos. They look amazing. As this trip is the result of Mum's bucket list, the group stands to one side as she and Dad walk onto the floor to a round of applause. She's wearing an ankle-length silvery dress with a lace bodice and sleeves; it's gorgeous and pairs perfectly with her little silver sandals. Mum has certainly taken the advice she was given to heart and looks beautiful. The music starts and Dad holds out his hand to her, taking hold and pulling her in with his hand on her hip as instructed. At the beat, he waltzes her round the room, never taking his eyes off her. I'm so proud of him. This wasn't his dream and I don't think he would ever have chosen to do it, but he's here and he's learned his steps perfectly to make his wife's dream come true. That's true love for you.

CHAPTER TWENTY-NINE: SINGLE LADIES

It feels like several weeks since we arrived home from Vienna but it's only a matter of days. The world certainly seems to be spinning far faster than it was before we left. I went straight back to work the afternoon the flight arrived as Charlie said the phones were ringing off the hook and indeed they were. Dance lessons and bucket lists are now driving our sales and people really have some strange things they want to do.

'I think I would rather die than do that,' says Charlie as we look at the details of one request.

'I think you'd die if you ever attempted it,' I tell him. 'A full-on heart attack if you ever looked down.'

We're staring at the Glass Skywalk, which is on the side of Tianmen Mountain in Zhangjiajie National Forest Park in China. It goes around the outside of this sheer mountain drop and is only five feet wide with a glass floor so you can see exactly where you'd plummet to your death. It is utterly terrifying.

'How on earth did they ever build something like that?' I ask.

'Why is the more pertinent question,' adds Charlie.

'Oh come on, guys, it'll be fun,' says Josie, looking over our shoulders. 'I'd give it a go.'

As she's not in the slightest bit disturbed by sending one of our clients to certain death, we leave her to arrange it.

It's the golf club fundraising do tonight and, reminding the others not to be late, I clock off exactly on closing to go and get ready. I know that I need to look gorgeous if I'm standing alongside the future chairman of the club and I've contacted the hairdresser who performed the miracle on Mum to work her magic on me.

Patty isn't home when I get back but she's left me a little note telling me to have a lovely time and she's signed the bottom with lots of kisses. She wants me to know that despite her misgivings, she's rooting for me, and I hug the note to my chest. I do my make-up, admiring the shine and bounce my hair now has; I've had a lot of fun in the past few days and I genuinely believe I look younger because of it. My frown lines have softened for a start, and as I smooth a little foundation across my forehead, I wonder whether that's the secret to eternal youth — simply having a good time. It certainly hasn't done Patty any harm. My dress is fresh from the dry cleaners having had a trip to Vienna with me. It seems to have soaked up some of that Austrian elegance, and as I step into my shoes I look at myself in the mirror.

'Not bad, Bo-Peep,' I tell my reflection. 'I'd certainly take you for a spin around the floor.'

Dad is picking me up, and on the dot of seven o'clock, he and Mum pull up and Dad honks the horn from the end of the driveway. Grabbing a shawl and my clutch bag, I hurry to meet them. I'm wearing my waltzing shoes, which aren't the most beautiful pair that I have, but I know that I can dance in them and hope there's a chance to show off my new skills.

'You look lovely, sweetheart,' Dad says to me as I climb into the back seat.

'We're like sisters,' adds Mum, which I know is a compliment.

'How often does a man my age get to escort two beautiful ladies for the evening?' Dad continues as he closes the door.

'Flatterer,' I reply. 'But keep it coming.'

It isn't a long drive and we get there just as Peter, Charlie and Josie are pulling up in their taxi. They don't look very happy though.

'What's up?' I ask as we approach them.

'Hiccup on the wedding front,' says Peter with a purposefully calm tone. 'Our preferred venue has double-booked and they've told us they can't do the date.'

'Can they do another date?' I ask.

'If we want November,' Charlie says. 'And I don't. Our honeymoon is booked too.'

This much I know as he frequently shows me pictures of the resort in Formentera.

'We could still go for a holiday but it won't feel the same,' he continues. 'I want to go as a married couple.'

I put my hand on his shoulder and tell him I'm sorry.

'We'll find you somewhere for the date you want,' I tell him. 'We'll scour heaven and earth and find somewhere completely fabulous — just you wait and see. You'll be glad that place was double-booked.'

He leans his head into me and I kiss the top of it. I've just promised a lot, but there must be a venue with space in March — it's not exactly peak season.

Ed and Caroline pull up, which means we're ready to head in. Peter walks over to Charlie and pulls the sides of his mouth up into a smile; the silly act makes Charlie laugh, so Peter and I link arms either side of him and strut into the golf club.

Kathryn has done a fabulous job; the club looks gorgeous. The small floral centrepieces and napkins are in the club colours of orange and green, which makes the room look fresh and inviting. The linen is crisp and the cutlery gleaming. When the basics are done well, I remember telling her at our meeting, there's no need to spend a great deal on decoration. I can see that she's taken this advice to heart. There's a little gift bag at each place setting, which excites our group until we open them and find a tiny bag of golf tees and some golf pencils provided by a sponsor. Happily, there's also an even tinier box containing two Belgian chocolates. Obviously, they don't last long around us.

'Why do golfers need little pencils?' asks Josie, holding one up and examining it as if it's an ancient artefact.

'To write down the scores as we're going round,' says a voice behind me.

It's David and I get up to give him a kiss on the cheek.

'The place looks terrific,' I tell him and he thanks me. I can see he's a little nervous.

'Thank you all for coming,' he says. 'It's always a bit nerve-wracking wondering if you're going to sell enough seats but we're completely at capacity. I even had to squeeze in another table for four at the last minute.'

He points to a corner where there are indeed four people looking very cosy.

'What should we do with the pencils and tees, given none of us play?' I ask him.

'Leave them on the table, I can always distribute them to the youth team or use them in lessons, they won't go to waste.'

We can see that the waiters are about to start serving, so I wish him luck and let him head back to his own table. Inevitably, as soon as he's gone, the questions start.

'So that's the one you've been spending so much time with,' says Josie.

'What happened to that Michael guy?' asks Mum.

'Oh, keep up, Mrs S,' Charlie tells her. 'He's mysteriously vanished.'

'Like in the Bermuda Triangle?' asks Mum.

'Exactly,' replies Charlie.

'Poor love,' says Mum, putting a hand on top of mine. 'You don't have much luck, do you?'

With Ed sitting only two seats away, my cheeks are blazing red and Peter comes to my rescue, telling them all to back off. I nod my thanks and then tell them that he's just a friend.

'With benefits?' persists Charlie, getting poked with the pointy end of a golf tee.

* * *

The meal goes well but the after-dinner speeches and dedications mean very little to our table and we don't understand any of the golf jokes. I look around at the group and see a couple of stifled yawns; over on David's table they're roaring with laughter and we could be on completely different planets. The auction and raffle get underway next, thank goodness, and at least the prizes aren't all golf related. The Mercury Travel voucher raises a decent sum and Charlie is asked to present it to the winner, then Caroline wins a rather nice silk scarf donated by a local boutique.

After this, the chairman stands and asks everyone to raise a glass to the organiser, Kathryn, and to the brains behind the evening, David. They read out the sum of money they've raised and it's enough for the work they need doing, so all the club members cheer even louder as the rest of us politely applaud. Kathryn is handed a bouquet of flowers and David a gold tiepin. Then there are photos of the two of them.

My table have gone back to talking about potential wedding venues but I'm watching the photos. I'm watching David put his arm around Kathryn, which is a perfectly normal thing to do when you're being asked to squeeze together for the picture, but it's the way he's doing it. He's leaning in so naturally and I don't think he's ever done that with me. Music starts up and David waves over at me to check it's okay before pulling Kathryn onto the dance floor. I simply nod and smile. My group are up the second the music starts, happy that the party has actually started. Only Caroline stays behind as Ed and Josie strut their stuff to 'Voulez-Vous' with the others.

'Penny for them,' says Caroline. I can feel her eyes boring into the side of my head.

'How do you know if you're kidding yourself?' I ask, nodding towards David and Kathryn.

'Do you think he's having an affair?' she asks.

I shake my head and tell her he genuinely is only a friend, and although I wondered whether it could be something more, he hasn't indicated that he's looking for that.

'At least not with me,' I add. 'And Kathryn is lovely. They look very natural together, but if there is a spark between them then I think it started tonight and not before.'

'And how does that make you feel?' asks Caroline in complete therapist mode.

I turn and smile at her.

'Are you coaching me again?' I say with a laugh.

'If it helps.'

I consider how I do feel and the answer is slightly sad. I tell Caroline this and she asks whether I'm sad for the loss of a potential relationship or the loss of David.

'Sometimes we just want to be in a relationship and, if we're honest with ourselves, we're forcing it — trying to make someone fit your life or changing yourself to fit theirs,' she adds.

I give a little snort as it's exactly what's been happening since I met David. My crowd are not golf club people and this is his passion. He'd be horrified with the Granny-Okies and would die of embarrassment if I ever got back up on the stage with them. We're just different people.

'If you find yourself thinking things could be great *if only* they'd change or *if only* you could become interested in the things they like, then it probably isn't going to work,' she says.

I take a deep breath and nod. Mum and Dad come back to the table and tell me they're going to head home but Charlie can fit me in their taxi if I want to stay. I blink away the prick of a self-pity tear and say that I'll come with them as I'm still quite tired after Vienna.

I pick up my shawl and bag then head over to David and Kathryn. I tell them the evening has been fabulous and that

I wish them every success with the future of the club. I give both of them a peck on the cheek then look David directly in the eye as I say, 'Goodbye.' He nods his understanding.

That pity tear threatens to return as I walk towards the door and hear the music slow down as the DJ plays a truly vintage track that I remember my mum listening to on the radio — 'Alone Again (Naturally)'.

CHAPTER THIRTY: SECRETS AND LIES

I wake after around four hours' sleep and feel worn out. In the sleepless hours, I veered from wondering whether I'm destined to be alone for the rest of my life to deciding that it wouldn't be the worst thing in the world. I made the mistake of flicking on my tablet and scrolling through the social media accounts of inspirational single women who're travelling the world with a campervan and a dog. They look deliriously happy staring out at sunsets with their mug of coffee nestled in their hands and their dog sitting calmly by their side. I guess they're all trying to demonstrate that it's the simple things in life that count, but after scrolling several of them, I wonder why they all use the same image? And who is taking the photo? Is it on a timer? If so, then it seems that they're going to an awful lot of effort to prove to people that they're happy alone. And how is their hair perfect if they live in a campervan? Do hairdryers work off grid? Then I wonder what these people smell like if they've been living in a van for several weeks. And how does the van smell with a dog living in it? Would the dog not rather be in a comfy basket at home? Interrogating their lives did take my mind off my own situation but didn't make for a restful night. At least I know that I won't be heading off to the motorhome shop any time soon.

Patty is positively fizzing when I get downstairs and into the kitchen. She's holding up the calendar, which has every day of the month so far crossed out in a thick blue ink.

'Oh my God, it's getting closer,' she says, pinning it back up on the wall. 'It seemed so far away when I got the call but here we are — four weeks to go.'

Of course she's talking about her imminent departure and seeing '*CRUISE!!!*' written in highlighter pen with heart shapes all around it on the same page as my dentist appointment makes it very, very real.

'You're going to be okay, aren't you?' asks Patty. 'I won't be away long, so you won't have time to miss me too much. You might even be more comfortable inviting David round if I'm not here sticking my size sixes in. How did last night go?'

I keep it simple and tell her that over the course of the evening, I realised that we really did have nothing in common so I told him we'd just be friends. It's mostly true.

'Wow, Bo — I'm really proud of you,' she says. 'It takes courage to trust your own instincts. Well done.'

Patty gives me a suffocating hug and I stay where I am until she's finished squeezing the life out of me.

'So what now?' she asks as I sit down at the kitchen table. 'You haven't exactly had a great start to the year when it comes to men, have you?'

I've never actually known Patty to be understated before but on this occasion she most certainly is and I tell her so.

'It's Michael that I don't understand,' she says, making us both a coffee. 'He seemed so friendly at New Year and then again when you got back in touch.'

'But then he stood me up, never gave me a reason why and I followed up on what Sarah said and confirmed it; he really is seeing another woman.' I grimace as I realise I've given away the new snippet of information I have.

'Really?' Patty of course leaps on it as she puts cups down in front of us and sits down with me. 'When did you do that?'

I could lie and say someone else told me the same thing (although this technically wouldn't be a lie as the neighbour told me) but I decide to get it all out in the open, that I went round to see what had happened.

'After all, Sarah might have been wrong and he could have been injured or in hospital.' I wrap my hands around the warm coffee and wonder if I look like one of those social media women. No dog, unfortunately.

'Although they do have phones in hospital,' Patty says. 'Unless, of course, he's had a head trauma and forgotten you completely. I advise you to cut your losses now, Bo.'

'You're all heart.'

'Do you have any clue who this woman is?' asks Patty, opening up Facebook on her phone. 'Does he have a social media profile?'

I genuinely don't know so she has a search but can't find anything. Then she looks up his company account but it's all very official with no personal photos at all.

'I don't like a man you can't stalk,' she says, putting the phone down.

'Let's take the advice you've just given me and drop it.' I sigh and, getting up, head to the cupboard, where there is crusty bread that might distract her. I cut a couple of slices and pop them in the toaster then gather together the butter and marmalade, bringing it back to the table.

'If he'd wanted to say anything to me, he'd have found a way.'

Breakfast is a slow affair this morning; after one round of toast we're on the second cup of coffee and I've managed to change the subject.

'Only a few weeks to go. Are you as ready as you can be?'

'I think so.' Patty nods. 'And the audience never minds if there's a little cock-up; we're all good at improvising.'

'Is there anything you want to do before you go?' I ask.

Patty gives me one of her looks, pulls up something on her phone and pushes it across to me.

'SeniorLove?' I say, looking at the happy septuagenarians staring out from the page.

'We still have one more item on your mum's bucket list, and as this one was my responsibility, I'd like to try and tick it off before I go,' Patty tells me.

'You want to *tick off* my mum having an affair?' I exclaim. 'It's not like making sure you have enough pairs of knickers, you know.'

'Which reminds me . . .' Patty is trying to make a joke of it, but sees the annoyance on my face. 'You said you'd trust me on this.'

'Only because I thought you wouldn't go through with it.'

'We have to, Bo,' says Patty, standing and clearing everything away. 'You know what it's like having an itch you can't scratch. If I thought for one moment your mum would ever leave your dad I wouldn't do this, but she won't. She'll get all excited at the thought of an affair and then want to be back home for her cocoa.'

'I hope you're right.' And that does sound like my mum.

'Now, call her and tell her we want to come and see her,' Patty instructs me firmly. 'Tell her that your dad has to be out for the duration.'

She heads upstairs to get dressed and I make the call. We're instructed to go after she's been to the supermarket because that's when Dad will be heading over to his friend's house to watch the motor racing.

'I can't bear all that noise here,' she tells me. 'It's like a hundred cats screeching over and over again.'

* * *

We arrive at Mum's late afternoon just as Dad is heading out of the driveway. He gives us a wave from the car and tells us to have fun. I feel like a complete traitor as I wave back. I might as well have the dagger in my hand.

Mum is standing in the doorway yelling that Dad should stay out all afternoon, that we have *girl things* to discuss. I'm devastated by the huge smile on her face.

'Come on in,' she says, pushing us through the doorway. 'The supermarket had loads of yellow stickers this morning. We're in for a treat.'

My mother is the queen of the bargain and her favourite hobbies are hoovering up free samples in food stores and loitering in aisles waiting for the assistants to mark down short-dated goods and give them a yellow 'reduced' sticker.

'I hope you haven't had dinner,' she says. 'There's a choice of Thai curry, fish pie or spaghetti carbonara — oh, listen to me, I'm like a gastropub with an exotic menu.' She holds up the single-portion ready meals.

I'm not sure I can actually eat with the guilt forming a lump in my throat, but Patty has no such qualms and opts for the curry. Mum picks the carbonara, leaving me with my least favourite dish of all time.

'You snooze, you lose,' Mum says to me, putting them all in the oven then directing us into the living room. 'They'll be twenty minutes, now tell me what this is all about.'

Patty sits down on the sofa beside Mum, shows her the dating app and explains what needs to be done. Basically, Mum needs to choose a photo that she's happy with and answer the questions about what she's looking for.

'Friendship or romance?' asks Patty.

'Definitely romance,' says Mum.

'Dark or blond?'

'Dark,' replies Mum. 'He has to have hair on his head but not in his ears.'

Patty snorts and says that there isn't really a section to input that.

'We'll say "well-groomed",' she suggests. 'That way he'll know he has to get any ear or nose hair trimmed.'

Mum is adding that he can't bite his fingernails or have a ponytail as I stand and head into the kitchen. I check on the progress of the delightful gourmet meals that seem to be bubbling along in their tinfoil containers.

'Ten minutes,' I shout from the doorway, looking in to see how they're doing. Mum and Patty seem to be having a deeply secret conversation and that worries me.

'What are you two conspiring about?' I ask, coming up behind them. They both jump out of their skins and rush to hide something.

'Nothing that need concern you,' says Mum. 'Why don't you set the table for us?'

She rubs my arm and stares up at me, letting me know that I'm expected to leave them to it. I shake my head and head back to the kitchen. I feel like Cinderella being banished by the ugly sisters.

The timer on the oven pings, so I shout that things are ready and risk third-degree burns extracting these floppy foil cases. I upturn each dish into a bowl and muse how very similar they all look upside down. Patty's curry is less yellow than Mum's pasta but the overall consistency is pretty similar.

'Would you like a glass of wine with this?' asks Mum, reaching into the fridge and pulling out a bottle of white. 'I think I will.'

'It might make it more edible,' I say, poking through mine in search of the one prawn that is so clearly depicted on the packaging photo. I feel an enormous sense of victory when I find it and spear it with my fork.

Mum pours us both a small glass and gets Patty a sparkling water as she's driving home, then sits down and starts eating.

'I think you did the right thing last night,' says Mum as she pats the edge of her mouth with a napkin. 'He wasn't your sort really.'

So that's what they were talking about; Patty has told Mum that I called it a day with David.

'I know.' I'm trying to sound like a grown-up. 'And it's not as if it had progressed beyond a couple of meals.'

'Well, if this dating app works for me then you might be able to give it a go.'

'It's for "seniors",' I reply. 'I'm not quite one of those yet.'

'You might be by the time you find a man,' says Mum with a huge laugh, getting a round of applause from Patty.

'Thanks a bunch, you two.' I smile. You really cannot wallow for too long with this pair.

'And trust me,' Mum continues, 'you had a lucky escape getting rid of a golfer. My neighbour three doors down went out with a golfer once and she said it was awful.'

'Why was that?' asks Patty. She really should know by now not to encourage Mum's tales.

'She was always up for hours before one of his tournaments.' Mum gives a weary shake of the head. 'That man had her up all night polishing his balls. He was never satisfied.'

Both Patty and I choke on our mouthfuls, trying to keep them down. Mum, of course, looks at us in all innocence but she knows what she's said.

We just can't stop laughing and every time one of us gets hold of herself, she looks at the other two and collapses into hysterics again. My sides and cheeks are aching when Dad comes back in through the door.

'It looks like you've had fun,' he says, kissing the top of Mum's head.

For a moment I'd forgotten the reason we came here and now I feel terribly guilty all over again.

CHAPTER THIRTY-ONE: IT TAKES TWO

Patty is up incredibly early the following morning — up and dressed while I'm still in my jammies having my first coffee of the day.

'You do know it's seven in the morning, not the evening, don't you?' I ask through a huge yawn. 'I thought stars of entertainment didn't do such ungodly hours.'

Patty isn't rising to my jibes. She grabs both my hands and sits me down.

'Jack's retiring,' she says with a wild-eyed gaze. I can't tell whether it's excitement, terror or bewilderment.

'He told me last night and I don't know how I feel. I'm scared and delighted at the same time. Does that make sense?'

I'd like to reply that not only does it make sense but that I managed to guess each of those emotions from just one look, but I don't. Instead I just nod and squeeze her hands as a good friend should.

'He's leaving in the summer when I complete my contract. So the Granny-Okies will be on board for his retirement bash and then after he sorts out things with his own house, he'll be coming here to live.'

Wow — no wonder she's stunned. Patty hasn't lived with a man since her husband died five years ago.

'He's coming to live here?' I ask.

'His family live in Lancashire, and although it's not a million miles away, I don't want to move from here. So eventually, yes, we'll be back here.'

It hadn't even occurred to me that my best friend might move away from me and, yes, Lancashire might be less than forty miles away, but it's not around the corner and that would make a difference. I miss her enough when she's away singing but the thought of her going permanently is too hard to even contemplate. In fact, I'm so distressed at the thought of Patty leaving me that the more pressing and obvious issue doesn't strike me until moments later. And then it does.

'I'm going to have to move out,' I say, leaving my jaw hanging open — stunned.

'No you won't,' Patty reassures me. 'You'll still have your own room. Although we might need to soundproof it.'

Patty nudges me and winks. That was probably the least reassuring thing she could have said. The very thought of being the third wheel in their love nest is too disturbing for words. I need to get off my backside and find somewhere to live. I've drifted for too long.

'I don't think there'd be enough soundproofing in the world,' I reply, trying to keep things light. 'In fact, if I moved next door I'd probably still hear you two — if the Zoom calls are anything to go by.'

'Oh, there's an idea — move next door!' exclaims Patty. 'I could buy some cockroaches and feed them through the letterbox, then we could make a cut-price offer when they're begging to sell.'

'Highly unethical,' I tell her. 'And there is no way I would ever move in somewhere there'd been cockroaches.'

'A ghost?' continues Patty. 'We could get up in the small hours every night and rattle some chains by the window?'

'That plan fails with either of us managing to get up every night.' I get a shrug of acknowledgement. 'No, this has been fabulous and I'm so grateful that I've been able to stay with you, but I do need to find somewhere of my own. I'll pop into the estate agents over lunchtime.'

'Just don't go to any photography studio viewings without me,' she says with a snort of laughter.

I shudder at the memory of what she's referring to. A viewing I made last year when I first started looking — let's just say that boudoir photoshoot will be etched on my mind forever.

'So the reason you're up early is just excitement?' I ask, getting back to the first newsworthy event of the day.

'Partly,' she says with a little sadness in her voice. 'And partly because I have to say goodbye to everything here that was Nigel's. I know I've moved on now but I still need to say goodbye to little things and make space for my new life.'

I rub her arm gently. She acts all big and blowsy but deep down my best friend is as soft as the rest of us.

* * *

In the office, Charlie is focussed entirely on finding a wedding venue that fits in with the honeymoon while Josie and I deal with customers.

'You could have the honeymoon first and come back tanned and relaxed,' Josie suggests during one of our coffee breaks.

I think that's a pretty good idea but Charlie obviously hasn't heard it as he scowls at the computer screen.

'If you continue like this,' I tell him, 'you'll have frown lines on your wedding photos and you won't like that.'

Those words horrify him into looking up and feeling his forehead, smoothing it down with the palms of his hands.

'Do you think I should get a little tweakment?' he asks us, now stretching out either side of his face.

'I think you should stop fretting,' I tell him. 'You know that Zoe's hotel has a wedding licence. I could still ask her if she has availability.'

I have offered this before but have been told, in the nicest possible way, that it's not really 'different' enough. I get that, I really do. But as my mother would say, beggars can't be choosers, which when you think about it, is an incredibly mean expression. However, it seems that Charlie has reached that stage as he reluctantly replies, 'I suppose there's no harm in knowing some dates.'

I promise to call Zoe as soon as I get back from the estate agents.

Mercury Travel is quite quiet today so I get off to lunch early and head along to the local office. I'll register online too but it's always best to talk things through personally. I firmly believe that if we want shops to stay on the high street then we have to use them as these offices buy lunch from local cafés, take clothing into local dry cleaners and buy dinner from the local shops. It can be a virtuous circle or a downward spiral and the choice really is ours. Happily, Chorlton loves its bohemian reputation and the streets buzz with customers.

'Angie Shepherd,' says the agent as he searches through his database. 'Aha, you were registered with us last year — so you never found the right place?'

'Not at the right time,' I tell him. I don't want to say that I wasn't ready for my independence and the warm embrace of Patty's home was far more appealing.

'I did like the duplex apartment in the converted mansion,' I say, instead sounding like a woman who has it together. 'I liked the space and the fact that someone else did the gardening.'

He smiles up at me and says as he types it in, 'Low-maintenance property required.'

After confirming my details, he hands me the particulars of a couple of properties, which I promise to look at and get back to him.

Leaving the estate agents, I actually feel a little lighter, that I'm ready to take control of my life. Taking control of my business life has not been an issue, I was jumping at the bit to get that in motion, but emotionally I seem to have ricocheted from one person to the next and I can see that now. It's time to stop being the pinball.

On my way back to Mercury I pick up lunch for the others and a bottle of champagne to take home to Patty tonight. It's fabulous news that she's found love and that Jack is moving in; my little family of friends is simply growing.

I walk in waving the goodies and am surprised to see Poppy O'Cherry sitting at Josie's desk. They turn and call out, 'I'll have the champagne but no sarnies, I'm on strictly no carbs.'

I give them a kiss on the cheek and ask what brings them into the office.

'Even drag artistes take holidays, darling,' they reply, adjusting the tailored pinstripe suit, which really emphasises their long legs right the way down to the shiny spats. Poppy would look like a gangster if it weren't for the wavy red bob wig.

'I'm going for a cross between mobster and moll,' they explain, catching my glimpse.

'Stunning — but here I was thinking that at the end of each evening you were just packed away in a magical trunk with your dresses,' I say, smiling.

'Wouldn't mind being packed away with his magical trunks.' Poppy nods towards the door where Peter is standing.

Charlie walks up to him and, looking exasperated, falls into his arms.

'What's up there?' asks Poppy.

I explain about the wedding plans collapsing and before I've put the full stop on the sentence, Poppy is up and out of their chair and standing in the middle of the room with their arms outstretched.

'Gentlemen,' they say. 'Do not despair, for your fairy drag mother is here to save the day.'

The guys look over wearily.

'Seriously,' continues Poppy. 'I'm a wedding celebrant, and you two lovelies shall have the most magical day or I wasn't crowned Ms Lovely Legs Butlins 2019.'

Poppy picks up a pencil from the desk and waves it through the air. I can almost hear the Disney sparkles follow its path.

* * *

The three of them move into the break room to continue the conversation, leaving Josie and I in the calm quiet of the shop.

'Do you think they'll go for it?' asks Josie.

'I don't know,' I say. 'As much as they like Poppy, I think they were aiming for romantic rather than theatrical.'

'I'd let Poppy officiate,' continues Josie and I look at her trying to hide a tiny surge of panic.

'Are you and Matt . . . ?' I ask.

'Noooo — but if we were, then I'd ask Poppy,' she says. 'It would be seriously cool.'

I know it's irrational but I'm hypersensitive to all my friends marrying and moving in together. I love them all dearly but am starting to feel like a spare part and would at least like to have something of my own before they're all settled down.

When Peter and Charlie emerge an hour later, they have broad smiles on their faces.

'It's all sorted?' I ask with eager excitement.

'Go on, tell us. What sort of wedding will it be?' asks Josie.

Poppy appears and simply swipes an imaginary zip across their lips.

'It'll be memorable, and you lot need to glam up to the nines,' is all they'll say before sauntering out of the shop, hips swinging.

I watch as Poppy strides along the high street, where literally everyone they pass turns to look and a few people ask for selfies. It really does take incredible bravery and confidence to be yourself.

Peter insists on Charlie coming home with him immediately, saying that he knows his fiancé is incapable of keeping any secrets.

'Damn,' says Josie. 'We were banking on Charlie breaking after one bout of tickling.'

'I doubt it would take that much, judging by his expression,' I add. 'You're just bursting to tell us, aren't you?'

He nods; his little cheeks are flushed and his eyes wide. This man is so excited he would have spilled everything the second Peter was out of the door.

We have a late-afternoon flurry of customers booking last-minute Easter breaks to keep Josie and I busy. As I arrange them, noting the dates, I realise Patty will be away and I'll be in her big house on my own. I know I need to make more effort with my other friends so that I can build a social life without her both for that month and for when she comes back with Jack.

As soon as we lock the door to the shop, I call Caroline and ask if she fancies going for a drink or to see a film one night.

'I'd love to,' she says. 'Not this week as Ed is whisking me away somewhere — can I call you when I get back?'

I say of course and hope that she has a lovely time.

Then I look up Sarah's number and check the time before calling her. It's nearly six so she should be closing up too by now.

'Hello, Angie,' she says, sounding breathless. 'How lovely to hear from you.'

It boosts my ego to hear that someone is really pleased I've called. Perhaps she's in the same situation I am and we can become best buddies. I imagine us strolling along the canal laughing together.

(I have a tendency to do this — one tiny indication that things are going well and I extrapolate to the nth degree. If the man in the florist smiles at me I instantly picture myself as his partner, fixing him a coffee at 5 a.m. before he heads off to the flower market. He always leaves me a rose on the pillow too. I think this flaw in my personality comes from believing my childhood book of fairy tales was in fact an encyclopaedia).

Anyway, getting back to Sarah, we exchange some pleasantries about how busy our days have been and then I ask her if she'd like to go out.

'Aggh,' she replies, bringing my best buddy dream to a crashing halt. 'I'd love to but you'll never guess what? I've got a date! Can I call you later?'

She sounds so happy that I shouldn't begrudge her and I don't. I repeat what I've just said to Caroline and after the call, scroll through my contacts. Yep — that's it confirmed. Every single friend I have is officially coupled up.

CHAPTER THIRTY-TWO: THE SPY WHO LOVED ME

'You need to bunk off for the afternoon,' my mum whispers down the phone.

'I can't,' I tell her huffily.

'Yes you can, you're the boss,' she insists.

'I'm a partner and that means I have to show responsibility, which means no bunking off.'

'Oh, so Charlie hasn't bunked off to sort out his wedding at all this year?' Mum makes a point.

'That's different, he's been badly let down,' I tell her. 'Besides which, a wedding is important and takes a lot of organising.'

'How do you know that reason I need you here isn't important?' Mum asks, not giving up.

'The last time you wanted me to bunk off it was because you'd found a freezer full of yellow-sticker turkey crowns but had no one to drive you home,' I remind her.

'They'd have come in handy for Christmas.'

'It was the Boxing Day sale.'

'Well, your father and I got an awful lot of curries and pies from them that year, but this is nothing to do with shopping and everything to do with you.' I can almost feel her prodding me from a distance. 'Now, get on down here — I'll meet you in the Three Swans on the canal.'

I sigh with despair as my mother puts the phone down on me. It's late in the afternoon and we only have another hour until closing, so I explain the conversation to Josie and Charlie and ask if it's okay to leave early. They're both happy and even excited by the idea.

'I wonder what scheme she's cooked up now,' says Josie. 'Do you think she's found something else to add to her bucket list?'

'Dear Lord, I hope not,' I tell them as I shut down the PC and collect my things.

'We want a full rundown in the morning,' Charlie yells as I head out the door.

* * *

The Three Swans is in a fairly idyllic location next to a lock. As I walk towards it from the car park, I notice flowers starting to bud and the air smelling fresher. Despite the fact that I'm meeting my mother, it feels good to be out of the office. I see a group of women on the canal bank striding along with walking poles; they're chatting and laughing as they walk and I wonder whether I could join something like that when Patty leaves. The thought of sensible boots and waterproofs would have her needing a lie down before she'd started. Then again, with the pace these women are going at, I'm exhausted just watching — maybe that isn't my new thing after all.

Compared to the late-afternoon sunshine outside, the interior of the pub is quite dark and I can't see Mum anywhere. Typical that she's dragged me out and isn't even here herself. She had to have driven here and that's surprising too — normally Dad or I would be called on to chauffeur. Unless she's on a date from that ridiculous website Patty signed her up to. I panic slightly, thinking my mum might be trying to get out of a dangerous situation, and grab at my phone, dialling her number.

Somewhere behind me the theme tune to *Mission: Impossible* starts playing very loudly and I spin round ready to ask them to turn it down when I see my mum skulking in a corner booth. She's wearing dark sunglasses with her phone blaring full blast. I end the call and the music finishes as I do. Mystery solved.

'You've changed your ringtone,' I say, walking towards her. 'I didn't realise you knew how to do that.'

'I got next door's grandson to do it for me,' Mum explains. 'Good, isn't it?'

'Distinctive,' I tell her. 'We'll always know whose phone is ringing.'

'Oh, it's only on for when you call,' Mum says.

'Why? And why are you wearing those glasses and that old trench coat? I thought you'd thrown it in the charity bag.'

'Get me a bitter lemon and I'll tell you everything,' says Mum, removing the sunglasses. 'I've worked up a bit of a thirst today.'

Thinking it'll be midnight before I get any information out of this woman, I nevertheless head to the bar and get us drinks and crisps. I know that this will be her next request and I'm not jumping up and down all afternoon. Mum dives into the snacks then takes a long sip of her drink and begins.

'I've been doing some detective work,' she says. 'I needed to be undercover.'

She taps the side of her nose and I gather that's why she's wearing that old coat. She once wore it to a murder mystery party when she went as the amateur sleuth.

'Nothing says inconspicuous more than a glamorous seventy-year-old with a purple handbag and an old coat,' I tell her.

'Nothing says inconspicuous more than a seventy-year-old, full stop,' says Mum. 'I could probably have gone around naked.'

I grimace at the thought but she does make a valid point, and after all, I never spotted her when I walked in.

'So why are you doing detective work?' I ask, thinking we should really get to the point before the pub closes.

'To save your love life,' asserts Mum. 'Someone has to do something and I'm probably best qualified.'

I pause, not sure whether I want to hear any more of this but also curious as to what on earth she can be up to. Not being a cat, I think I'm perfectly safe to let the curiosity win today.

'Go on,' I tell her cautiously.

'It makes no sense to me,' she says. 'That Michael fellow being keen one minute and spooking you the next.'

'Ghosting,' I say, but she brushes it away with a 'whatever'.

'I saw the pictures from New Year and he looked really happy,' she continues. 'You all looked as if you were having a roaring time and I can't believe that a man on his own doesn't want a little more of that.'

She isn't telling me anything I didn't know or hadn't thought.

'We did have a good time but it happens, Mum,' I tell her. 'You might have looked at pictures of me and David and thought we were having a good time but neither of us really were.'

'Anyone with half a brain could have seen that,' replies Mum. 'Not sure why it took you so long to figure it out.'

There's tough love and there's my mum's love — which would have Bear Grylls crying in his coffee. I don't mention that Patty had it figured out too. There's always a bit of competitiveness between my mum and my friend as to who knows what's best for me. Apparently, I have no clue.

'Shall we get to the point?' I ask, hoping to avoid a dissection of that particular failed attempt at a relationship.

'Anyhow, as I said, it didn't make sense to me and I decided I'd try to get to know him better and work it all out.' She pauses and somewhere in the ether there's a drumroll just for her. 'So I followed him.'

'You did what?'

'I put him under surveillance to find out what on earth was going on,' Mum repeats as if it's a perfectly normal thing to do.

'When did you do all of this?' I ask.

'Last night and then today,' she tells me. 'Your dad came with me last night although he didn't know why I was doing it. He thought he was just having a nice trip to the pub. Michael's never met me or your dad so there was no danger of him recognising us, if that's what you're bothered about.'

There are many things that bother me about this situation and that was on the list but fairly low down. My mother being outed on one of her schemes would probably do her good.

'Do you want to know my findings?' she asks, pulling a little notebook from her handbag. I simply shrug and let her go ahead.

'Nineteen hundred hours, suspect leaves his house and gets into a taxi,' she begins. 'I know he's not a suspect but I wasn't sure what else to call him.'

'Wasn't Dad suspicious that you were waiting outside someone's house?' I ask.

'I told him I had my reasons,' replies Mum. 'He knows not to ask when I say that.'

This much I know. Throughout my life, when Mum has done something weird or wonderful and I've asked Dad about it, his weary reply has always been, '*Oh, you know Mum — she has her reasons.*'

She could probably be caught digging a body-sized hole in the garden and Dad would accept this explanation. I'm distracted for a moment wondering whether her having an affair falls into this category.

'Are you okay?' asks Mum, bringing me back to the present.

'Yes,' I tell her then ask the other question on my mind. 'How did you know where he lived?'

'He's on Cross Road where you used to live and he has a cat with white paws that sits in the window,' Mum says as if I'm crazy to ask. 'I wouldn't be much of a detective if I failed at the first hurdle.'

The cat often stayed at my house and Mum would definitely have recognised her, so I concede this. It's a good point, well made.

'We pursued the suspect to this pub, where he ordered a pint and a gin and tonic then sat over there by the window.' Mum points out the seat in question.

'So, he was meeting someone,' I say. 'And a G&T probably means it was a woman.'

'Hold on there, Miss Marple,' Mum tells me, wagging her finger. 'Technically, the suspect was meeting someone and a woman entered the pub shortly afterwards.'

'Did you recognise her?' I ask.

'No, but she was quite plain looking,' Mum says. 'No one would have given up my daughter for her.'

As much as I hate the denigration of any woman, I'm slightly boosted by Mum's little compliment. Yet again, I know how shallow and needy this makes me appear.

'It sounds as if he has, Mum,' I tell her, mentally pulling on my big girl pants. 'And I'm happy for him. I just wish he'd had the courage to tell me.'

'Getting ahead of yourself again, Angela. I'm not finished yet.' Mum pulls herself up tall in the seat, cradling her hands in front of her like a judge. 'You see, I don't think there was anything going on between them. There was no spark.'

I tell her all about Richard Branson's advice and how a spark isn't everything — love takes time to build and is about doing small things together. She waves my sage's advice away with one hand.

'He should stick to vacuum cleaners,' she says.

'That's Dyson,' I tell her. 'Branson does space flight.'

'Even more useless,' she replies. 'Now, shall we get back to the point?'

I nod and tell her I'd love to.

'Little things give it away,' Mum continues. 'Look around this pub now and tell me who is having a good time and who isn't.'

I do as I'm told and see those little things — the brush of a hand, the holding out of a chair, the genuine smiles and laughter. Those having a good time share food easily and seem to flow around each other like waltzing on the dance floor — it's easy and effortless. And on the other hand, the silent sitting opposite each other glued to their phones, the folded arms and pursed lips. I know all of this as I used to watch other couples all the time when I was out with my ex. We used to guess which ones would last and which wouldn't. Mum has made her point and I tell her so.

'So, tell me what you saw with Michael,' I ask.

'I saw a keen woman — constantly reaching out to touch him on the arm and laughing at whatever he said. I also saw an indifferent man — or maybe the look was confused?' says Mum. 'He looked puzzled when she kept laughing at him and he certainly didn't like being touched. I asked your dad what he thought and he said that it looked as if the bloke couldn't wait to get away.'

'How long did they stay?' I ask.

'Well, after she'd finished her drink, she got up to buy a round and he obviously just ordered a half-pint,' Mum reads from her notes.

'Two things to note there,' says Mum but I'm way ahead of her.

'He didn't leap up and insist on buying the drink and he didn't order a pint because he didn't want to extend the evening.'

'You're learning, sweetheart. Then, when the woman was in the bathroom, he took out his phone and rang someone. When she returned he held the phone up as if he'd just got a message and had to go. The woman looked crestfallen but seemed to be making other suggestions. He just kept shaking his head and stood up. She leaned in to kiss him and he quickly presented the side of his cheek.'

I'm liking the sound of all this, but just because he was with someone he didn't gel with that night doesn't explain why he ditched me without a word. I say all of this to Mum.

'I know,' she says thoughtfully. 'And it could be that this is who he is; you said he was widowed, so maybe he's just trying out a number of women to find someone to replace his wife. He might be extremely efficient at sussing them out and when he knows it won't work just cuts his losses instantly. At least he doesn't string them along.'

'He doesn't explain why it's over either,' I remind Mum.

'Well, Operation Edith isn't finished yet,' she says.

'Edith?'

'From *Downton Abbey* — she has the worst luck in love ever,' Mum tells me, clutching her palm to her chest. 'Even worse than you.'

'Gee, thanks.'

'No need,' she continues. 'I'm going to continue this surveillance for the rest of the week and I will get to the bottom of what happened between you even if I have to lock him up in the cellar and shine a light in his eyes.'

'Mum—' I start to protest but she gives me a wave of the hand.

'No need to thank me,' she says. 'It's no bother at all.'

CHAPTER THIRTY-THREE: WITH A LITTLE HELP FROM MY FRIENDS

'She's right, you know,' Charlie says as Mum explains her stalking episode to everyone in the Mercury Travel shop the next day.

And by everyone, I do mean that. Poppy and Peter have, well, *popped* in to see Charlie about the wedding, a customer managed to get herself locked in when we hurriedly closed up shop and Patty is here because she has very little else to do while waiting for her ship to sail. Add myself, Dad and Josie to the mix and we almost have a full house.

'If you're interested, you would definitely offer to buy the next drink,' says Josie. 'You'd probably suggest sharing a bottle of wine.'

Murmurs of agreement echo from everyone.

'And yet he hasn't been in touch,' says Poppy. 'Angie could be right and he's just trying a few women on for size. Must be difficult after a bereavement.'

'It is,' says Patty. 'But I don't remember dating lots of different men — did I?'

She looks over at me and I shake my head. It was rather the opposite actually. When her hubby died, Patty became a recluse for quite some time. Hard to believe that now.

'Tell us the timeline again.' Charlie has pulled our whiteboard out of the break room. He wipes off our sales targets and instead draws a horizontal line like you see on detective shows.

'New Year's, you brought him to the party and he seemed to have a good time,' he calls out. 'As evidenced by this photo.'

He pulls out his phone and shows everyone the picture of all of us at the party.

'Yep — that smile looks genuine,' says Josie, getting nods from everyone. It appears that they have all become experts in behavioural psychology as well as selling holidays and entertaining on stage.

'Then,' continues Charlie, 'there's no word from him for how long, Angie?'

'A week,' I tell the room to gasps and whispers of '*that's a long time if you're keen*'.

'*But,*' I interject quickly, 'when I did call him, it turned out that I hadn't given him my number and he didn't know Patty's address.'

There's a collective sigh of relief as Charlie jots these details on his whiteboard. It's as if the office is watching some B-movie unfold.

'So he now has your number and you arrange to meet,' he says. 'At the tea shop on the canal.'

'So sweet,' says the customer. Everyone turns to face her as we'd forgotten that someone came in to spend money. She blushes at the attention and tries to make herself smaller in the chair.

'But he doesn't turn up,' says Patty. 'And he doesn't message or call to say why.'

A group '*Ooooooh*' this time. I think this B-movie might be *The Twilight Zone* — that's what it feels like.

'And he hasn't done since?' confirms Charlie, looking at me. I nod as he writes this down too.

'Nope,' adds Patty, 'and when we were in the Lake District at the end of January we hear that he's seeing someone, although we don't have that confirmed.'

'But if he wasn't keen on the woman he met yesterday, that couldn't be the person he was supposedly seeing back then — what stopped him calling between then and now?' asks Poppy, tapping a well-manicured nail against their lips.

'We can rule out him having fallen in the canal or being dead,' says Mum helpfully.

'But not a bump on the head and total amnesia,' adds Josie even more helpfully.

'Amnesia's not real,' says Patty. 'It's just a helpful plot device.'

Everyone stares at the whiteboard and the gap in time that can't be accounted for.

'Could he have lost your number again?' asks Dad in his kindest voice. 'I'm forever losing things. He might have stuffed your number in his pocket and then put those jeans in the wash.'

'He put it straight into his phone,' I say, squeezing his hand.

'Well, maybe the phone was in his pocket and that went through the washer,' he continues and Mum picks up that line of thought.

'That could be it,' she repeats. 'Poor man hasn't got a woman around; they're always doing daft things without us.'

'You know, we really aren't,' Charlie tells her haughtily. 'I've done my own washing for forty years without incident.'

I don't want this to turn into a battle of the sexes and I don't actually want it to last a minute longer, so I tell everyone that even if there had been a washing machine mishap, Michael would still have been able to contact me through the shop. I tell everyone that I'm grateful for their concern but I'm happy to let matters rest.

'No chance,' says Mum. 'You deserve an explanation.'

I protest that I don't need one.

'I'm quite curious though,' says Charlie, getting agreement from everyone. 'I say we let Mrs S keep up the surveillance and report back later.'

Dad looks over at me and I shrug defeat. In solidarity he says that he can't continue as he's busy. Mum throws him a furious look which I know means no supper for at least two days.

'I'll come with you,' says Poppy. 'He's never met me.'

'How on earth are you going to look inconspicuous?' asks Mum.

'Wait and see,' they say, linking arms with her. 'Just you watch — we'll be the next Mulder and Scully.'

The reference is lost on Mum and I can't see how hunting aliens has anything to do with Michael but I let it go.

We clear everyone out of the shop including the customer, who promises to come back in a couple of days for an update. I suggest to Patty that we head over to the wine bar to decompress.

'I have a better idea,' she tells me, pushing me towards a waiting taxi.

'Not Clubbercise again — please,' I say. 'I'm not sure I could cope with that.'

'Don't worry, neither could I,' Patty says as the taxi heads in the opposite direction to home.

We pull up outside a small social club on the edge of town. As we park I notice the other Granny-Okies are there too. Kath and Sheila hug us like old friends and say they've reserved a table at the front.

'Front of what?' I ask, looking at the place and guessing that the front of the room and the back aren't that far apart.

We walk in and I'm right. It's a tiny venue with a small stage at one end. The kind of club where comedians might debut and get heckled off stage, where punters would later brag that they saw such-and-such when they first started out — forgetting completely that they gave them a hard time.

Patty buys a bottle of wine for us and we sit at a small round table that does indeed have a scrap of paper with the word *Reserved* on it. It's a weekday and the place isn't exactly heaving so I doubt it was needed, but Kath seems excited. And then I guess why.

A pull-out poster stand is dragged onto stage announcing an act playing tonight — Getting Wetter, a tribute to Wet Wet Wet.

'Just wait until you see Marti Pellow,' gushes Kath. 'He's just like the real one — absolutely gorgeous.'

Now I'm a little excited too — who hasn't had a crush on that handsome man at some point in their life? Although I'm not sure about that name.

Patty tells the girls that I need cheering up, which means I have first dibs on the Mr Pellow lookalike. I catch a glimpse of *over my dead body* on Kath's face so quickly assure the girls that I want nothing to do with any man tonight. Kath looks slightly appeased but I guess she'll keep a close eye on me. The first bottle of wine goes down far too quickly so Sheila and Kath get up to buy another. I know it's a work night and I should be doing my best to stop it turning into a wild session, but right now I don't care.

'What do you think happened?' Patty asks me while we're alone. 'Assuming you don't believe the amnesia or dead in the canal theories. Why do you think he hasn't called?'

I have of course pondered this and as I thought Michael was such a nice man, I can only think of reasons that play to that image.

'Well, I've never lost a spouse like you both have,' I reply, choosing my words carefully. 'But when my divorce was finalised, people kept telling me to move on and I started to feel like a failure because I wasn't sure I was ready.'

'I remember,' says Patty. 'I felt that way too.'

'So perhaps, coming to the New Year's party was Michael bowing to pressure from other people. He tried to move on but realised that he wasn't ready.'

'But why not just tell you that?'

'Because it sounds weak,' I say. 'He may even have had a really nice night but then he got home and felt guilty. It's kind of difficult to explain that to someone you've just met.'

Patty doesn't have time to respond as the girls arrive back with an ice bucket and a fresh bottle of Pinot Grigio. As our glasses are topped up, I notice that the room is filling and it's pretty much all women. Kath is going to have far more competition than me tonight.

The lights in the room go down and the one stage spot lights up. There's a whoop of delight from the audience behind us and Kath adjusts her hair. At the opening bars to one of the band's biggest hits, some of the ladies rush to the front of the stage ready to start dancing.

The other band members appear to a muted response, which I guess they must all be used to now, and then Marti appears and everyone goes wild. And with good reason. This man is extremely handsome and has that broad smile that made the real Marti very popular.

'Sweet Little Mystery' is their opening track and immediately everyone is dancing like it's 1987 again. Kath and Sheila are up immediately, elbowing their way to the front, but Patty and I are happy to sway along from a seated position.

'Are these guys repped by your agent?' I ask Patty when there's a break between songs.

'Yes, and they're on the cruise ship too. They're doing the whole summer though.'

'Kath will be happy about that,' I comment with a laugh.

'To Kath getting wetter,' says Patty, raising her glass to clink. I can't because I've snorted with laughter so hard that the sip I've just taken is threatening to come down my nose.

The band run through a medley of their biggest hits, ending with 'Goodnight Girl', where Marti really works the audience, walking into them and taking the hand of one lady then the next. He twirls them romantically then kisses their hand before moving onto the next. They all seem to love this, and happily for Kath, he reaches her last and brings her up onto the little stage. For the instrumental at the end of the song he pulls her into a close slow dance, which she evidently enjoys. As it ends, he bows to her and helps her off the stage then turns to the audience and blows kisses to them. They erupt with applause, proving that a man with manners can flirt with multiple women in one night and get away with it.

I've had a lovely night and tell the girls this as I say goodbye. Patty is still inside having a word with Marti and the band but comes out shortly afterwards.

'Checking their terms and conditions?' I ask, knowing that Patty is pretty hot on ensuring she gets as good a room as anyone else.

'Something like that,' she says in a vague, dismissive way.

Our taxi pulls up and we head home. On the way I can see that she's messaging Marti but she won't tell me why.

'Just business,' she says. 'You'll see soon enough.'

CHAPTER THIRTY-FOUR: HOMEWARD BOUND

With the mystery of my vanishing love life now firmly in the hands of others (so it seems), it's good to get a phone call that enables me to grasp hold of my own destiny without any outside interference.

'Ms Shepherd?' says the voice on the other end of the line. 'We have something you might be very interested in.'

And indeed I am. It's the estate agent telling me that an apartment has just come up for sale. They haven't advertised it yet but they expect lots of interest when they do. I know that's just the sales pitch — I do it myself. I tell customers that I can't hold an offer price much longer or I can't guarantee the deluxe suite unless they book today. We all do it and I'm not fooled, but I am extremely keen because when they email through the address, I know that it's the mansion house that I saw and loved last year. I hold my voice steady as I arrange to view it early that evening and ask them to hold off advertising it if they can. This is me also playing the game as I'm guessing if it's just come on their books, they haven't done the floor plan or the detailed description so there's no way it'll be advertised before the evening.

I'm going to be on tenterhooks all day but fortunately there's no chaos occurring in the shop. Mercury Travel is a happy place today; Charlie is singing to himself as he types away confirming bookings, and he's making lots of them thanks to that cheery disposition. Customers seem to be swept up in his joyfulness and say yes to all of his suggestions. Added to this, he tells us that his wedding plans are going very well but he won't reveal the details to anyone and he's revelling in the secrecy. He has told us that the dress code is 1950s glamour, which is both easy and flattering so I'm delighted. Josie and I have guessed that he's going for a *Mad Men* theme as that's one of his favourite TV shows, but his lips are sealed. Whatever it is, I hope he has some of those crystal champagne coupes. I think they're so elegant but have always been too afraid to buy a set, knowing that I'll likely break them within weeks. Come closing time, I tidy up promptly and tell the others that I have to go. They wish me luck and look as if they're about to settle in for a post-work coffee and chat. I sincerely hope it's going to be about the wedding but I daresay my life will be discussed too.

This evening, I don't care. I'm on my way to see a place I would have been terrified to live in last year. Terrified because back then I felt it was too good for me; all I had was a failed marriage and a fledgling business to my name. I remember feeling a fraud just looking around the place. Now things have moved on. We won the Business Award I coveted and Mercury has a fabulous reputation with five star reviews all the way. Okay, so the relationship stuff seems to roll from bad to worse, but I can't wait for all the stars to align, can I? Perhaps I'll start to succeed in love when I'm in my own place but if I'm destined to live alone then this is the kind of place to do it.

I reach the address in Didsbury and turn into the grounds. Grounds!!! I'd have grounds! I don't think I'd ever tire of saying that. I'll have a huge lawn that someone else looks after — how perfect. The estate agent's little electric car is already there, so after parking up, I do a little tidy-up in the mirror to check that I look like a woman who means business and then stroll assertively towards her, holding out my hand for her to shake. We walk through the grand doorway into the beautiful Georgian hallway and through to the apartment that is for sale. Opening the door, I get a frisson of excitement running right through me; it's a mirror image of the one I fell in love with last year. It has the high ceilings, spacious rooms and period features that I remember, and a fireplace where I pictured my Business Award trophy sitting. I look around with the agent and then on my own, opening the French windows to the private patio, now completely able to see myself living here. I feel calm and at home — as if this place has been waiting for me to feel ready.

'Okay,' I tell the agent. 'What's the asking price?'

She tells me what they're thinking of putting it on for and it's higher than last year but still within the limits of my divorce settlement. I nod sagely and try to look as if I'm considering what she's said but there's no point in me pretending — I want this place.

'I'll give you five thousand more, cash, with no chain and I'll allow the vendor to set the moving date, but I need my offer accepted today with no further viewings permitted,' I tell her assertively.

She looks slightly startled but agrees to call the vendor and I stand tall, prompting her to do it right now. She moves into the grounds so I can't hear the conversation, while I sit on the huge sofa imagining that I live here already. The agent comes back into the room ten minutes later with a big smile on her face, so I know it's a done deal.

'They've accepted your offer,' she says. 'Congratulations, Ms Shepherd, you have a lovely new home.'

After signing some paperwork I head to the shop and pick up a bottle of champagne. I feel fabulous that I've actually done something for myself at last. And none of my friends or family were around to encourage or otherwise. It's as if I've taken the stabilisers off my ability to make decisions. All the way back to Patty's I sing Helen Reddy's 'I Am Woman' over and over again and I yell that I'm *strong*, that I'm *invincible*, and I know this time I'm not faking it.

I've watched cartoons where the main character is in full flow — doing something they love or just running fast and then all of a sudden they have to screech to a halt as they hit an obstacle in their way. This happens when I walk into Patty's still singing and holding out the bottle of champagne. I feel my whole being screeching to a full stop as I see the faces of Patty, Poppy and Mum staring back at me. I find myself glued to the spot feeling like Wile E. Coyote just waiting for an anvil to fall on my head.

'Thank goodness you're back,' says Mum. 'We have news.'

I hold the champagne bottle aloft and tell them I have news too but that's ignored. Patty takes the champagne and says she'll chill it while I hear what the others have to say.

'So we've been on surveillance,' begins Mum as they sit me down on the sofa and surround me. 'Poppy was surprisingly good actually — they went in a flat cap and dowdy old man clothes and nobody paid a ha'penny worth of attention, did they?'

'Told you I was good,' says Poppy.

'Just tell me what you found,' I say wearily.

'It's interesting.' Patty reappears from the kitchen and reassures me.

Mum gets out her little notepad and clears her throat.

'At one fifteen, suspect and his work colleague park their van and have lunch in the park,' she says. 'We did start following him before this but he was in some office block all morning and we couldn't see what he was doing.'

'You needed a pass to get in, otherwise we would have tried,' adds Poppy, getting a nod from Mum. How such an unlikely alliance formed will probably baffle anyone who doesn't know my family.

'Suspect had cheese sandwiches without *any* salad,' declares Mum as if this is a groundbreaking finding.

'How close did you get?' I ask.

'Poppy has binoculars,' explains Mum. 'You can see in the windows right across the street with them. I know what I'm asking for next birthday.'

'The key point here,' Poppy says, picking up the thread, 'is that we think if there was a woman around, she'd probably have bought salad and made him put it in his sandwiches.'

'He might not like salad,' I suggest. 'Or, here's a theory — maybe he makes his own lunch even though he has a girlfriend.'

'No need to be uppity,' says Mum. 'You may not like the thinking but I know people and that was not a female-made sandwich.'

'Is there anything else?' I sigh.

'Oh yes,' declares Mum. 'I'll skip past the following him all afternoon and into the supermarket where he bought microwaveable meals for one as you'll probably have some snarky remark about that. We'll get onto the key discovery.'

'Please do.'

'I stayed in the car park while your mum followed him around the shop,' says Poppy. 'Just in case she lost him and he came out early.'

'We had the phones on so we could alert each other,' adds Mum, absolutely loving all of this.

'When he came out, he sat in the seat of his van and made a phone call before he left,' continues Poppy. when you have that phone on. 'Well, we were standing quite close by, and we heard that call in its *entirety*,' says Poppy with a flourish. 'He called you.'

I sit stunned and eventually say, 'Me?'

'That's right,' adds Mum, reading from her notebook. 'We wrote this down afterwards but we both heard it:

'Angie — Michael again. Really sorry to keep calling you like this but I'm worried and do wonder if everything is okay. I know you said not to bother you but if you could call back and let me know whether your friend Patty is recovering, I'd love to hear from you — and just in case you've lost it, my number is . . .'

'Are you sure?' I ask the wall of faces now staring at me. 'I haven't had any calls from him at all. Maybe it's someone else he's calling.'

'Someone else called Angie with a friend called Patty?' asks Patty.

'I promise you that's exactly what he said,' says Poppy. 'Somehow, he's using the wrong number.'

'How? I gave him my number and called him from it,' I say.

'Don't know, but it's the only explanation,' says Mum. 'He obviously thinks that you're ignoring him.'

'What are you going to do?' asks Patty. 'Call him?'

'No,' I say, channelling the strong woman who has just bought a beautiful apartment. 'No more mixed messages, I'm going to go round to his house and talk face to face. If he's out, I'll wait. If he has a female visitor, I'll take two minutes of his time then leave them to it. I want this cleared up once and for all.'

'Can we come?' asks Mum, getting a very firm 'No!' from everyone in the room.

I want to stop the speculation about what the possible reason behind this mystery could be so I wrestle myself from the sofa and head to the kitchen, emerging with the champagne and four flutes. It stops the conversation.

'I have news too,' I tell them as I place everything on the table and begin to undo the metal tie and take off the muselet. I twist the bottle rather than the cork but it still flies off, hitting the ceiling, rebounding and ricocheting off Mum's head. I honestly couldn't have aimed better and we all burst out laughing at the astonished look on her face. I pour glasses and hand them out, raising mine and telling them, 'I bought an apartment today.'

They all put down their glasses to give me a hug of congratulations and then start plying me with questions. It was Mum who first spotted this mansion house so she's taking credit but I don't care. I promise to hold a housewarming party, and a garden party and New Year. I only hope the neighbours are a friendly bunch with all these celebrations going on, and that's before Charlie and Josie have put their requests in.

Even though I plan to confront Michael tomorrow, I won't worry about that tonight — what will be, will be. Now, I'm simply celebrating being ready to move on. I raise the champagne flute to my lips as Patty toasts me and my new apartment. As I take a sip, I promise myself one thing — I'm going to buy those crystal champagne coupes. After all, I'm worth it.

CHAPTER THIRTY-FIVE: CALL OFF THE SEARCH

'You should definitely put a chaise longue there — just because you can,' says Josie at work the next day.

I'm proudly showing them pictures of my new apartment and they're cooing over them as if they were baby photos, which I guess they are to me.

'Right, ladies,' says Charlie, checking his watch as he gets up. 'Guess it's time to open the doors to all those bookings. We need a great day to set us up for an even greater evening.'

It's Charlie and Peter's hen/stag night tonight. We tried to think of a portmanteau that would work but neither of them liked 'hag' or 'sten', so we're sticking with using them both and changing them randomly. Charlie's friends are heading out with him and Peter is out with his, then we're all meeting up in a nightclub.

'And remember,' he says, wagging a finger at us, 'I want this to be fun but tasteful. Absolutely no firemen jumping out at me.'

Josie tuts and says, 'When did stag dos become so sanitised? Anyway, we've booked a policeman.'

Charlie looks horrified until he realises she's kidding and I promise him that there are no strippers whatsoever booked for tonight.

We work a full and busy day and are closing up when Mum calls me in a fit of excitement.

'I've got a match!' she screams down the phone.

At first I haven't a clue what she's talking about.

'He wants to meet me tonight,' she says, and the penny drops that it's a dating match. I'm struck silent with despair but she doesn't seem to notice.

'I know that meeting on a stag do isn't the best way to start something, but it'll make me look fun and if anything goes wrong or I don't like him then I just need to signal over to one of you,' she says, obviously having thought this out.

I sigh out loud and tell her that I didn't think she'd actually be going through with this item on her list. I tell her to think of Dad and how he would feel if he knew.

'After all,' I say, 'how would you feel if he did the same and wanted an affair? You'd be really hurt.'

'He'd never do that,' she says. 'Besides, I've told him.'

'You've what? What did he say?'

'He wasn't best pleased.' Mum is probably understating the situation. 'But Patty had a word with him and then he agreed that I'd be better off getting it out of my system. I've only ever known your dad and sometimes things do need shaking up a bit.'

I sincerely hope that if I ever find someone else, I won't want to 'shake it up' as I approach my eighties. I hope we're happily drinking cocoa and watching cosy mysteries together, but if she's really cleared this with Dad then I know I can't stop her.

'You'll be wearing a rainbow flower garland and headdress,' I remind her. That's Charlie's dress code — all black except the garlands. It's easy to do and a huge relief as I've seen many a hen party in the most ridiculous get-ups.

'But that's good because I won't have to worry about what to wear,' Mum continues. 'Honestly, I think it's a godsend that it's all planned out. I know where to meet him and how long he can have before we move on to the nightclub.

It's perfect — I don't know why more first dates aren't held on hen parties.'

Patty would love this logic and Mum is right — if she's determined to go through with this then it's better that we're around and even better that he sees her crazy family as that will have him running a mile. I must find out what Patty actually said to Dad.

I don't tell Charlie what's going on — he's worried enough about this evening going well. Instead, I just wave him goodbye and tell him I'll see him later. I know he'll now spend hours getting dressed and yet he'll look just the same only smell sublime. As no one will be looking at me, I'll get changed and be out in a flash — right now, I have something else to do.

Thanks to Mum's surveillance, I know exactly when Michael gets in from work and I'm heading over there to get to the bottom of this. I drive to Cross Road and park up opposite his house then wait. Pretty much on the dot of the time in Mum's notes, Michael's van appears and pulls into his drive. He gets out and pulls a folder from the passenger side then opens the door and heads in. I watch all of this and realise that I still feel a pang of affection. His front garden is as immaculate as ever and now abundant with spring flowers that I know he'll have planted with care. My heart starts beating faster and I wonder whether I'm doing the right thing. Am I about to humiliate myself with a man yet again? After all, I have form. But if I don't do this then:

1. I will never understand why he seemed keen one minute and ignored me the next.

2. My mother will come round and ask him herself — and that will be even more humiliating.

I have to do this.

I get out of the car, hoping that none of my old neighbours are watching and if they are that they don't recognise me. I walk calmly up to Michael's door, practising my opening sentence and pause before pressing the bell.

The ten seconds or so it takes him to open the door feel like ten years, but then, there he is, and I watch his expression move from hassled to surprised to delighted.

'Angie!' he shouts, pulling me into a hug then quickly releasing me. 'Thank goodness, please come in. That is, if you want to?'

He looks as nervous as me as he holds his hands firmly by his side. My opening sentence has long since vanished; I simply nod and walk in. I don't sit down but instead turn to face him.

'I wanted to check that you were okay,' I say in as neutral a voice as I can muster.

'I'm okay,' he says. 'What about you and your friend, Patty — how is she?'

Okay, I think, *so the call Poppy overheard seems to be valid so far.*

'She's fine,' I tell him. We're both treading very carefully here and I'm hoping to work out what is going on before him.

'It's just, when you told me not to contact you because you needed to spend time with her, I thought . . .' Michael looks to the ground then back up at me. 'Well, I thought it might be very serious and I know that when my wife was first diagnosed, we didn't want to hear from anyone.'

He thought Patty had cancer?

'It's understandable,' he continues. 'But I've been through it and if you ever need a shoulder to cry on or just tea and a chat, I'm here.'

Okay, this is weird and we need to stop beating around the bush.

I sit down on the sofa and he follows my lead.

'Patty is absolutely fine,' I tell him, getting a surprised look in return. 'When did you get a message that she was ill and why did you think it was from me?'

'Because it came from your number,' Michael replies. 'The new number you got after you lost your phone.'

'But even if I had lost my phone, you can transfer a number,' I say, trying to put this jigsaw together but unable to see the picture on the front of the box.

'Okay,' he says sheepishly. 'I know that but you said you weren't that tech savvy so I wasn't sure if you knew it — sorry.'

He looks so ashamed of himself that I can't stop myself from laughing out loud. As I do so, he joins in and it clears the air.

'I can't work out most of the settings on Patty's combi-oven but I can switch phones without losing my number,' I reassure him. 'Let's try and understand what happened, shall we? Starting with you standing me up at the café.'

He opens his mouth to protest but then closes it and calmly says, 'I was on my way to the café, really looking forward to it, when a friend of yours calls and tells me that you've had to cancel because of a personal issue.'

'Which friend?' I ask, and he replies that they didn't say.

'Then later, I get a message from a new number saying you've had to change yours and I should replace the number in my phone with that one. Obviously I did that,' he continues. 'I messaged to ask how you were but you didn't reply.'

I'm astounded by all this and tell him I did none of these things.

'I've messaged your new number a couple of times suggesting we meet up whenever you were ready but you didn't reply to them either. I called the number and left voicemails but again no reply. Then, you sent me a message saying that Patty was seriously ill and could I stop calling as you were dedicating all your time to her.'

'Wow,' I reply. 'This is elaborate. I swear to you, I haven't heard from you and didn't contact you because I thought you'd just lost interest.'

'Never.' He shakes his head. 'I sent you a Valentine's card with gnomes on it hoping you'd know it was me and get in touch, but you didn't. Then I saw pictures of you dancing and at a fancy golf club evening. I have to be honest — I was jealous and angry. I thought you were stringing me along.'

'And I came by here one night and was told you were out with a woman,' I tell him.

'The only woman I've been out with is an old friend of my wife's,' he replies. 'And I do it out of respect for her loss but I honestly wish she would move on and let me do the same. I still really like you, Angie.'

'And I like you,' I tell him.

We sit quietly and I contemplate all that I've just heard. It's obvious that someone has been trying to keep us from getting together but we both want to give this a go.

'Can I see the number you were given?' I eventually ask and Michael stands to get his phone out of his pocket then hands it to me. I go through his contacts and find my name.

'Call it,' I say, handing it to him. He does and it goes straight to voicemail. It's an automated response so there's no clue as to who is behind this.

Almost immediately after the call, he gets a message saying that this fake Angie is busy. My skin crawls to see my name appear on the phone and know that someone is pretending to be me.

'Give me the number,' I say. 'They might pick up to a number they don't know.'

I call the number and after a couple of rings, the person picks up.

'Hello? Who is this?'

I recognise the voice immediately and suddenly it all falls into place.

'Sarah?'

'Angie? Oh god.'

'Sarah, I'm here with Michael and I think we need to talk.'

* * *

We meet in the park and as we watch her approach, I feel as if I'm in some Russian spy movie. I invite Sarah to sit at a picnic table and ask her to explain everything.

'I've loved him for years, ever since I lost my husband,' she blurts out through snotty tears. 'Jenny and Michael took me in, we went everywhere as a threesome, so when she died, I presumed it would move on to just being the two of us. I knew I could look after Michael better than you ever could and that's what Jenny would have wanted, I'm sure. If I lost Michael to you I'd have nothing, so I called him from my colleague's phone while you were in the bathroom at the café and then I got the idea for everything else later. I bought one of those pay-as-you-go phones to send the other messages. I didn't think you were serious enough about him and hoped you'd hit it off with David.'

She looks up at Michael and says, 'We could have made a go of it.'

Kindly, he puts his hand on top of hers and tells her that it wouldn't have worked as he sees her as just a friend. I look on, thinking that's particularly generous as I'd have pulled her hair out.

'The book club?' I ask.

'I just wanted to keep tabs and know what you were up to.'

'And *The Salt Path*?'

'Jenny and I read it together when she was first diagnosed.' I can hear the sorrow in Sarah's voice as she speaks. I'm not quite sure how it's happened but in this moment I'm actually feeling sorry for her. When I first met Sarah, I thought of my own situation this time last year; how lost I was and how much I needed a friendship circle of my own. I invited Sarah into ours and I know I would have done anything to make her welcome. I've been badly deceived, and although Sarah's actions had no regard for my feelings, I do understand them. I'll be happy when I never have to see her again, but I feel sad for her rather than angry.

I'm ready to leave and get up from the bench but Michael stays seated. I hear him tell Sarah that she'll meet someone soon and, when she does, he'll be so happy for her. Sarah gets up and walks away; we both watch to make sure she has.

'Gosh, that was tough,' I tell him.

'She's still grieving,' he says. 'But as long as we're okay, we can watch out for her going forwards. Agreed?'

'Agreed,' I say, then link into his arm as we walk; I feel relief at being able to leave this scene behind us. 'Now for a very important question — do you have a black sweater and jeans?'

'Of course, why?'

'Because we're going to rekindle this relationship the way it started. With a party.'

CHAPTER THIRTY-SIX: DON'T STOP THE PARTY

When I walk into the bar with Michael there's a cheer from my friends as well as some odd glances. I can tell they're all itching to ask what happened but are being polite while he's by my side. The politeness is unusual from this lot but welcome right now.

'We're on champagne to start,' says Charlie, putting a rainbow-coloured Hawaiian garland over our heads then pouring us each a glass from the bottle on our table. He leans in to give me a kiss on the cheek and whispers, 'I want to know *everything*.'

'Maybe I'll tell you later,' I reply with a wink. 'But maybe not.'

My mum clinks her glass with Michael's and says, 'Good to finally meet you. I thought you might be a figment of my daughter's imagination until I started following you. She used to have pretend boyfriends when she was a teenager so it wouldn't have been a surprise.'

I watch Michael's face try to process all of that and can't help but laugh. I link arms and guide him gently away from her.

'She started following me?' he asks with a puzzled frown on his face.

'It's a very long story but let's just enjoy the night.'

Charlie's party includes me, Patty, Zoe, Mum, Josie and now Michael while Peter's has Ed, Caroline, Matt, James and Dad. Sensibly we head to a restaurant after the champagne, where we have a private room upstairs on the mezzanine level to ourselves. I let Josie and Zoe sit either side of Michael, while at the other end of the table, Patty and Charlie have me surrounded, ready to interrogate. I tell them everything while we eat and they're as astounded as I was.

'She seemed rather quiet and normal at the book weekend,' says Patty.

'Just goes to show, never trust quiet or normal,' adds Charlie, clinking glasses with Patty. 'At least with the loud crazy ones you know where you stand quite quickly.'

I look around the table and especially at my mother, who is drinking a Pina Colada through a novelty straw shaped like a penis, and find myself agreeing with Charlie. None of us brought penis-shaped straws, so goodness knows where she got it from. She is looking gorgeous tonight, and I know it's because she's meeting her date later. I guess she'll ditch the straw by then. Changing the subject, I ask Patty if she thinks this date is wise.

'It's better that she meets him when we're all here,' she says. 'We can keep an eye out and intervene if needed.'

'I wished so hard that we could just forget this. I hoped it would just go away,' I tell her.

'I realise that, but we both know your mother and it isn't going to,' says Patty. 'And I wasn't having it happen while I was away. I definitely want to see this.'

'It's not funny, Patty — these are my parents we're talking about.'

'Trust me, Bo,' she says, putting a hand on my thigh and squeezing it.

* * *

When the food is finished and the plates are cleared away, Charlie declares that we're playing a game of 'Never Have I

Ever', where he'll read out a statement and if you *have* done this thing then you have to take a sip of your drink. I look over at Michael and wince at him — I guess we're going to get to know each other very quickly and very publicly. Charlie pulls a piece of paper from his jacket pocket and unfolds it.

'Okay,' he says. 'An easy one to start us off — never have I ever accidentally set something on fire.'

I immediately take a sip, expecting everyone else to follow suit, but no one does.

'Be warned, Michael,' Zoe laughs. 'My mum's ability to flambé every meal is legendary.'

'Oh, tell me everything,' he says. 'Forewarned is forearmed.'

There follows a rapid-fire description of every cooking disaster I've made, including forgetting to take the disposable barbecue out of its cardboard wrapper and causing a major campsite incident when Zoe was thirteen.

'I've improved a lot since then,' I protest with a huge smile on my face. Not because of the stories but because Zoe and Michael seem to be getting on quite well.

'Next one,' continues Charlie. 'Never have I ever laughed so hard I've wet myself.'

Everyone takes a drink to that one and Mum adds, 'But it doesn't matter if you're wearing your Tena Ladies.'

To which everyone roars with laughter and probably some do indeed wet themselves.

The game continues and I discover that Michael has never:

1. Skinny-dipped
2. Joined the mile-high club
3. Done a runner from a restaurant

But he has:

1. Been attracted to a cartoon character (Jessica Rabbit — hasn't every man?)
2. Eaten something on holiday not knowing exactly what it was
3. Fallen in love on a first date

He looks over at me as he's sipping his drink to that one and I hope he's thinking of that New Year's party. Of course, the group asks him about it, but he simply says that a gentleman never tells.

I think Charlie might have chosen some of those statements knowing that I'd done them, so I'm feeling a bit fuzzy at the end of the game. I ask for a jug of water, and although everyone tells me I'm being boring, they all take a glassful.

In the pause, Mum suddenly leaps up with her phone in her hand.

'He's on his way!' she shouts out excitedly. 'My date's on his way. I'd better go freshen up.'

I sit dumbfounded as both Zoe and Patty head to the bathroom with her. Charlie rubs my arm and tells me to trust them.

'I can't just sit here and let this happen,' I tell him, making to get up and follow them. Charlie gently restrains me and again emphasises that I need to trust them.

'It'll be okay,' he says, staring right into my eyes.

It's obvious something is going on and I'm not party to it. I try to breathe calmly and reassure myself that if Zoe is involved then it can't be that bad. She wouldn't put her gran in any sort of danger and she wouldn't knowingly upset her grandfather. I just wish I could be absolutely sure.

Mum emerges with her entourage and reads her phone, declaring that he's here and waiting at the bar. I immediately try to get up again and once more am restrained. Patty tells Mum she looks lovely, while Zoe tells her to have fun but simply head to the bathroom if she feels at all uncomfortable. They then leave her to head down the stairs to the bar on her own.

'You have to tell me what's happening,' I tell Patty when she gets back to the table. I'm now not only worried, I'm angry that this has gone so far.

This time Zoe comes over to me and puts her hands on my shoulders.

'Give her ten minutes and then we'll go take a look,' she says. 'I promise Gran is okay.'

Charlie tries to keep the conversation light for those ten minutes but everyone can tell the humour is forced and I'm practically destroying my hands as I chew my fingernails off. Michael doesn't take his eyes off me but he can't get close as Charlie and Josie have him surrounded. I see him check his watch and declare, 'Okay, that's close enough to ten minutes. Angie needs to know her mum is safe.'

'Let me just check something,' says Patty, getting out her phone and reading something. 'Okay, let's go take a look.'

I try to remain calm as I scrape back the chair. Michael heads straight for me and holds my hand as we all head to the balcony of the mezzanine and peer down to the bar. The lighting is dimmed down there but I can see Mum sitting at the bar with her back to us. Opposite her is a man who looks awfully familiar.

'Is that . . . ?' I turn to Patty.

'Marti Pellow,' she says, nodding. 'Or Dougie Campbell as he's known to his friends.'

'Dougie doesn't have quite the same ring as Marti does it?' says Charlie. 'Although he's quite handsome.'

'Greyer than I remember,' I add.

'He always retouches the old roots before he gets on stage,' Patty says. 'I thought he'd be better off keeping it grey for this gig.'

'Gig? You mean you hired him?' The penny has now dropped.

'Of course,' she says. 'His brief is to have your mum running back into the arms of your dad.'

'Not sure how that's going to work,' I say, relieved that this isn't a real date but still not sure how he's not going to leave Mum wanting more; they both seem to be talking and laughing amiably. 'They look quite happy at the moment.'

'Watch and wait,' says Patty again, checking her watch.

* * *

Marti aka Dougie clicks his finger for the barman to come over and orders another drink. When it arrives he appears to be asking Mum if she'll pay. I can see she looks surprised but gets her purse out and taps a card on the reader. Marti downs his drink quickly and then as Mum is sipping hers, he gently runs a finger down her arm. Mum gives a little shiver and I can't tell whether she's enjoying it or not. Then Marti adjusts his seat so that he's closer to Mum, very close in fact, and I can tell from her body language that she's not comfortable.

'He's not going to distress her just to put her off dating, is he?' I ask. 'I don't want the evening to end badly.'

I'm thinking not only of Mum but of this stag night — surely Charlie doesn't want to spend his evening watching a woman being humiliated?

'It won't,' he whispers to me.

Marti puts his hand on Mum's leg and at that moment, the door to the bar bursts open and the other stag do walks in with Dad and Peter striding side by side at the front. Their group costume is evidently cowboy as Dad is in a huge Stetson with a holster slung low around his hips. He looks just like Mum's hero — Gary Cooper in *High Noon*.

Dad walks up to Marti and stands directly in front of him, legs astride.

'Son,' he says. 'I ain't looking for trouble, but if you don't get your hands off my woman then that's exactly what you're gonna get.'

Marti looks him up and down then snorts, 'You and whose army?'

He stands and goes to take a punch at Dad. Dad grabs his fist and quickly pulls that arm behind Marti's back, pushing him out of the bar. Dad returns and walks up to Mum, then pulls her out of the chair, dips her down backwards and kisses her — just like in the movies. As I'm watching all of this, I have a tiny tear of joy in my eye.

We all erupt into cheers and a round of applause, then more champagne appears and the entire entourage take a glass. We toast true love and I give Patty a huge hug of thanks.

It's soon time to move onto the nightclub, but once outside the restaurant, Mum and Dad tell us that they're going home for an early night.

'And I'm going to make him keep the Stetson on,' says Mum with a wink as their taxi arrives.

'Argh, too much information,' I tell her as I kiss them both goodnight.

Walking along with Patty on one arm and Michael on the other, I feel as happy as I have been in a long time.

'So it was all a set-up and Angie's dad knew about her bucket list?' Michael asks.

'He did,' Patty says. 'He was the one who told us that it was probably his fault as he hadn't been very romantic recently. He forgot their anniversary.'

'It's not their anniversary until July,' I say puzzled.

'The anniversary of their first date, apparently,' says Patty. 'They went to see a Gary Cooper movie.'

'Hence the costume,' says Michael. 'It's a good job the other group were in cowboy outfits.'

'We weren't until Patty and Zoe hatched their plan,' Peter tells us. 'We were going with the garlands too until then.'

'Then Angie's mum did me a favour too,' says Charlie, leaning into Peter and adjusting the Stetson. 'I do like a man from the Wild West.'

CHAPTER THIRTY-SEVEN: TIME OF MY LIFE

The hour of the wedding finally arrives and I'm nervous as I help Charlie adjust his bow tie. I'm his best woman today and couldn't be more thrilled. There are no speeches so my only official duty is to get Charlie there on time and try to keep him busy for the day. The happy couple decided on an evening event so that it would feel like a party from the outset, and that's a great idea but it could have resulted in Charlie and me spending all day fretting about things that could go wrong. Anticipating this, I booked us into a day spa for a relaxing massage and facial. We still spent the day fretting but thanks to some medicinal mud we don't have the wrinkles to show for it.

I researched the 1950s theme and quickly realised that the fashion was knockout so I've fully embraced it. I absolutely love my dress, which has an hourglass outline and Bardot neckline. I've also got the long black gloves, small clutch and killer stilettos to complete the look and feel like a sexy Audrey Hepburn. I might not be able to walk in a couple of hours but for now even I feel good. Charlie is in a vintage tuxedo which doesn't look too different from modern versions except for the small bow tie and lapels but he is radiant. I stand back and look at him affectionately; the slimline cut of his suit works perfectly and he seems to shine from the top of his immaculately coiffured head to the tip of obsessively polished shoes.

'You look fabulous,' I tell him.

Dad comes to pick us up and hands Charlie a small box. Charlie opens it and he looks up at Dad with delight in his eyes.

'They're gorgeous,' he says of the mother-of-pearl cufflinks.

'They're genuine 1950s and they're our gift to you,' says Dad. 'So you have your something old.'

Charlie hugs Dad and we hurriedly change the ones he's wearing. We're heading out of the door when Charlie suddenly says, 'Wait, I don't have anything borrowed.'

His 'blue' is the lovely thistle buttonhole, his new is his entire outfit, Dad has just provided the old, so I'm with him on this — he has to have something borrowed.

'Got it,' shouts Patty from the other room. She rushes in with a watch box. I'm stunned as I know what's in it.

'This was Nigel's,' she says, holding back the emotion. 'You never knew him but I'm sure you would have loved him, and besides which, you've certainly looked after his missus these past few years.'

It's the watch she gave Nigel for their wedding, a simple gold face and black leather strap. It's perfect. Charlie picks it up and gently caresses it. It has an understated elegance not often seen in modern-day timepieces. It doesn't count steps.

'Oh, Patty, are you sure?' asks Charlie as a tiny tear appears in Patty's eye.

She nods and pats her eyes gently.

'Just don't go skinny-dipping in it and have it back by midnight. Now hurry up before you ruin my mascara.'

Charlie puts the watch on then gives Patty a peck on the cheek, being careful not to disturb her make-up. The four of us hug then Patty heads out to the waiting car with Mum and Michael while Charlie and I get into a ridiculously huge Cadillac with Dad. It feels so over the top but I'm loving this and I think our car might just explode with the excitement radiating from us.

The guys still haven't revealed the theme for today and it's no clearer when we pull up to the venue they've chosen — Marianne's dance studio. I recall her saying that they held parties and weddings here but wonder why the guys have chosen it.

'Curiouser and curiouser,' I say to Charlie.

We meet up with Charlie's parents outside and I leave him in their care while I head into the ceremony room with my family and Michael. I honestly didn't know what to expect — after all, we've been given a dress code and there's a drag artist officiating — but this room is amazing, with fairy lights twinkling all around the perimeter, a four-piece band in the corner playing melodic versions of songs I remember Mum listening to on the radio and a stage at the far end with a simple wedding canopy at the centre. There's a red-carpet aisle which winds its way to the side stage stairs and chairs arranged in a semi-circle facing it. There are no sides to choose — the families are together.

We take a seat in the second row as I don't want to miss any of this. When everyone is seated there's a buzz unlike any other wedding I've been to where it seems to go deathly quiet. I guess that's the church effect. Then suddenly, there's a hush and I look around for what is happening and see why the room has stopped breathing — Jackie Kennedy Onassis is walking onto the stage. Obviously not a reincarnation but Poppy O'Cherry channelling that most famous of style icons, complete with bouffant auburn hair, cherry-red shift dress, pearl set and pillbox hat. They stand with their gloved hands in front of them and music starts up at the back of the room. It's a musical version of a 1950s tune and I do know it from somewhere but without the lyrics I can't quite place it.

'What's this song from?' I whisper to Michael but he shrugs.

On my other side, Patty smiles and tells me I'll work it out soon enough.

'You know, don't you?' I ask, slightly miffed.

She raises her finger to her lips and tells me to shush.

We all stand as the guys walk down the aisle and onto the stage together. I can see that they're both a bit nervous and Charlie is practically clinging onto his very-soon-to-be husband. Poppy clears their throat and begins the ceremony completing all the official parts simply and without fuss. Incredibly for a six-foot-tall Jackie Kennedy, they manage to fade into the background and not outshine the grooms.

'And now,' says Poppy, addressing us, 'Peter and Charlie have written their vows to each other.'

The guys angle slightly so they're facing each other but also the congregation (or audience — I don't know what we are outside of a church). Charlie begins with words that I've never heard but have seen practised. Many an hour he's spent reading them over and over then closing his eyes and seeing if he remembers them — I've watched his lips move for days now. Again, those words are familiar and one or two hang like clues waiting to be revealed.

'. . . waiting for so long . . .'

'. . . take each other's hand . . .'

There are a few giggles as some people finally get it and Patty asks me if I know the theme yet. I'm livid with myself but cannot grasp it.

Peter's vows seal it.

'When I first saw you, you were dressed in a tattered old wedding dress just to entertain your friends and I was scared. Not because you were pretending to be a ghost, but I was scared of walking out of that room and never feeling again the way I felt right then.'

It's my favourite line.

'*Dirty Dancing*,' I whisper to Patty and she nods.

'I declare you husband and husband,' says Poppy from the stage. 'You may now seal it with a kiss.'

The room stands and cheers as the guys embrace; we converge on them with confetti and party poppers as they walk down the stage staircase while around us the event staff move all the chairs to the side and waiters dressed in holiday camp blazers arrive with champagne (in coupes!) and canapés. I rush to congratulate the boys.

'I love the theme,' I tell them. 'Although technically it was supposed to be 1963, not the fifties.'

'I knew you'd know,' Peter says, smiling.

'I couldn't say 1960s or everyone would come in horrible hippy clothes,' said Charlie. 'And everyone wore fifties fashion in the movie.'

I admit they did and manage to give them one kiss each before they're swamped by everyone else.

I stand back and bathe in their reflected love. Michael approaches with champagne and I hold that glass as elegantly as I can. The golden champagne glistens off the crystal-like fairy dust. I'm back in that Disney movie and everything is perfect.

'May I just say,' Michael begins, 'that you look absolutely ravishing tonight. Stunning, incredible, beautiful . . .'

I kiss him on the cheek, then thank him. Mum and Dad are with Poppy so I pull Michael over to find out what they're saying.

'Have you ever thought of running for prime minister?' Mum is asking, and of all the things I imagined she might be discussing, this was not one of them.

'Do you think I'd get elected?' asks Poppy, raising a perfectly shaped eyebrow towards me.

'Well, I was just thinking we'd get the best of both worlds,' Mum says. 'If you have to deal with tough nuts you can channel Margaret Thatcher, and if it's a cosy chat people need then you could probably don a sweater and pipe for Harold Wilson. Then when you're visiting the US president you could wear this — they wouldn't be able to resist you.'

'You've got a point there,' says Poppy, 'but I'm not sure about the old man get-up. There haven't been any truly stylish male prime ministers, have there?'

'You could be the first,' Mum continues. 'I'd vote for you.'

And with that she walks off, leaving us all bemused.

'You have a lovely family,' says Poppy. 'They're all slightly crazy.'

'But that's the best sort, isn't it?' adds Michael and we all raise a glass to that.

I watch Michael as he makes Poppy laugh with stories about his own family and I marvel at how well he's fitting in. I shouldn't be making comparisons but I can't help it, and I know that David would not have enjoyed today. Some guests approach and ask Poppy for a selfie so we leave them to it.

The music changes from jive tunes to a slow dance and the band starts playing one of my favourites from the movie — 'She's Like the Wind'.

'Oh, I love this,' I tell Michael, pulling him into the centre of the floor. 'And Patrick Swayze, but you'll do for now.'

He smiles and says he's very thankful for that. He pulls me close and we sway together for three blissful minutes. Although the room is full of lively chatter, a quiet stillness descends over me and I realise it's contentment. I don't know what will happen next for Michael and me but in this moment, surrounded by my family and friends in all their glory, I am completely happy.

Over by the band there's movement and as our song finishes I see Patty standing with them behind a microphone.

'Okay, everyone, it's the moment you've all been waiting for,' she shouts with a huge smile on her face. 'Please clear the dance floor.'

We all move to one side and the intro to *that* song starts up; I am delirious with excitement. Patty starts to sing the words that were in Charlie's vow. A spotlight beams into the centre of the stage, where Marianne stands. She's joined by Felipe and together they do the mambo moves from the final scene of *Dirty Dancing*. Their footwork is spectacular, rocking forwards and back with little toe kicks, and the way they hold their upper bodies is so strong and defined. Felipe's muscular arms are accentuated even more by the lighting.

'I'll have him sent to my room gift-wrapped,' says Poppy from behind me.

'Join the queue,' I reply.

It gets to the part of the song where Felipe jumps off the stage and dances down the aisle then turns back to the stage followed by the whole dance school. Now Peter is up front with him and he's changed into a Patrick Swayze style tight black T-shirt and he looks buff. He has evidently been rehearsing, as he does all the right moves and reaches the stage, where Charlie now stands with Marianne. He saunters down the steps to Peter and they twirl together for the finale.

Patty tells everyone to get up and we don't need much encouragement. In moments, we're a frenzy of all dance techniques and none. Felipe and Marianne move between the guests, leading them through some moves and making everyone feel like a superstar. The chorus reaches its crescendo and the room links arms, forming a circle around the happy couple, bellowing out the lyrics, and like everyone else, I truly am having the *time of my life*.

CHAPTER THIRTY-EIGHT: AU REVOIR

'To Patty.' I raise my glass and the rest of the table does the same. We're gathered for a goodbye meal and now toast the wonderful woman who leaves us bright and early tomorrow morning. It feels like more than a fond farewell. The first quarter of this year has had so many ups and downs, it's almost like a reboot for all of us. When Patty comes back, Jack will be with her, I'll be moving on and we'll have newlyweds among us. I hope that the rest of the year runs at a much slower pace.

'Thank you,' Patty is saying. 'I know how much I'll be missed, but it's only for a short time. I'll be back and checking up on you all before you know it.'

We cheer and beg her not to go.

'I must,' she says with the back of her hand to her forehead in mock dismay. 'For my audience awaits.'

'And more importantly,' shouts Kath, 'so does Marti Pellow.'

She gets a playful dig in the ribs from Sheila.

'Oh, I don't think I could ever look at that man again.' Mum grimaces. 'I'll have to switch the telly off when they're doing those eighties shows.'

'It taught you a lesson though, didn't it?' says Patty. 'You already had the man of your dreams.'

'Oh, I always knew that,' Mum says, snuggling into him.

'Especially when I'm in the Stetson,' adds Dad.

'TOO MUCH INFORMATION!' yells both Zoe and I in unison, getting a laugh from everyone.

'Now, talking of lessons,' continues Patty. 'It's been quite a year and I want to be sure that you all don't fall to pieces while I'm away, so I've jotted down some advice for each of you.'

We all spontaneously put down our glasses and look up at her like obedient students.

'Ed and Caroline,' she begins. 'Please don't invite any more would-be stalkers to join the book club.'

The group laughs together.

'That was strange,' says Ed shaking his head. 'Sarah seemed so nice initially.'

'Do you know how she's doing?' asks Zoe.

'Apparently very well — she's taken up with the barman of the Rose and Crown,' Caroline says. 'He told me the other day when I was in there to reserve the book club table for the rest of the year. They're smitten, so I hear.'

'It didn't take long to get over you, Michael,' says Patty. 'Unless she's just biding her time.'

She gives me a look of mock horror as she speaks, but the very thought of Sarah stringing along someone else while she lies in wait actually terrifies me.

'You'll have to find a new venue if she moves in with him,' says Mum.

Mum seems to have read my mind — I don't think I'd ever trust that a drink she served me wouldn't be laced with something nasty. I had really wanted to put all thoughts of Sarah behind me, so if she does become a fixture at the pub, I'll ask Caroline if we can move the venue for the book club. I shake off the sense of dread that threatens to ruin the moment.

'Now, Josie and Matt.' Patty picks up her thread again. 'To you I say this: if you're ever going to take relationship advice from one of your bosses — make sure it's Charlie.'

'Oi!' I exclaim. 'I'm not that bad.'

The sympathetic looks around the table show no one is going to agree with me on that. Michael leans into me and tells them, 'Some things are just worth waiting for.'

He gets a cheesy groan and a couple of bread rolls thrown at him.

'Zoe and James,' Patty continues. 'Don't work too hard, look after your gran and maybe find some time to make Bo-Peep a grandmother.'

Zoe blushes and puts her head in her hands.

'I am in absolutely no hurry to be a grandmother,' I reassure her.

'And I'm not being a great-gran,' adds my mum. 'That sounds far too old.'

'Okay,' says Patty. 'Then just have fun practising for when the time is right.'

Zoe shouts out, asking the ground to swallow her up, then tells Patty to kindly move on. As if conspiring to rescue my daughter, my phone rings and I know it's a video call from the guys. I try to hold it up for the table and we all wave excitedly at them.

'Wow,' says Josie. 'That place looks stunning.'

'It is,' gushes Charlie. 'It's my absolute dream location.'

They wish Patty the best of luck and ask her about the setlist.

'We've added your song,' she tells them. '"Time of My Life"— I think it'll go down a storm.'

'Not the best word to use in relation to a cruise.' Peter laughs. 'But I agree, I can just see you all doing that. It's a shame Felipe isn't there to show everyone the moves.'

'There's a dance instructor on board who'll work with us on some simple group choreography,' Patty says.

'Sounds fabulous, but don't have such a good time that you don't want to come back,' Charlie shouts.

'Never,' says Patty. 'You're my family.'

We all wave goodbye and Patty turns to me. I'd almost forgotten that I haven't received any words of wisdom yet.

'And as for you, my gorgeous girl,' she says, reaching out and grabbing hold of both my hands. 'Take care of the house, invite Michael around as much as you like but don't disturb the nanny-cams as they're beaming directly into my cabin so I can keep an eye on you.'

Everyone laughs except me.

'Kidding!' she continues. 'You two have a great couple of months, just make sure that you don't do anything I wouldn't do.'

'Is there anything?' asks Michael, laughing.

'Not really.' She looks over at me with a faint smile. 'Now, who'd like another glass of wine?'

* * *

At three o'clock the following morning, Sheila's car pulls up and I help Patty haul her cases into the boot. It's freezing and I'm standing there in gardening clogs and pyjamas. The girls mutter about how they're going to fit all of this stuff into a small cabin and I recall that the below-deck accommodation isn't huge.

'We'll just throw yours overboard, Kath,' says Sheila. 'If it works out with Marti you won't need it.'

'Very true,' Kath says. 'You'll have to be a duo.'

They banter happily and when everything is in, Patty turns to me and we embrace in the tightest, warmest hug.

'I'll miss you,' she says.

'It's not for long, and if it gets too bad just click your heels three times,' I tell her.

And with a final cuddle, my best friend gets into the car and I wave until I can no longer see her. I breathe in the fresh air and head back inside.

Time to get my own life back on track.

THE END

THE CHOC LIT STORY

Established in 2009, Choc Lit is an independent, award-winning publisher dedicated to creating a delicious selection of quality women's fiction.

We have won 18 awards, including Publisher of the Year and the Romantic Novel of the Year, and have been shortlisted for countless others. In 2023, we were shortlisted for Publisher of the Year by the Romantic Novelists' Association.

All our novels are selected by genuine readers. We are proud to publish talented first-time authors, as well as established writers whose books we love introducing to a new generation of readers.

In 2023, we became a Joffe Books company. Best known for publishing a wide range of commercial fiction, Joffe Books has its roots in women's fiction. Today it is one of the largest independent publishers in the UK.

We love to hear from you, so please email us about absolutely anything bookish at choc-lit@joffebooks.com

If you want to hear about all our bargain new releases, join our mailing list: www.choc-lit.com/contact

ALSO BY HELEN BRIDGETT

SERENITY BAY
Book 1: SUMMER AT SERENITY BAY
Book 2: CHRISTMAS AT SERENITY BAY

PROFESSOR MAXIE REDDICK FILES
Book 1: ONE BY ONE
Book 2: WRONG SORT OF GIRL
Book 3: MY SISTER'S KILLER

THE MERCURY TRAVEL CLUB
Book 1: THE MERCURY TRAVEL CLUB
Book 2: THE HAPPINESS PROJECT